Swirl Secrets

Swirl Secrets

Honey

www.urbanbooks.net

Urban Books, LLC
300 Farmingdale Road, NY-Route 109
Farmingdale, NY 11735

ISBN 13: 978-1-62286-210-8
ISBN 10: 1-62286-210-4

First Trade Paperback Printing October 2019
Printed in the United States of America

10 9 8 7 6 5 4 3 2 1

Distributed by Kensington Publishing Corp.
Submit Orders to:
Customer Service
400 Hahn Road
Westminster, MD 21157-4627
Phone: 1-800-733-3000
Fax: 1-800-659-2436

Dedication

This book is dedicated to my one and only child, my son, Solomon Berewa III. I also dedicate this one to my parents, The Honorable Judge and Mrs. William C. "Billy" Randall. You three are the wind beneath my wings and the source that inspires me to continue to soar higher and higher.

Acknowledgments

I give all praise, glory, and honor to God for blessing me with the gift of creative writing and the talent to tell great stories.

Thank you, SB3, for your love, unwavering support, and patience you always extend to Mommy when I'm on the grind. Every book I write is another installment in the legacy I'm building for you. You are the reason for my success. I love you more than I love myself.

To my husband of nearly fifteen years, I say thank you from the bottom of my heart. Solomon, I couldn't write full time if you weren't such a mighty man of valor. You hold our family and me down, and I'm eternally grateful for your sacrifices. I know I get on your nerves when the house is a mess, and I order pizza instead of sometimes cooking because I'm in 100 percent creative mode. Thank you for understanding me, getting behind my vision, and supporting my plight to reach the top. I love you, baby.

Mama and Daddy, you have supported me through thick and thin from the very beginning, and you've always believed in my dreams. Thanks for everything you've poured into me. I love you two dearly.

Kwamah, you are any auntie's dream. No matter what, you always have my back. Thanks so much, nephew.

To my siblings, Dawn, Lance, Shirley, and Nikki, I say thank you. We are the Fabulous 5 for life because we're stuck together like glue. Mama and Daddy did a great job raising us and teaching us the valuable lesson of always sticking together. I love y'all crazy Negroes to pieces.

Acknowledgments

Dawn and Nikki, you two deserve a special shout-out for involvement in my writing process. I couldn't do what I do without you. Much love!

To every member of the Randall, Fults, and Berewa families, I say thanks and God bless you. I'm proud to be a part of such strong people.

Thank you, Selinda, for being such a great attorney and handling my business. You are my sister from another mister until death.

I am blessed to have the greatest literary agent on the planet in N'Tyse. Girl, I owe you so much. You believed in me right out of the gate. Thanks for making my dream come true.

Dawn, Nikki, Ashley, Deborah Anne, Katanga, Valentia, Christan, and Cherell, you ladies are the dream team of screeners. I love you all endlessly for what you do for me. Hugs and kisses!

A shout-out to Central High School (Macon, Ga.) class of '86. We're the baddest class in the universe—hands down. I am blessed to be a member.

Chapter One

Tyson

"Woo-hoo! Take it off, Mr. Chocolate! Take it off!"

"I w-want . . . want to see that l-looong choc . . . chocolate snake, b-baby," a thick brunette with multiple piercings and tattoos slurred. She was intoxicated beyond the max.

The rowdy bachelorette partygoers burst into a drunken fit of laughter and started chanting, "Take it off! Take it off! Take it off!"

I never knew white chicks could be so damn *ratchet.* These girls were wild as hell. The bride-to-be and I were the only two sober people in the entire room. Shit, even Precious, the overly pampered poodle, seemed smashed. I peeped her little ass in the corner barking and jumping up and down like my striptease was making her little pussy wet too. That was fine with me as long as I was stacking paper. A poor and struggling law school student needed all the money he could get his hands on.

Actually, I was a long way from poor, but I wanted the extra money. And I enjoyed the thrill of controlling a room full of women with my body. Anyway, I rolled my hips and grabbed my crotch when my *insane* light bill popped inside my head. The climate was changing in the ATL in mid-October. The temperature was dropping lower with each passing day as the weather transitioned deeper into fall. I couldn't have my pretty baby girl freezing in her crib. That's why daddy was about to turn up the heat on these silly-ass, desperate white chicks.

I removed the loose bills from my black silk bikini briefs and stacked them into a neat pile without missing a beat to Ginuwine's "Pony." I turned my ass to them broads and shook it like a salt shaker. They went *loco!* I swear I could smell pussies creaming throughout the room. I did an exaggerated version of the snake in slow motion all the way over to the table where I had placed my moneybag. I dropped my stack inside as I rolled my hips. I did a quick about-face and grabbed the waistband of my briefs teasingly. Screams rose to a deafening decibel. I had the girls eating out of the palm of my hand. Some were actually licking their lips and salivating. Without warning, I pulled at the snatch-away sides of my drawers and gave them what they wanted. When the fabric hit the floor, it sounded like Sunday morning at a black Pentecostal church. Chicks were screaming like crazy, waving their hands in the air, and convulsing out of control.

"Damn, I'd like to taste that big dick," a redhead screamed.

An exotic-looking snowflake with violet eyes and midnight hair pushed through the crowd with a bottle of Jack Daniel's in her hand. She stumbled toward me and stared at my dick for a moment as if she were inspecting it. She raised the bottle of whiskey to her full lips and took it straight to the head for a looong swig. Then, in an accent I wasn't familiar with, she informed me, "I'm about to call my gynecologist because I'm going to need emergency surgery before the night is over. I want to ride you all the way to the equator and back."

The pot had been stirred. The women started cheering, cussing, and hooting like dirty, old men. I shook my head and inched backward with sweat dripping heavily from my brow.

"Where's a fucking yardstick? I want to measure that baby!" Rhea, the chick who had introduced herself to me as the bride's cousin, shouted at the top of her voice.

A few intoxicated snow bunnies lunged toward me. I backed away quickly because I didn't want *Thunder* to get handled to the point of injury. Some of the females were bold enough to reach for my junk. It was times like this when I needed a bodyguard. I moved farther away and smacked my thighs as I thrust my hips upward with force like Bobby Brown used to do back in the day. I was stroking in the air with Thunder swinging back and forth and side to side. My well-toned pecs and abs were shiny like new money because I'd oiled them just right. I threw my head back and did a slow belly roll, giving my newfound fans a better view of the long and thick python dangling between my thighs. I knew what I'd been blessed with. Hell, I impressed my damn self sometimes. My dick was my moneymaker, and that was exactly why a wicked amount of bills was lying on the floor all around me. A couple of loose dreadlocks that had escaped from the rest of them I'd secured at the back of my head with an elastic band were swinging in my face as I went in for the kill. I was humping and bucking these white chicks into delirium.

"I want to kiss it!"

"Let me touch it! Let me touch!" The blond babe with blue eyes fell to her knees at my feet. "Please, let me touch it!"

I stepped back again. I was kind of scared until I looked into the steel-grey eyes of this one chick who seemed fascinated, but she was maintaining her cool. Make no mistake about it. She was lit up like a Christmas tree. I had watched her throw back tequila shots like a dude just minutes before I started my routine. Almost in delayed time, she floated forward and placed her petite body between her shameless friends and me with her arms outstretched. It was like she was trying to protect me. The bride pushed the button, shutting off the music on the Bose system.

"The party's over, ladies!" Miss Grey Eyes yelled over the loud boos and hissing in the room. "We bridesmaids have a group appointment at Bubbling Brook Spa at eight o'clock sharp in the morning. Let's call it a night so we can sleep off all of the booze we've consumed."

As the crowd of women began to disperse, she turned around in circles, searching for something on the floor. She found my briefs, picked them up, and handed them to me without saying a word. I watched her eyes crawl from my face down to my chest . . . and lower. When her grey orbs reached my dick, she drew in a quick breath. She exhaled it slowly before she swallowed hard.

"I have one question," she whispered, filling my nostrils with the harsh smell of tequila.

"I'm listening."

"Is it real?"

"Huh?"

"Your penis . . . Is it *real?*"

"Touch it and see."

Time, silence, and curiosity held us in place, staring each other down. The dare had been tossed. She'd been bold enough to ask the question, and I had returned her boldness with the invitation to find out. I was a future attorney. Evidence always solved the case. And I had *hard* evidence for her ass.

Instead of satisfying her curiosity, she reached into her bosom and pulled out a white envelope. "I'm Mallorie, Bridgette's maid of honor. Here's the rest of your fee. Thanks for coming. Have a good night."

I removed the damp envelope from her hand and smiled. Fear caused Miss Grey Eyes to spin on the balls of her feet and get the hell away from me in a hurry. She headed straight to the bar in the corner of the room. I was amused that she needed a drink. After all, she had just shut down the party for the rest of the guests. I guess she was about to try to drown the lust and temptation I had stirred up inside of her.

I heard Genesis crying the moment I entered the apartment. I dropped my duffel bag on the floor, rushed over, and removed her from Pilar's arms. I also grabbed her bottle of breast milk mixed with formula. "I got her. Go back to bed. Daddy can take care of his princess before he starts looking over case files."

I didn't expect a "thank you" or even a greeting from the mother of my child, but either one would've been nice. Pilar was a *trip*. After a failed eight-year relationship, a baby, and six months of living together for the sole purpose of coparenting our child, she could at least be civil. But I guess that was too much to ask for from a bitter woman. It's funny because *I'm* the one who should've been bitter. Pilar's ass had cheated on me during my second year in law school. Yeah, almost two years ago while I was busting my ass, trying to stay ahead of the pack at Emory University School of Law, she was out screwing around with a big dumb-ass motherfucker named Chad. She was slick with her shit back then, and I was too busy even to notice any damn thing. The only reason why I found out was that she'd gotten knocked up and didn't know if the other cat or I was the father.

Pilar's pregnancy was a painful waiting game for me. The experience was a fucking *nightmare*. There I was, going to doctors' appointments with my high school sweetheart, looking at sonograms, and shopping for a baby that I wasn't even sure was mine or not. But I wanted to do the right thing, just in case. Where the hell was Chad? That stupid bastard was MIA. He didn't give a shit about Pilar. She had risked the relationship we'd started when we were 16-year-old sophomores at Excel Academy for a sleazy affair with an asshole.

No one knew better than Pilar did about my dreams to become the next Johnnie Cochran. I had to prove a point to my low-life father. I needed to show him that even though he had left my mother, sister, and me devastated for a white woman, we could still rise. I was going to be a more successful man, father, and attorney than he ever was. I had shared all of that with Pilar. That's how come I couldn't understand why she would mess around on me. Our future together was looking bright.

Anyway, she *did* cheat on me with an Arena Football League player from the Jacksonville Sharks named Chad Morris. Pilar and everybody else thought that punk was going to the NFL for sure. Well, his ass ain't. He broke his neck trying to show off for some pro scouts in a throw down against his team's archrival, the Orlando Predators. He made a full recovery, but no NFL or Canadian teams will give him the time of day. They consider him damaged goods. I don't take any delight in his unfortunate life-changing injury because the dude could've been paralyzed according to his doctors. The main fracture was a sliver of an inch away from his spinal cord. Although he didn't deserve it, God had watched out for that buster.

Chad's injury happened a couple of months after Genesis was born, so he'd had plenty of time to check in on Pilar during her pregnancy to make sure she was okay, but he rarely ever did. And it served her unfaithful ass right. I was on my job the entire nine months, knowing there was a fifty-fifty chance that the baby wasn't even mine. But I was there when Genesis was born. Chad was calling Pilar's cell phone periodically while she was in labor, no doubt praying like hell that he wasn't the father.

Luckily for me, my daughter entered the world looking just like her daddy. Chad's worries were squashed the instant I laid eyes on my pretty little princess. That bulldog-looking son of a bitch was too damn ugly to make a baby as beautiful as Genesis. But, of course, a paternity test was performed immediately, and it confirmed that I was indeed the father.

I upgraded from a studio apartment to a two-bedroom spot and moved my daughter and Pilar in with me when they were released from the hospital. That back-and-forth-from-Mommy-to-Daddy shit wasn't an option for my baby. I was determined to raise Genesis as a hands-on, ever-present father, unlike Tyson Maxwell Senior. That fool had skipped out on both of his children. I didn't want to be anything like him. Although at the time I couldn't stand the sight of Pilar, I was in love with our daughter. We've been living together as a family for six months. It's a dysfunctional one, I must add, but a *family,* nonetheless.

Genesis and I share the master bedroom. Her crib, changing table, and dresser are in my sleeping quarters. Because Pilar doesn't work, she cares for our daughter most of the time while she takes classes toward her master's in sociology online. I'm a hustler. In addition to my internship with the Fulton County District Attorney's Office, I work some weekends for a landscaping company and strip at private events for *ladies only.* And they're usually white women I'd never see again. With my multiple incomes, I pay the rent, all of the utilities, and buy groceries. Plus, I maintain health insurance on my daughter and keep her dressed in brand-name clothes. Pilar doesn't contribute a dime to the household. She does take excellent care of Genesis, though. I have to give her credit for that.

Chapter Two

Mallorie

I couldn't get the vision of that sexy black stripper out of my mind. I was sexually frustrated even after masturbating with my trusted vibrator, treating myself to the orgasm of the century while thinking about him. I was still horny as *fuck,* though. How the hell could that be? There was something about black men in general that turned me on. They seemed so rugged, dangerous, and in command—Nothing at all like Collin. Mr. Chocolate made my panties wet the moment I caught him staring at me. I was forced to take a few shots of tequila to numb my pulsating clit.

Back in undergrad, I had watched plenty of porn flicks with black men in the lead roles. I used to fantasize about sucking a big black dick before having it rammed so far up inside of me that it'd exit through my mouth. I have often wondered how it would taste on my tongue and what it would feel like sliding in and out of my cunt. After my brief encounter with Mr. Chocolate, I was more curious than ever.

His dark fudge skin was as smooth as silk. And his tall, athletic body told me he worked out often enough and counted calories whenever necessary. He stood a few inches above six feet and was packed with muscles in all of the right places. The thick, long, male muscle between his thighs was my most favorite part of his body of all. It was a *monster*. Besides that, I was drawn to his full lips accented by a neatly groomed, curly mustache.

That deep baritone voice of his made me shiver when he dared me to touch his dick before he smiled, displaying a set of perfectly straight, white teeth. I couldn't get the vision of him out of my spinning head. I was drowning helplessly in a sea of lust over him.

Since I couldn't sleep, I left my bed and stumbled into the kitchenette for a drink. I was still pretty tipsy, so I don't know why the hell I was pouring myself a glass of vodka at three o'clock in the morning. All of my suite mates were asleep. We had raved and lusted shamelessly over Mr. Chocolate for a couple of hours once we checked into our lavish executive suite at the W Hotel. *Damn!* I wish I had touched his dick when he dared me. It wasn't that I didn't want to. I just couldn't force myself to do it with a dozen pairs of eyes watching. Every girl who'd attended the party knew I was engaged. Oh, but if he and I had found ourselves in a private place like in the bathroom, an elevator, or a closet, I would've done more than touch it. I would've *tasted* it and probably hopped on it for a wild ride too.

I gulped down the liquor in three long swigs and coughed through the burning sensation in my chest. My buzz crashed down on me quickly, as if I really needed to sink further into intoxication. I was drunk, bored, and horny out of my mind. And it was all because of the one thing my father, the great and accomplished Attorney Joseph C. Whitaker, had always preached to every other unattached female and me in our family to avoid at all cost—*a black man.*

Ever since I was old enough to know the difference between blacks, whites, Hispanics, and others, I've heard my dad's sermons proclaiming that the corruption of mankind was the direct result of the very existence of black men. According to Daddy and his three self-righteous brothers, who are also fellow attorneys in the law firm of Whitaker, Sons, and Associates, which was founded by my unapologetic racist grandfather, all black people are beneath the lowest level of the food chain. And they have no legitimate place in a civilized society. Slavery had been a blessing to the worshippers of Allah and other so-called pagan gods, who had been rescued from the underdeveloped, poverty-stricken continent of Africa. Slave traders had done them all a favor by bringing them here shackled in chains like cargo on ships to the land of milk and honey to teach them how to work hard for a living and introduce them to the God of Abraham, Isaac, and Jacob of the Old Testament. Black people are just ungrateful. After all that European Americans have done for them, they want more . . . and more. Shame on them all.

Uncle Frederick often says to his brothers' delight that if Africans had been left on their own soil, they wouldn't know the difference between the White House and an outhouse. Every time he spits such foolish venom, I want to whip out my voter's registration card to show him, Daddy, and the rest of the lynch mob that I am a proud liberal who contributed to the historic election of our country's first African American president. Yes, I secretly campaigned and voted for Barack Obama in 2008 and 2012. My choice had nothing to do with how fine, towering, and sexy I thought he was. I simply liked his message. And I'd longed to see a black man and his family residing at 1600 Pennsylvania Avenue in Washington, D.C.

I poured more vodka into the glass and guzzled it down before I tiptoed back to my bed. The heavy buzz would knock me out until it was time for me to rise and dive headfirst into my maid of honor duties. Bridgette was so lucky to have found a hunk of a man like Blake. He was good-looking, rich, successful, and all into her. He was exciting, too, and quite funny. He would make Bridgette happy for the rest of her life for sure.

Collin, on the other hand, could barely keep my juices flowing during sex. How the hell was he supposed to make me happy for a lifetime? And why had I accepted his ring and agreed to marry him after such a lackluster and predictable proposal? I guess I'd done what had been expected of me.

The night my beau of three years dropped down on one knee and asked me to become his wife in front of our families, friends, and associates should've gone down in history as the most special birthday I'd ever had. But that was not the case. My twenty-fifth birthday will forever be remembered as the day I finally did something to make my mother happy and proud that she'd given birth to me. Before then, I had always felt like I was only a disappointing afterthought that had slipped into the family right before Sarah Spaulding Whitaker transitioned into menopause.

My brother, Godfrey, has always been the apple of her eye . . . her pride and joy. He still is because he's *perfect*. He was the ideal student in high school, college, and law school. He never dated beneath our family's standards. His wife, Katie, is a prim and proper socialite who came from one of the wealthiest and most influential pedigrees in Atlanta. And she's very beautiful with a tiny size-two figure even after giving birth to my nephew, Garrett. Godfrey is perfect. His wife is perfect. Their son is perfect. My brother has a fucking perfect life.

I, Mallorie Elizabeth Whitaker, have always felt like the family's disgraceful failure. Nothing I've ever done was good enough. I didn't get into Emory University School of Law like Godfrey or the other gang of lawyers in the family because my admission score wasn't high enough. So, to my parents' displeasure, I'm a student at Georgia State University College of Law. I consider my current situation another disappointment on my long list of previous ones. It was awful enough that I'd lost my virginity at the age of 15 in the back of my boyfriend's father's car with blue, flashing lights from a police cruiser illuminating our naked bodies. My dad wrote me off that night when he picked me up from the police station after Wilson and I were arrested for public indecency and other embarrassing offenses. Our relationship and the shell of one I had with my mother have been strained ever since.

Family ties only got worse between my parents and me my senior year in high school when I refused to go to the prom with Carlton Benedict Junior, their trusted date of choice. I wanted no part of that chauvinistic nerd. I didn't give a flying fuck who the hell his father was, what he owned, or how much he was worth. Carlton was a jerk who didn't have an adventurous bone in his body. He had ambition all right, and would no doubt become a wealthier and more renowned real estate mogul than his father. But he couldn't light my fire even if he had tossed me inside of an erupting volcano. So I went to the prom with Juan Castillo and had a blast. And, yes, he fucked me like it was our final day on the planet afterward.

After Juan, my taste for ethnic men intensified to a brand-new level. Maybe I was acting out in rebellion against my parents, or I might've been born with jungle fever. The jury is still out on that one. There's something I know for sure: I wasn't attracted to white guys back then, and they sure as hell don't give me a rush now. In college, I sampled a cultural smorgasbord of men from a cute little Asian to an Italian stud to Ahiga, the Native American. I was never fortunate enough to gain the

attention of a black man, which was and still is my most
desired fantasy. But God knows I have tried. I guess my
flat booty is the antiattraction to *brothas*.

The sweetest juice I've ever tasted flowed from an ex-
change student from Saudi Arabia named Moiz. He and
I met in a philosophy class during my sophomore year,
and he rocked my world twenty-four hours later. He was
my favorite fling of all because he was emotionless and
always in control. I never had to worry about him getting
mushy or romantic on me. He liked to fuck me senseless
and compensate me for my time and attention with his
rich father's money. I, in return, had no problem with it.
We never acknowledged each other's presence in public
settings, especially not on campus. Our interaction was
limited to his condo in Buckhead and my apartment
near Georgia State's campus. We fed each other's fleshly
hunger regularly, leaving our bodies empty of sexual
fluids and energy until he graduated and returned home.
I probably never cross Moiz's mind today, but I think of
him often because he was the best fuck I've ever had.

Two years after my Saudi Arabian boy toy exited my
world, I met Collin. Of course, I wasn't attracted to him
the least bit, but he was a really nice guy. We used to hang
out from time to time, but we kept it friendly. It was cool
to have a "decent" date to all of the high society events
my family attended around Atlanta back then. Mother
fell in love with Collin's white-bread, all-American, con-
servative character. It was funny because he didn't come
from money like we did, but she ignored that. As long
as his name wasn't Tyrone, Pedro, Cho, or Mohammed,
she didn't give a damn. Those ocean-blue eyes and
curly blond hair of Collin's earned him a space in Sarah
Spaulding Whitaker's good graces. Soon after their first
meeting at a holiday gala, Mother started pushing me to
take my relationship with Collin to the next level. After

all, I wasn't getting any younger, and it would be hard to find a suitable candidate for a husband with all of the studying I'd be doing in law school at Emory.

Like an idiot, I slept with Collin, connecting us as a couple. Yeah, he got inside my panties, but I didn't get into Emory. So, I attempted to balance off yet another one of my many failures with what my mother considered my only accomplishment. I committed an unlimited amount of time and energy into my bogus relationship with Collin and maintained good grades at GSU's law school for *common scholars*. Now, I'm on the verge of graduating with my Juris doctorate, and in about six months, I will become Mrs. Collin Cartwright. *Yippeee!* Ain't life grand? I am going to marry a guy who I only love as a friend and share no chemistry with. There is no sexual tension between Collin and me whatsoever. There never has been. I'm not even physically attracted to him despite his good looks and fit build. He ain't my soul mate, and I am not the woman he deserves. My God, he could do so much better.

It's sad because Collin loves me to pieces and tells me often via Skype, FaceTime, in emails, and text messages I receive from him from the Republic of Côte d'Ivoire. He's in the West African nation serving as an interpreter for the United Nations and teaching English to school-age children. I'm expecting him home for a brief visit during the holidays just in time for the lavish engagement party Mother has insisted on hosting in our honor on Christmas Eve. My ability to snag a husband has been her life's delight and planning my $50,000-plus wedding has reversed her age by thirty years. I'm only going to force myself to go along with the façade and pretend to live happily ever after because I want a baby or two. Marriage must always precede the baby carriage in my family. Plus, Collin will make a damn good father. He has a natural rapport with children. They all seem to adore him. Collin Junior and little Isabella Emily Grace will be no different.

With my marriage to a wonderful and successful guy rapidly approaching, and visions of babies crawling and cooing flashing inside my head, why aren't I happy? My heart holds more enthusiasm for Bridgette and her plunge into matrimony tomorrow afternoon than my upcoming nuptials. I feel trapped and suffocated by the dreams of Collin and my parents. I'm not ready to be any man's wife. I still want to party, see more of the world, and explore my sexual options without inhibition.

I closed my eyes and allowed my fantasies to marinate in my psyche as the expensive vodka carried me into a restless sleep.

Chapter Three

Tyson

"Where're you taking her?"

I counted to ten slowly, trying my best to keep from cussing Pilar's annoying ass out early on a Saturday morning. Every spare moment I could steal away from studying and working has always been reserved for Genesis. I couldn't think of any reason why this morning would be any different. I released a pissed-off breath. "I'm about to take her to IHOP for her favorite Rooty Tooty Fresh 'N Fruity pancakes before we head to the park to people watch. Would you like to hang out with us?"

Pilar frowned, smacked her lips, and rolled her eyes *hard* in that order before she walked off. Hell, I guess that meant she wasn't interested in spending family time with baby girl and me. And if she thought we were going to cry, she was terribly off the mark. Genesis and I were used to being a duo. We did the grocery and household shopping together all the time. It was normal for us to get our praise on as a two-piece at Metropolitan House of God too whenever my grandma sends out the search squad looking for us. We always pull up in that little storefront church late but fly as hell to watch the show. Genesis bobs her little head and claps her hands to the beat of the loud drums, B3 organ, and steel guitars that remind me of music straight from a luau in Hawaii. All of that shouting, falling out, and speaking in tongues scares my baby sometimes. It cracks me up, though. I *do* believe in that type of carrying on because I was taught all about it as a child. But now that my mama is a die-hard, Koran-toting, no-pork-eating follower of The Honorable Minister Louis Farrakhan, I feel split between two religious worlds. I have one foot in Jerusalem and the other one in Mecca. Sometimes, I don't know if I want to shout hallelujah or as-salaam alaikum. And I bet some barbecue ribs would taste hella good with a slice of bean pie.

I attached Genesis' car seat to the top of her fancy jogging stroller and made sure she was strapped in securely. I was about to wheel her outside into the cold weather when I heard Pilar's bedroom door slam shut and her light footsteps creeping up behind me. I turned around to find her fully dressed and bundled up for the chilly morning air. Without a word, we left the apartment as a unit of three and headed for my ecru Jeep Laredo.

Pilar's smooth peanut-butter complexion turned crimson before my very eyes when the group of young ladies pushing strollers loaded with precious little ones walked away. I had felt her light brown eyes shooting fire at me the entire time I was exchanging diarrhea remedies and stain-removing methods with the young mothers. Pilar could've joined the conversation if she'd wanted to because Genesis is her baby as well as mine. She had kept her ass planted on the bench because of her unjustified jealousy. I am *not* her man. Our relationship ended three days after I found out she was expecting and there was a possibility that I was *not* the father. Plainly put, Pilar and I are not romantically involved, and she has no right to keep dibs on me. I am free to do whatever the hell I choose to do with whomever whenever I want. There was no reason for her to be pissed off because I had held an innocent conversation with a group of women no matter how pretty two out of the three of them were.

"You may hate me, but you *will* respect me as the mother of your child, Ty," she snapped as soon as I sat down on the bench next to her.

"What did I do that was disrespectful to you?"

"I'm not stupid. You were flirting with the chick with the corkscrew curls right in my face. What you do when Genesis and I aren't around is your business, but don't you dare bring hoes all up in our daughter's face. And I don't want to watch you put the moves on other women either. I should've stayed home."

You damn sure should have! I was tempted to scream, but I refused to raise my voice in Genesis' presence. "I was not flirting with any of those ladies. They all were rocking huge diamonds on their left ring fingers, *especially* the cute one with the corkscrew curls. Besides, I don't pick up chicks when our daughter is with me. That's something I do during my personal time. Now, get out of your feelings and stop pretending like I'm your husband instead of your baby's father."

I got up and walked away, pushing the stroller with my daughter strapped inside. She was kicking and babbling her little heart out as the cool autumn wind blew in her face. Thank God she didn't realize how dysfunctional her family was. No child deserved to be trapped in the fucked-up mess her mother had made of our lives. No matter how hard I tried to pretend that our situation was cool, reality had a way of slapping me in the face. Still, I was determined to keep the three us together under one roof until I came up with a better plan. I ain't going to lie. There have been times when I've wanted to tell Pilar to kick rocks. *Seriously*. My sister, Khadijah, and my militant mama would help me out with Genesis for sure. But I believed every little girl deserved a mommy if she was a decent person. Pilar may have been a disgraced cheater, but she was a damn good mother. So, I would continue playing house with her for the time being.

I have often wondered what's going to happen when I find the perfect chick to kick it with on the regular. Will it be cool for me to bring her to the crib for dinner or allow her to stay the night for a *grown-folks'* sleepover? And what if Pilar hooks up with some dude? Will I come home from work one night and find him butt-ass naked in my kitchen fixing yuca en escabeche? I ain't sure about how our unit is supposed to operate whenever a new lover enters the scene.

As it stands, I do all of my adult activities outside of the home. I spend time with females at their cribs. I have an active sex life, dividing my goods and services between a few different babes who are all aware of my situation. Although the only things that Pilar and I share are Genesis and the apartment, I respect her enough not to rub my personal life in her face. Hell, she knows my sexual appetite and preferences better than anyone else. She knows damn well I'm getting it in with somebody. She can't prove it, though. And what if she could?

Even though I had loved her since the tenth grade, and I'd had every intention of marrying her, I wasn't totally faithful during our relationship. I used to get me some strange coochie every now and then for the adventure of it. It wasn't right, but I couldn't help myself. I truly believed it was a *man thing*. Regardless, I did what I did, but I only got caught *once*. During my sophomore year at Morehouse, Pilar got wind that I was fucking this majorette from Morris Brown College. So, she and a couple of her Spelman College girlfriends launched a full investigation that came to a head at my apartment early one Sunday morning when I was supposed to have been in Birmingham, Alabama, with the debate team. Instead, I had been locked up in my place all weekend long with Tyra Battle doing all kinds of ungodly freakiness. Pilar was pissed and hurt when they barged in on us, but eventually, she forgave me after weeks of me begging her like Keith Sweat to take me back. From that point on, I practiced more discretion whenever I tipped out on her. That was how come I never got caught again.

I guess Pilar's fling with Chad had been Karma paying me a visit to punish me for my past sins. Why didn't I forgive her like she eventually forgave my ass after she'd found me butt naked in my kitchen with that majorette? Because I'm a *man*, damn it! Cats like me don't forgive women for cheating. It's against our genetic code. We're proud creatures. A black woman is not supposed to betray her man's trust. Pilar had crossed the wrong damn line, and now, our lives were totally fucked up as a result.

"Where is Pilar today?"

I handed Genesis a cookie and smiled at her before I looked across the table at my mama. "We dropped her off at home before we headed this way."

"Good. I don't like that girl, and she don't like me. Let her keep her ass in her territory, and I'll do the same."

"Grandma called me Monday," I announced, eager to steer the subject away from Pilar. "The church is having Family and Friends Day tomorrow. She was telling me about the big dinner the mothers are going to serve. I promised her Genesis and I would be there."

"You just keep right on believing in Jesus if that's what you want to do. White folks have had us fooled for over a thousand years. Before they kidnapped our ancestors, bound them in chains, and brought them to this country in ships like animals, our forefathers used to turn to the east five times a day and pray to *Allah*. Crackers beat our original religion out of them and forced them to worship the white man's God."

I wasn't about to get into another religious debate with Dr. Aminata Shahid. I was smart enough to choose my battles, and going back and forth with my mama in a never-ending argument over Jesus versus Allah would be insane. She believed what she believed, and so did I. I was born and raised in the Pentecostal church, but I embraced lots of the Islamic teachings. But my mama wouldn't be happy until my name was Tyson X, and I had sworn off swine for life.

She had been that way since I was 8 years old, which was two years after my daddy had left her, Khadijah, and me for his skinny, blond, blue-eyed mistress. Since then, Mama has harbored relentless, insurmountable hatred in her heart for white people in general. In Dr. Shahid's opinion, all people of European descent were devils. They have been and forever will be the cause of every war in the history of the world regardless of which continent it had been declared and fought upon. Her extensive research has caused her to conclude that so-called white Christians have manipulated and brainwashed minorities worldwide, stripping them of their culture, land, and resources, resulting in overwhelming poverty, disease, and bloodshed everywhere on the planet except for America.

I'll admit that some components of my mama's philosophy bear the truth, but for the most part, she's just plain ole prejudiced. And her feelings are rooted in my father's infidelity and subsequent abandonment of our family. My mama *hates* him, his wife of seventeen years, and my stepsister, Bailey. She resents Tyson Senior's success as an accomplished trial attorney and civil servant in the community because he was a failure as a husband and father to his first family. I'm over him, though, and so is Khadijah. His absence in our lives caused us to strive harder to reach our goals in order to show him that we didn't need him. But it left our mama bitter and cold.

Chapter Four

Mallorie

My clit jumped and hardened every damn time I saw Blake's lips latch on to Bridgette's in a sizzling kiss. It was a good thing I had decided to wear panties to the wedding. Otherwise, there'd be a slow trickle of hot sex liquid running down my thighs. I couldn't remember the last time a man had kissed me into a preorgasmic state. Blake was drinking from Bridgette's mouth like it was a fountain flowing with sweet and sticky honey. After his pronouncement of marriage, the priest even seemed to have experienced some kind of sexual charge from watching the newly married couple swap spit and mate with their tongues at the altar. Now, we were two hours into their very lavish reception, and they were *still* playing kissy face. *Go get a fucking room already.*

I looked around the ballroom before I focused on the dozens of couples on the dance floor wrapped in each other's arms, swaying to the music. The light rock band Mr. Higgins had hired was mediocre at best. I was expecting the best for his little princess's wedding reception. God knew he had shelled out major bucks on Bridgette's dress, flowers, alcohol, and catering. I couldn't imagine why he had hired a band that was more suitable for a middle school prom. I sighed and took a sip of champagne. My parents weren't going to spare any cost for my wedding. Mother wouldn't dare think of it. Hell, I wouldn't be surprised if Bruno Mars or Maroon 5 had been contracted to sing as I strolled down the aisle. But it wouldn't make very much of a difference to me. My wedding day was going to be all about my *mother*. I was sure it would be just as special for Collin as well, but only another expensive bill for my dad.

"Would you like to dance?"

My eyes fell down to stare at the hand that had been extended to me before they climbed higher. Ascending quickly up from his waist and higher to his chest, chin, and eyes, they finally took in the entire face. *Not bad,* I silently assessed. His brown eyes matched his wavy hair. I had always been a fan of a decent set of teeth. Therefore, I was impressed with his. Overall, the tall, good-looking stranger was cute. He was too slim for my preference, I must add, but he was cute, nonetheless.

"Would you like to dance?" he asked again as I gawked.

"I'd love to."

I wasn't a Justin Bieber fan. I was more partial to Justin Timberlake, but I felt awful for the often troubled Canadian-born singer at the moment because the band's lead singer was committing a heinous homicide on his hit, "I'll Show You." But I placed my hand in the unknown gentleman's hand anyway and allowed him to lead me to the dance floor. I wasn't much of a dancer because I had no rhythm or coordination. My mysterious dance partner enfolded me in his arms and guided our bodies in a smooth swaying motion to the beat of the music. He seemed content dancing in silence with no intention of introducing himself or asking me my name. But I wanted to know who the hell he was.

I tilted my head back and looked up into his deep brown eyes and smiled. "I'm Mallorie."

"I know."

"And how would you know that?"

"You're Bridgette's maid of honor. Your name was printed on the program."

I allowed him to twirl me around as if I were a ballerina and draw me close to his nearly six-foot, slender frame again. "Are you a relative or friend of the bride?"

"Actually, Bridgette and I dated a very long time ago. We've kept in touch over the years as *friends,* of course. Anyway, she sent me an invitation, and here I am."

Silence followed that surprise revelation while the band totally destroyed the ending of the song. Bridgette's nameless ex-boyfriend and I danced to two more slow tunes before he released me from his arms and escorted me to the bar on the opposite side of the ballroom.

"What would you like?"

"A shot of tequila would be fine, but I'd like to know the name of the person I'll be drinking with first."

"I'm Adam . . . Adam Warren."

"It's nice to meet you, Mr. Warren. I'll take that shot now."

My eyes fluttered open slowly at the sound of deep and throaty snoring. I sprang to the sitting position in bed when tiny bits and pieces of last night tumbled through my memory. Two things stood out slightly clearer than everything else. I had drunk an oceanful of tequila, and I'd accepted Adam Warren's invitation to join him in his hotel room for more drinks and conversation. What I couldn't recall was how I had ended up naked in his bed. I raked my fingers through my hair, racking my brain for clues. All of a sudden, I cringed as my mind floated back to me giving him a blow job before I'd even removed my satin lilac bridesmaid's dress. *How much fucking tequila did I drink last night?*

I jumped up and started searching everywhere for my panties, dress, and shoes in the thick darkness. Everywhere my bare feet stepped, they landed on pieces of plastic that made soft crunching noises. One clung to my right sole. I lifted my foot to see what it was. Imagine my horror when I discovered a condom wrapper, which seemed to have been one of many, was stuck to my foot. Well, at least we had practiced safe sex. It was too bad I couldn't remember if it had been great sex or not. Judging by the several empty condom packages on the floor, we'd fucked up a shameless storm. A vision of Collin appeared in my head. I felt awful. He didn't deserve a fiancée like me. I touched my engagement ring with my right hand. The cool platinum setting brought back memories I had no business reflecting on in the aftermath of a fuck fest with another man who happened to be a stranger.

I closed my eyes in a desperate attempt to erase Collin, my unfaithfulness, and my engagement ring from my thoughts. I needed to get the hell out of Adam's room and sneak into my own without waking my suite mates. I didn't have the strength or mental capacity to face them. I wasn't a creative or convincing liar by any stretch of the imagination. It often made me wonder what kind of lawyer I was going to be. All attorneys were professional liars. I was far behind in my future craft, but I figured I would learn how to taint the truth someday very soon.

"Are you leaving?"

I froze, unsure of what to say. Hell, yeah, I was about to flee Dodge, but I didn't want it to seem like I was one of those loose women who had only spent time with him for sex.

"I didn't want to wake you. I was going to leave you a note and my number. Some members of the wedding party are going to meet for breakfast in the morning. The maid of honor is expected to be there." I laughed nervously for no reason at all. I guess I was embarrassed.

"I understand. And I'm sure you wouldn't want anyone to see you leaving my room in the morning. The rumor may find its way to your *fiancé,* right?"

"If you knew I was engaged, why did you come on to me?"

"You're engaged, and I'm married. Your fiancé obviously didn't attend the wedding, and I left my wife and kids back at home in New Jersey. We had a good time. I won't tell anyone about our little secret. What's the big deal?"

"You bastard!"

I slid into my panties, seething before I ran into the bathroom with my dress and one of my shoes and slammed the door. I swiped the wall with my free hand, searching for the light switch. When I turned it on, I came face-to-face with myself in the mirror. I hated what I saw. I stared at a pretty girl with such a big heart. I knew I was a good person, but I often made the dumbest mistakes. Last night, I'd made a *huge* one. I turned on the faucet, cupped my hands to catch a few water drops, and splashed them on my face. I slipped my dress on and tucked my shoe under my arm. When I stepped back into the bedroom, Adam was holding my other shoe and my purse. He smiled when I snatched both items and growled at him in anger.

It was funny how I had missed his arrogance the night before. Then again, I may have been too toasted to recognize it. He was a tall, tanned, and attractive man. But he was a jerk—and a married one with children at that. He leaned against the wall and folded his arms across his bare chest. He was as naked as the day he was born, but I was too pissed and humiliated to notice or be impressed.

I tucked my other shoe and evening bag under my arm and stormed past him. His cocky snickering almost made me turn around and punch him in the stomach. But even though I had acted like a sleazy whore last night, I still thought of myself as a lady. Ladies didn't throw punches, but they did suck off and fuck random strangers, I supposed.

The best man winked and gave the couple a thumbs-up. "Have fun, you two."

"Take lots of pictures!" one of the bridesmaids shouted.

"And make me a grandbaby!" Mrs. Higgins yelled before she blew a kiss.

The small crowd smiled, gushed, and wished the new-lyweds well before they took off for their fourteen-day honeymoon in Paris. I giggled and waved with a myriad of emotions stirring within. I was happy for Bridgette, my good friend of six years, but at the same time, I was jealous of what she and Blake shared. I wanted what they had, or at least I *thought* I did. I longed for a man who could set my body on fire with his eyes. I wanted a lover who would never grow tired of having his way with me day in and day out. And in those times when we weren't in bed feasting on each other's bodies, I wanted us to be thinking about it. I wanted the whole nine yards, but not just yet.

Blake fired the engine of his red BMW and peeled out of the parking lot of the W Hotel. I smiled and waved one last time, fighting back tears of joy as well as those of sadness. I wanted to be genuinely excited for them, but I was of a different breed. The things that usually brought joy to most women my age and socioeconomic status did absolutely *nothing* for me. I loved adventure.

I was an explorer and a risk taker by nature. For spite, I had often bucked against the norm and all forms of tradition and predictability just to piss off my family. I was intrigued by mystery and the abnormal. I was drawn to any and everything that was deemed forbidden. I was indeed the black sheep of my family and the oddball amongst my friends.

Chapter Five

Tyson

I lifted Genesis at arm's length to check out my hair-styling skills. She smiled at me and drooled with a sparkle in her big brown eyes. "You look just like your nana, baby girl. Daddy picked out your itty-bitty 'fro to perfection. It matches my militant mama's."

I secured my daughter in her swing and turned it on to its slowest speed. She looked like an African baby doll all decked out in her kente cloth jumper and black boots. The solid gold studs in her tiny earlobes shaped like the continent of Africa really stood out. Overall, my baby reminded me of a beautiful little princess from the Motherland. I grabbed my cell phone and snapped a few pictures of her before I started getting dressed.

Mama was on her way over to pick up Genesis so they could spend the day together while Pilar studied. I wouldn't be surprised if she'd be able to enunciate the words "cracker" and "white devil" perfectly by nightfall. I chuckled at the thought. I wanted Genesis to be proud of her race and culture, but I didn't want her to be a racist or a bigot. My mama needed to keep all of her hate to herself. I was all about black pride and preserving our rich heritage, but I wasn't down with annihilating the white race or any other race for that matter.

I turned my back to my daughter, untied my towel, and bent down to step into my drawers. Pilar appeared in the doorway of my bedroom just as I pulled my boxer briefs over Thunder. I saw a hint of a smile touch her full lips as her eyes took in what used to belong to her and *only* her. She missed my dick. I noticed the longing in her light brown orbs. If I were to ask Pilar to let me make love to her, she would oblige me in a heartbeat. Our sex game used to be on point. She knew what I liked, and I knew how to turn her all the way out. We used to try to please each other so good to the point that we never failed to wear each other out. Pilar's freakiness used to put a cat to work, and I always delivered.

I swear I injured Thunder one night in undergrad when we were on spring break in Daytona Beach, Florida. Pilar and I had smoked some weed they call loud on the beach, and it gave us the crazy munchies. After we pigged out at the Waffle House, we went back to our hotel room and fucked like a pair of wild rabbits on steroids. Man, I was in that pussy all night long in positions that would've confused celebrated yoga instructors and any physical therapist on the planet. When I woke up the next morning, we were in the bathtub without any water, and Pilar's ass cheeks were on the side of my face. I don't know how the hell we had ended up twisted around each other like two pretzels, but it was *insane*. Thunder was sick, though. He was red and swollen. And he had a *fever*. I ain't lying. Pilar tried to nurse him back to health with an alternating method of treatment of ice cubes one hour and warm wet cloths the next. It didn't help.

My dick was out of commission for the rest of our stay in Daytona. It was tender to the touch, and it even hurt whenever I took a piss. There was no rash or discharge, though. Pilar thought a little head action would make it feel better, but it didn't. I cried like a little bitch when she covered Thunder with her hot, wet mouth because it hurt like hell. I went to the emergency room as soon as we returned to the A. The attending physician laughed at me after his exam. All tests for sexually transmitted diseases came back negative. The doctor told me the only thing wrong with my penis was it had been used too much in a rough manner over a short period of time. I simply needed to give it a break.

Pilar released a fake cough, yanking me from a memory in our past together. "I'm going to the library to study now, but I'll be back before your mother returns with Genesis."

"Oh, nah, I'm going to pick her up from my mama's crib after I leave the courthouse this evening. You don't have to rush back. Take your time."

"Okay. I'll see you this evening then. There's a tuna casserole in the fridge. I woke up early this morning before daybreak and made it. There's a mixture of breast milk and formula on the top shelf next to it. I puréed some fresh squash and spinach for the baby too. Don't forget to give it to your mother."

I nodded, still standing in place in just my drawers, feeling somewhat uncomfortable. I had no idea why, though. I got butt naked for strange white women all the damn time. Pilar was the mother of my child, and she was as familiar with my body as she was her own. I shouldn't have been feeling some type of way because I was half naked in front of her. I was tripping.

"Cool," I finally said to end the awkward moment.

"I'm so sorry, sweetie," I mumbled as I bent down to pick up the folder and documents from the floor. "I was in a rush and not paying attention to where I was going. Please forgive me, ma'am."

"It's fine. I was out of it too. My mother says I act like I'm lost in space sometimes."

I handed the young lady the folder and court documents. I smiled at her when our eyes met and locked. Then I nearly choked on air when I recognized her face.

"*Mr. Chocolate?*" she shrieked, clearly in shock.

"Hey, lady, you've got to chill with that." I looked around the busy third floor of the Fulton County Courthouse and noticed a few pairs of eyes watching us. I cupped her elbow and gently pulled her to her feet. I guided her off to the side, out of the way of nonstop body traffic.

"What . . . what . . . What are you doing here?"

I ain't no criminal about to appear before a judge if that's what you're thinking.

Yeah, that's exactly where her mind was. Her steel-grey eyes that had checked out Thunder thoroughly Friday night told me so. I had to set her ass straight. "Believe it or not, I'm a law school intern in the DA's office."

"Get the fuck out of here." Her voice was low, but it was far too animated for my comfort.

"It's true. What you witnessed Friday night was just my side gig. It's also a very well-kept *secret* that I wouldn't want to go public, especially around here. Do you feel me?"

"Oh, yeah, sure, I totally feel you. Your secret is safe with me."

I stuffed my free hand inside the pocket of my suit pants and studied her face closely. She was a cute white chick with long dark brown hair that I'd mistaken for black under the dim lighting at the bachelorette party. Her pointy nose and thin lips gave her a girlish look so unlike the lustful drunk I had encountered Friday night. "What's *your* story? Why are you running around the courthouse colliding with people?"

"I'm a law school intern too."

"With a firm, I bet."

"Yeah, I'm with Brown and Shackleford."

"You're stomping with the big dogs, huh?"

She giggled. "I guess so."

"I'm Tyson Maxwell Junior," I said, extending my hand.

"I'm pleased to meet you," she returned, shaking my hand. "My name is Mallorie Whitaker. So, what law school do you attend?"

"Emory."

Her eyes almost popped from their sockets. I believed she was surprised at my answer, but I couldn't figure out why. I think I was offended. I wondered why it was so hard for her to believe I was in my final year at Emory University School of Law. *Is it because I'm black?* I wanted to ask her bony, white ass. The spirit of Aminata Shahid had jumped inside of me and was about to take over. Mallorie must've sensed it because I watched her countenance transpose within seconds.

"That's great. Emory is an excellent school. I attend Georgia State."

I nodded, realizing what had just happened. Mallorie was shocked shitless that a young black stripper had been smart enough to get into a law school like Emory. Hell, she didn't know the half of it. Not only had I been accepted to Emory, but I'd also earned admission to Harvard, Princeton, and Yale among others. The only reason why I had stayed home to attend Emory was that I didn't want to be separated from Pilar.

I smirked and cocked my head to the side in sheer ghetto-style arrogance. "Was GSU your first choice of law schools?"

"No, it wasn't. *Emory* was, but I didn't have the LSAT score."

"I'm sorry to hear that," I lied straight through my teeth, feeling victorious. "Hey, I've got to run, Mallorie. It was good to see you again."

My head snapped quickly to my left when someone tapped on my window, snatching me away from my music. I was usually more observant in the parking deck, but I had allowed Tupac's "Trapped" lyrics to take my mind someplace else. The dude was a legendary musical genius with a socially conscious mind. Man, he'd departed life way too soon, but his impact on the urban community would never die.

I was surprised to see Mallorie standing next to my ride, smiling and waving. I rolled my window down. "What's up?"

"I was about to get in my car when I noticed you sitting here. Are you done with work for the day?"

"Yeah. I was just killing some time before I head to my mama's house to pick up my daughter."

"Wow! You have a *kid?*"

"Yeah, I have a 6-month-old baby girl. Her name is Genesis," I told her, tilting my head toward the picture of my princess on the dashboard.

Mallorie leaned in closer and stared at my baby's smiling face. "She's beautiful."

"Thank you."

"Well, I won't keep you from your daddy duties. I just saw you, and I wanted to say something." She offered me a business card. "If you ever feel like talking about the law or anything else, give me a call. Maybe we could meet for lunch."

"Cool." I stuffed the card in my breast pocket before I started my engine. "I'll see you around."

I backed out of my parking space and drove toward the exit of the deck. Through my rearview mirror, I saw Mallorie unlocking the door of a silver, late-model Mercedes GLE Coupe. More than likely, she was a spoiled and pampered rich chick who had been given everything her heart desired. But not even money had secured her a slot in the law school of her choice. Wealth was a good resource to have, but it couldn't buy happiness or a whole lot of other things.

I didn't have much, but my life was cool enough for right now. My plan after law school was to land a job at a reputable law firm, defending innocent, accused criminals and make globs of money. I wanted to purchase a home with a huge backyard so Genesis could play and entertain her friends in a secure environment. I was going to give her the world. I wasn't sure how Pilar was going to fit in, but she would be somewhere close by.

Chapter Six

Aminata

I took my time walking to my front door from the den. I wasn't ready for my grandbaby to leave. I had enjoyed her so much. She was pretty and smart, just like her nana. Sometimes, I wished Tyson would get rid of Pilar. Then he and Genesis could move in with Khadijah and me. But I had to give my son his props. He wanted to raise his daughter in a family setting. He wasn't anything like his trifling-ass father. All that fool had ever done for my babies after leaving them for that white devil was throw checks at them. *I* did everything else. Sure, he used to show up and stick out his chest at special events whenever Tyson or Khadijah was honored for one accomplishment or another, but that was it. I, Dr. Aminata Shahid, am responsible for the success and productivity of the two Maxwell children. And I will shoot anyone in the heart who'll say anything different.

I unlocked my door and opened it.

"Dang! What took you so long to get to the door, Mama? It's cold out there," Tyson complained, crossing my threshold.

"Boy, don't come in here questioning me. Genesis and I were watching TV in the den."

"I hope y'all were watching something suitable for kids. She doesn't need to watch any more Farrakhan sermons or Malcolm X documentaries."

"My grandbaby will watch whatever the hell her nana wants her to watch whenever she's in my home. But to ease your mind, we were watching Sprout, sir."

I walked toward the den with Tyson a few steps behind me. When we entered the room, Genesis looked up, smiled, and started kicking her little feet. She was a daddy's girl. I loved the bond Tyson and his daughter shared. It was quite special.

"Hey, baby girl. Your daddy missed you." He released the restraints and lifted Genesis from the bouncy chair. "Did you miss Daddy? Did you?"

"No, she didn't miss you because she was with her *nana.*"

I sat down on the leather sectional, and Tyson joined me with Genesis in his arms.

"Was she a good girl?"

I nodded. "She always is. I love spending time with her, Tyson. If you would take out the trash and move back home, I would see my grandbaby every day."

"Mama, please don't start. You know the deal."

"Yeah, I know you're struggling to keep a roof over your head, and Genesis' too, while that *whore* gets to live carefree. I understand that you want the baby to be raised in a two-parent household, but you're cheating yourself, son. You need to work out a new arrangement because your current one is jacked up."

"I'm not going to put Pilar out on the street, Mama. And I refuse to allow her to move to New York or Jacksonville and take my baby with her. That's not an option. I know my present situation ain't perfect, but it's the best I can do for now. Stop worrying. After I finish law school, things will change. I promise."

"*Humph,* I damn sure hope so because I want you to meet a nice and successful young lady to settle down with. Then you can give me some more grandbabies *after* you put a ring on it. The burden is all on you because Khadijah ain't thinking about getting married or having babies any time soon. She's one of those *contemporary* women driven by her career and money."

"Yeah, Khadijah is going hard on her career path to becoming a doctor. I'm proud of my little sister. But I want to get married and have two more kids. I just hate the idea of having a wife and a baby mama. My dream was to have a traditional family, but—"

"That skank screwed it all up."

"Pilar ain't no *skank,* Mama. Yeah, she cheated on a cat, but she's a decent person outside of that. And remember, she's the mother of your only grandchild. Y'all need to find a way to get along for Genesis' sake."

"I don't have to get along with that heifer. All I need to do is love my grandbaby and spoil her rotten. Her mammy can go straight to hell."

The room fell silent. Tyson James Maxwell Junior was not about to have this conversation with me because he knew I would eat him alive on the subject of Pilar Turk. He was also aware of how stubborn and set in my ways I was. I despised Pilar, and there wasn't a damn thing she or Tyson could do about it. I was more hurt by the whole cheating slash who's-the-baby-daddy scandal than my son was.

Pilar and I used to be down like saggy pants back in the day. The girl stopped eating pork two weeks after she met me. And she went natural, leaving Dark and Lovely, Mizani, and Dr. Miracle in the wind because she wanted to rock an Afro like mine. When she caught Tyson screwing that majorette from Morris Brown on his kitchen counter, I took her side during the fallout. But our sister-girl bond went straight to hell when I found out she'd slept with that ignorant-ass football player behind my son's back. It shredded my heart to pieces. I wanted to strangle that heifer with my bare hands for hurting Tyson. My boy was devastated. I was worried he was going to lose his mind over Pilar's whorish behavior.

He was happy but scared when she first told him she was pregnant. The idea of becoming a father actually intrigued him, and he had begun to embrace it. But three days later, Pilar shocked Tyson shitless when she hit him with the confession. She had been creeping with a Negro who was too damn dumb even to spell *cat*. And then she was so stupid that she had rawdogged it with the illiterate son of a bitch, placing my son and herself at risk for Allah only knows how many sexually transmitted diseases. A nasty tramp . . . Anyway, Tyson is Genesis' father, she's my grandbaby, and Pilar is still a worthless trick. Case closed.

The sound of Tyson's cell phone chiming to notify him he had a new text message yanked me from my thoughts of Pilar. It was probably her checking up on him like he was her husband. I watched him as he checked his phone while he bounced Genesis on his knee. His facial expression confirmed my suspicion. It was Pilar.

Tyson stood up and stuffed his cell phone inside his coat pocket. "We're about to head out, Mama. Pilar bought the baby a new movie, and she wants us to watch it together before she crashes for the night. Plus, I need to look over a few case files. I'll call you tomorrow." He kissed my cheek.

"I hope you'll bring Genesis over next Wednesday even if Pilar isn't busy studying. Just bring her anyway to spend time with her nana," I said as I packed her diaper bag.

"I'll try."

I watched Tyson bundle the baby in her pink Eskimo coat before he wrapped her in a blanket. He was such a good father, and it made me proud to call him my son.

I walked him to the door. "Bye-bye, Nana's sweet baby. Come and visit me again soon." I kissed her chubby chocolate cheek and hugged her daddy.

"We'll see you later, Mama. I love you."

"You *are* my love, Tyson."

My land line started ringing as soon as I closed the door. It was probably my mother, and Allah knew I didn't feel like talking to her. Don't get me wrong now. My mother is my heart, but she gets on my last nerve sometimes. The old-school, no-nonsense, Pentecostal evangelist is loving and kind, but she's constantly in my business and always preaching to me about the Jesus she raised me on. I hurried to the kitchen to grab the phone.

"As-salaam Alaikum."

"Wa-Alaikum-salaam," the sexy, velvety voice returned.

My coochie caught a heartbeat. "Brother Dafiq, how are you this evening?"

"I'm blessed, my sister. And you?"

"I am well. Thank you."

"There's an African art exhibit, poetry performance, and fashion show coming to the Cobb Energy Performing Arts Centre Saturday night. It would be my honor if you would allow me to escort you there after we enjoy dinner at Bezoria."

Dafiq was a sweet, accomplished, and very attractive Muslim man who'd been sniffing after me for a couple of months now. I liked him enough, but I didn't trust myself to be alone with him. It had been so long since I'd been intimate with a man that I doubted we'd make it to the event. Hell, as horny as I was, his car probably wouldn't leave my driveway. I could see myself straddling the man and molesting him repeatedly. Oh, I would *make* him take this pussy.

"Sister Aminata, are you still there?"

"Um . . . Yes, yes, I'm here," I stammered after his voice rescued my mind from the gutter. Praise Allah for the interruption.

"Well, would you like to go out with me?"

Baby, I want to go out, in, above, and under with you! my body screamed, but my mind warned me to beware. "Can I give you my answer tomorrow? I need to check in with my son. Grandmother duties often keep me busy. Call me this time tomorrow evening, and I'll let you know."

"Sure, I'll give you a ring. Have a good evening, my beautiful sister."

"Thanks and same to you."

Chapter Seven

Tyson

The movie Pilar had bought for Genesis was amazing. The characters were very colorful with weird and squeaky voices that captured the baby's attention and held it. The music was lively with catchy lyrics, and the graphics were unbelievably vivid. Genesis was fascinated and totally engaged until she became hungry. She always got cranky whenever it was time for her to eat. I volunteered to warm up some mashed potatoes with gravy and spinach for our little princess.

When I returned with the food, a spoon, and a feeding bib, Pilar was breastfeeding Genesis without a nursing cloth. I'm a man, so, of course, I stared at the scene. There was something damn near erotic about watching a beautiful woman openly nurse a baby. In my opinion, breasts were a defining feature of the female anatomy. They greeted a man only seconds after a woman's face, and usually before her butt, thighs, and vagina made his acquaintance.

I watched Genesis suckle the firm and soft nipple of her mother's left breast, extracting milk from it into her body for nourishment. It sounds like a simple and innocent act of human nature, doesn't it? Well, for me, it was anything but. I had sucked that same breast and its match a million times over eight years for an entirely different purpose than my daughter. I was more than familiar with the taste, texture, and scent of both taut nipples and areolas. I also remembered Pilar's reaction each time my tongue, lips, and teeth made contact with the smooth tip of each fleshy mound.

I cleared my throat to make my presence known and in an attempt to steer my mind away from the past. Pilar tore her eyes away from the baby to stare at me. She smiled, and I felt like I was in the early stages of a sexual shakedown. *Is she trying to seduce me?* Thunder stiffened. I didn't have a definite answer, but I did know that if enticement was Pilar's intention, I wouldn't allow it to happen. I quickly placed the plate of food and other items in plain view on the coffee table right before I left the room without saying a word.

"Yo, Maxwell, you've got a phone call up front. I tried to transfer it, but it bounced back."

I swiveled around in my chair to face Stan, another law school intern, and pointed with my finger to the phone pressed against my ear. I was talking to Khadijah. That's why he hadn't been able to transfer the call to my direct line.

"Should I take a message?" He walked closer to my desk, leaned in, and whispered, "It sounds like a *white* chick. She didn't offer her name."

"Khadijah, I've got a call on another line that I need to take. I'll hit you back later. Maybe we can meet for lunch tomorrow if you're not too busy. Anyway, I'll call you this evening."

I ended the call with my sister and stood. I felt Stan's curious eyes all over me. He was so damn nosy for a man. I ignored his silent query, brushing past him on my way up front to answer the general line.

"This is Tyson Maxwell."

"Good morning. It's Mallorie Whitaker. Remember me? I *literally* ran into you at the courthouse yesterday, and I gave you my card in the parking deck."

"Yeah . . . Um, what can I do for you, Ms. Whitaker?"

"Actually, I was hoping *I* could do something for *you*."

I laughed nervously. "Really?"

"I'd like to take you to lunch this afternoon if your schedule will allow it. Do you think we could meet at the Busy Bee Café at one o'clock?"

"What do you know about the *Busy Bee?*"

"Oh my God, it's like one of my favorite restaurants. I *love* soul food. You do too, don't you?"

"Yeah, I do. Will this be a business lunch or is there something else on your mind, Ms. Whitaker?"

"Let's allow it to play out, and then you decide. So, is it a done deal? Will I see you at one or not?"

"I'll be there."

It wasn't hard to spot Mallorie in the popular soul food joint the moment I walked in. She wasn't the only white chick there, but she stood out like a crooked tooth in a tan designer business suit as she sat scrolling through her iPad. She was a white speckle in a sea of mostly blackness, but she looked comfortable in her present surroundings.

"I apologize for being late. Traffic was kind of slow," I told her as I removed my suit coat. I draped it over the back of the chair across from her, sat down, and held her gaze.

"It's fine. I arrived a few minutes early to answer some personal email messages. I don't have much free time during the day to do it."

"Yet, you found time to call and invite me to lunch out of the clear blue sky. What's up with that, Ms. Whitaker? Shoot it to me straight."

"I like you, and I'd like to get to know you better."

I nodded, fully understanding that this rich white girl, who was used to having anything she wanted, had just propositioned me. "Do you want to get to know Tyson Maxwell Junior better or *Mr. Chocolate?* They're two different cats, baby. Don't confuse them."

I could tell that images of my performance and our brief standoff Saturday night flashed before her grey eyes by the way she squirmed in her chair. Even the memories set her body on fire. She reached for the cup of water on the table in front of her, spilling a few drops before she brought it to her lips for a deep swallow. A red hue had covered her cheeks out of the sheer embarrassment of me calling her out.

I sensed that Ms. Whitaker wanted to play the swirl game. She damn sure wasn't trying to date a cat or take him home to meet the parents. Shit, she didn't know whether I was married, divorced, or even heterosexual. This entire meeting was all about *Thunder*. He was stuck inside her brain. Our chance encounter at the courthouse yesterday had turned out to be her lucky day. In her mind, it had given her a second chance to possibly do what she'd been too afraid to do at the bachelorette party when I'd challenged her.

"Which one are you interested in?" I pushed.

"Both."

"I told you I have a daughter. You saw her picture. How do you know I'm not married or engaged to her mother?"

"You don't wear a wedding band. And I don't know *any* woman who would allow her husband or fiancé to be an exotic dancer. So, I'm pretty sure you're single."

She's bold and observant.

"Correct. But my situation is a little complicated because I'm a single dad."

"And how would becoming involved with me further complicate your situation?"

"Whoa! Whoa! Whoa!" I said, holding my hand up and shaking my head. "Who said we were about to become *involved?* That would be hard to do anyway since you've promised to take the ultimate stroll with another man." I peeped that phat-ass piece of ice on her left ring finger more intensely. "*Damn,* girl, how many carats is that thing? I could prepay my daughter's full ride to college with the money ole dude spent on that."

Yeah, she wasn't the only observant one. While executing her bold plan to call a cat and invite him to lunch so she could offer him some ass on a sly, she had forgotten to remove her engagement ring. I guessed her horniness had surpassed common sense and her ability to pay attention to personal details.

"Okay, I *am* engaged to be married in six months, but like your situation, mine is also complicated. You see—"

"Nah, sweetie, there's no need to paint me a picture. Your life is your private business as is mine. Whatever is going on or *not* going on between you and your fiancé is not my concern. I'm ready to order now," I announ-ced, waving to get a server's attention.

I ordered fried chicken, collard greens, baked macaroni and cheese, corn bread, and sweet tea. Mallorie preferred baked chicken with the same veggies, side items, and beverage as mine. We ate mostly in silence, commenting only on how delicious our meals were. I was trying to wrap my mind around her proposed idea that we could somehow hang out together although she was engaged, and the mother of my daughter and I resided under the same roof, coparenting. No, Mallorie didn't know the complicated details of my home life, but she sure as hell knew she had a fiancé.

"He's working abroad," she blurted out, interrupting my pondering.

"Huh?"

"Collin, my fiancé . . . He's working in the Republic of Côte d'Ivoire. He's been there for three months now."

I didn't believe in psychic powers or telepathy and shit, but Mallorie sure as hell had read my mind. Now, I knew her game plan. She wanted to play in all of this chocolate while her vanilla knight in shining armor was away making money to buy boulder-size diamonds and expensive designer suits for her ass. My interest was piqued. Plus, I had always been curious about picking cotton. Tyson Senior had turned his back on his entire family for a lifetime in the snow. What was there about white women that often made brothas lose their minds and sell their souls to the devil? I was tempted to find out.

Mallorie glanced at her high-priced watch and then placed her fork on her plate of leftovers. "If you're not busy tonight, meet me at Connections Bar on Peachtree at eight."

"I'll see what I can do. Remember, I'm a single father of an infant who still wakes up for a feeding and a diaper change every three to four hours."

"Where is her mother?"

I pushed my chair back and stood. I dropped more than enough cash on the table to cover our bill and the server's tip. "I told you it was complicated. But she's around." I put my jacket on.

"Thanks for coming."

"It wasn't a problem. I had to eat something. The Busy Bee is always on point."

Chapter Eight

Mallorie

I had grown frustrated looking at the entrance of the bar every five seconds. He wasn't coming. I should've known better. I had been officially stood up by my fantasy man. That's exactly what Tyson aka Mr. Chocolate represented—my longtime fantasy. He was everything I had ever desired in a man. He was over six feet tall, dipped in fudge, and beyond handsome. I loved his dreadlocks and muscular build. And his midnight eyes gave me chills. His nonchalant demeanor told me he was confidently wrapped in that smooth chocolate skin. And he was smart. He'd gotten into Emory, but I hadn't. He was *fascinating*. I wanted him to let his guard down long enough to indulge me in an intelligent conversation before taking me on a wild ride to sexual utopia.

Unfortunately, it wasn't going to happen tonight. It was almost nine o'clock, and Tyson was nowhere in sight. I drained my Long Island Iced Tea, which was now weak due to the melting ice cubes. I had been nursing it for nearly an hour while I waited for Tyson to show up. I placed a ten-dollar bill on the bar counter and grabbed my coat.

I exited Connections feeling a little disappointed, but I wasn't exactly surprised that my night was about to end with me alone in my cozy Buckhead condo. Looking back on my behavior, I had totally hunted Tyson down and thrown myself at him by calling him on his job and inviting him to lunch. I felt like punching myself in the face. The poor guy probably thought I was desperate or a fucking psycho. I was an engaged woman who had boldly all but offered my cookies to a man I knew nothing about. I shivered just thinking about the opinion he must've formed about me.

I looked up in time to see a cab coming down the busy street in my direction. I stepped closer to the curb and threw my hand in the air, waving like a maniac. "Taxi! Hey!" I watched it drive past me without a single passenger inside. "Damn it."

"Yo, Mallorie, are you leaving?"

My stomach did a triple cartwheel at the sound of his voice. I did a slow about-face, trying my best not to put my excitement on display. "I thought you weren't coming."

"I had to write a brief, bathe my daughter, and rock her to sleep."

"Cool. I understand. Who's watching her now?"

"You ask too many questions." He looked over my shoulder at the bar. "You owe me a drink because you invited me here. I don't usually hang out on weeknights, but now that I'm here, I've got a taste for some Hennessy."

I spun on my heels and retraced my steps back to Connections. I heard Tyson's footsteps close behind me. I headed straight to the bar. We sat on a pair of vacant bar stools side by side. I ordered a double shot of Hennessy for him right away. A few seconds of comfortable silence passed before we even looked at each other. I wasn't sure what was on his mind, but I was glad he had shown up after all.

"I'm going to watch you drink. I'm done. One or two per night is my limit on weekdays. But on the weekends, I let my hair down."

"Oh, I've seen you in action, baby. You drowned your-self in tequila at the bachelorette party."

"I was celebrating."

"Whatever."

The bartender placed Tyson's drink in front of him, and he picked it up and took a sip. Our conversation took off, beginning with politics. We had very similar political views on most of the major issues. Our opinions on organized religion were vastly different, though. The law was our common ground. We spent over two hours dis-cussing various cases we'd worked on at our respective internships and historical events in our country's judicial system. Close to midnight, I was more impressed with Tyson than ever. A handsome, intelligent man with acute insight into the law was a complete turn-on.

Before I could stop myself, I blurted out, "Let's go hang out at my place."

He shot me an unreadable look that made me feel like a fool. "It's late, Mallorie. I have court at nine o'clock in the morning. I need to head back south to Camp Creek so I can crash."

"My condo isn't that far away. And I don't expect you to stay long. I'm having fun because you're great company. I don't want the night to end just yet."

I guess my pitch to prolong our time together was convincing enough. Tyson stood from the bar stool and waited as I settled the bill. When I was done, he walked toward the exit, and I followed him.

"I parked over there."

I looked in the direction where he was pointing. I had arrived in an Uber to avoid traffic. "Let's go."

Everyone has a wish, but not all wishes come true. Only a few of us have been or will ever be lucky enough to live out our most desired fantasies. I was going to become Mrs. Collin Cartwright in April for sure, but before I did,

I wanted to fulfill my ultimate fantasy. I refused to depart life without experiencing what I had always dreamed about. I figured it would be better to satisfy my craving before I got married than to find myself in a sordid interracial affair down the road. Tonight was filled with promising possibilities. I only hoped that Tyson would be willing to take me to a place I had never been before. I longed for the journey to find out what was on the other side.

"This is my ride," I heard him say as he stopped in front of a Jeep Laredo.

"This is a nice SUV. I meant to tell you that yesterday."

"It's not as nice as yours. I saw what you're pushing in the courthouse parking deck." He opened the passenger's-side door for me.

I got inside of the vehicle and waited for him to join me before saying, "I had nothing to do with the kind of vehicle I drive. It was a surprise Christmas gift from my dad last year. I would've preferred a more sensible and less-expensive car."

"Well, let me know whenever you're ready to trade with me. You can have this thing *and* the note too."

I was relieved when Tyson turned on his stereo system as we cruised toward Buckhead. The soulful sounds of R&B surrounded us and eased my nervousness. The wild and crazy girl who had practically begged a man she knew very little about to come to her condo had cowered in a matter of seconds. All of a sudden, I felt shy and awkward. I couldn't think of a single thing to talk about, so I just mumbled the directions to my condo and made hand gestures, telling him which way to turn.

As we got closer to my building, my breathing became so irregular that I thought I was in respiratory distress.

But I wasn't asthmatic, nor did I suffer from any other air-restricted conditions. Anxiety had a grip on me. I was having second and third thoughts about my intentions. I didn't think I could go through with my plan to seduce Tyson, and there were a thousand reasons why. The main ones were that he was a stripper who I'd only met a few days ago, and I had a *fiancé*. And I couldn't remember if I had condoms in my house or not. *Why the hell hadn't I considered those reasons before I invited him to my place?*

It was too late to turn back now, I realized, as the vehicle pulled into a parking space behind my building. Tyson turned off the engine and looked at me. I had no idea what he was thinking. I chanced a glance in his direction with my heart racing close to the speed of lightning. I unbuckled my seat belt with trembling hands and then reached for my purse on the floor. I heard Tyson's door open and close a few seconds later. The next thing I knew, he was standing outside my door, holding it open for me.

We walked quietly toward the entrance of my building side by side. I smiled at Pablo, the third-shift security guard, but he ignored me as he threw suspicious eyes at Tyson. The young Latino toy cop had never seen me bring any other man besides Collin into our building. And tonight, I had the audacity to come creeping home with a mysterious *black man*. I could only imagine what thoughts were running through Pablo's head.

On the elevator ride up to the ninth floor, I caught a severe case of the butterflies. I felt like a thousand pairs of tiny wings were fluttering around inside my belly. I looked into Tyson's piercing eyes, the windows to his soul. I wanted some sign to confirm that we were on the same page. I needed his nonverbal consent that it was okay for me to fulfill my most erotic fantasy in his arms

tonight in my bed. But I saw nothing. His eyes maintained a dark and mystifying depth that seemed endless.
I had never met a man—white, black, or other—with such
an emotionless nature. Tyson's demeanor fascinated
me—but it horrified me at the same time. I wanted him, if
only for one night, but I also wanted to run far away from
him to save myself from myself.

My body jolted involuntarily when the bell chimed,
alerting us that we had reached my floor. Tyson stood in
place with his back against the wall watching me watch
him. The elevator doors swung open. I exited and walked
slowly down the hall. As usual, it was quiet on my floor.
The only sounds I heard were our footsteps advancing
closer and closer to the uncertainty that awaited us
behind door 916.

Chapter Nine

Tyson

Mallorie gave me *the look* before she exited the elevator. Any cat who'd played around in as much random pussy as I had over the past year knew that look. I could spot it from a mile away. It was just strange that I had never allowed myself to get close enough to a white chick to know they had mastered *the look* too, just like sistas. Mallorie's eyes were glossed over with lust and shiny like a pair of new silver dollars. She wanted me, but she would have to spit it out in plain English before I would dare go there. I didn't have time for guessing games or missing clues. And I damn sure didn't want to catch a race case. If Mallorie wanted me to fuck her, she was going to have to ask for it. The situation was already crystal clear to me, though. She had a fantasy to fulfill, and I was just plain damn curious. The overwhelming desire to explore the forbidden and the unknown often led us down paths that we'd never dare to take otherwise.

"Welcome to my humble abode," she announced after she unlocked her door. She rushed to the keypad on the wall a few feet ahead to disarm the security system.

I closed the door behind us and stood in the middle of the foyer checking out my surroundings. Her place was tight, but I hadn't expected anything less. She'd reeked of wealth and privilege from the night I spotted her overdosing on tequila. She'd obviously been born with a few silver spoons in each hand. But even all of Daddy's money couldn't buy her some things. It sure couldn't buy her *me*. She'd sought me out on her own. And I'd bet her pops wouldn't approve of her actions any more than my mama would appreciate me being in a white girl's crib. But Mallorie had initiated our coming together, and I was about to do us both a favor *if* the terms met my satisfaction.

"Tyson," she called my name softly on a faint breath as she walked toward me. "I've never been with a black guy before."

"Is that your mission tonight? Is that why you invited me here?"

"Yes."

"Why?"

"Because if I don't have you right now, I'll die."

It was *on* after that. Her aggression was a new thing for me, but it gave me a testosterone rush that shot straight through the roof. The shit turned me on. When she pushed my back against the wall, my dick turned to stone in anticipation of my first dip in the snow. She yanked at the zipper of my jacket until she got it down and then peeled the leather from my body. Her small, soft hands eased under my sweater and T-shirt, caressing my pecs and abs. At first, when she licked my nipple, sending warm vibrations throughout my body, I felt light-headed. But that tiny spark was nothing compared to the sensations that shot through Thunder when she fondled the length of him through my jeans. He jumped and bucked against the zipper as hard as granite, fighting to get out.

I didn't help Mallorie undress me. If she wanted what was underneath my clothes, she was going to have to work for it. And the girl was putting in the work with her hands, busy snatching, pulling, and unfastening everything in her downward path. When she finally freed my dick from my jeans and boxer briefs, I felt a slight chill sting my exposed flesh. But soon, heat struck me, causing my blood to simmer as Mallorie stroked and explored Thunder in awe, like the black dick was a new discovery to mankind. I opened my eyes and looked down when she dropped to her knees. She teased the head of my penis slowly with the tip of her hot tongue while she continued palming it up and down in a steady rhythm.

I should've been the one humming and growling because *she* was putting the moves on *me*. But all of the moaning and purring in the room was coming from deep within Mallorie's soul as she worked her magic on me. Without warning, she covered the first few inches of Thunder with her mouth and swallowed the remaining length of him gradually, inch by inch. She didn't even gag when the head hit the back of her throat, touching her tonsils and beyond. She moaned and tightened her jaws around my meat and pulled hard with perfect suction. Her salivary glands exploded, secreting a gush of warm moisture. The inside of her mouth and her throat were hot, tight, and sloppy wet.

Mallorie slurped, moaned, and sucked, pulling me in deeper. My dick eased in and out of her throat in a slow yet consistent rhythm. And with each inward motion, her tongue slithered like a snake against my sensitive, engorged muscle. My dick got lost inside her mouth, completely out of sight each time she sucked me in. I watched in awe, and my body tingled all over. My dick felt like it was about to explode. The sounds of Mallorie slurping and moaning mixed with the sight of Thunder sliding in and out of her mouth intensified the sensations traveling like electricity through every muscle in my body. My blood was bubbling like hot lava, and my heartbeat exceeded the speed of sound. I felt a nut mounting like a deadly tidal wave. I couldn't contain it. The oncoming force was overpowering, and I was too damn weak.

"*Uggghhh! Oh shit!*" My heart paused as I released every ounce of semen from my testes into the warmth and wetness of her mouth.

Mallorie continued sucking my dick and twirling her tongue all around it. The slurping changed into loud guttural gulps as she swallowed the heavy surge of come. She finally gagged, and I was afraid she was choking. But I was in euphoria, ejaculating more of what felt like gallons of baby-making sperm. I was hissing and cursing through the best nut I'd ever busted until I heard a gurgling sound. The suction that Mallorie's lips and jaws had on Thunder decreased as her head jerked backward.

"Are you okay?" I asked, out of breath but feeling like the king of the world in my postorgasmic state.

Mallorie nodded that she was all right, but she was coughing terribly and gasping for air. Her face was fully flushed as tears streamed down her cheeks. When I knelt to see what was wrong with her, I saw semen dripping from her nostrils and spilling down her lips. Spittle oozed from the corner of her mouth. My sexual high instantly fizzled away. Mallorie had almost choked while she was giving me head. I felt terrible.

"I'm sorry. I didn't mean—"

"It's okay," she croaked, still gasping for air as semen, mucus, and saliva dripped from her nostrils and mouth.

I snatched my underwear and jeans up over my thighs, hips, and penis before I pulled her to stand. "Maybe you need a glass of water. Where's your kitchen?"

"It's down the hall to the left." She went into another fitful round of coughing.

I hurried down the hall and hung a left. It was dark, so I scanned the wall with my fingertips, searching for the light switch. I found it and flipped it on. The bright lights illuminated an all-white kitchen with stainless steel appliances and a matching center island. The faces of the cabinets were made of glass, allowing me to see their contents. I found one housing the glasses and removed a crystal goblet. I opened the fridge and found a bottle of spring water. I removed the lid and poured some into the glass. After placing the half-empty bottle on the counter-top, I left the kitchen and rushed back to the foyer. But Mallorie wasn't there.

"Mallorie! Where are you? Are you okay? Mallorie!"

I made giant steps toward the back of the condo, passing the kitchen. A sliver of light peeping from under a door to my right caught my attention. I tapped on it three times. I hoped the chick hadn't died on me. I had never experienced anything like this before. I knocked again. Seconds later, I heard movement on the other side of the door, and I breathed a sigh of relief. Thunder and I hadn't killed her after all.

"Mallorie, I brought you a glass of water. Can you let me in? I want to make sure you're all right."

The door opened slowly. Embarrassment had fully covered her girlish features. She looked toward my face, but she avoided eye contact. "I'm fine." She took the glass of water from my hand. "Thanks. Come in."

I followed her into the spacious suite decorated in pastel pink and cream. A fancy round bed gave the room a chic Hollywood vibe. It was huge and enticing. I'd only seen such a unique piece of furniture on television. I was impressed, but I refused to let her know it. She had changed from her sweater and skirt. An Atlanta Falcons jersey—more specifically, Matt Ryan, their quarter-back's jersey, now hung loosely on her petite frame. The hemline stopped at midthigh. I planted myself in the middle of the thick cream carpet while she sat on the bed Indian-style and sipped the water.

"What happened?"

She lowered the glass from her lips and swallowed. "I guess I choked. That has never happened to me before— *ever*."

"Are you good?" I asked, checking my watch.

"I'm fine. But you're not about to leave, are you?"

"Yeah, I think I should. It's late, and you just scared the shit out of me. Now that I'm sure you'll live, I feel like it'll be okay to leave you."

"But I don't want you to go yet. We didn't finish."

"Mallorie, maybe the little mishap tonight was a sign that you shouldn't be creeping on your fiancé. It ain't cool for you to be getting it in with another dude while you're rocking his engagement ring. How would you feel if you were to find out he was across the water slaying African pussy for breakfast, lunch, and dinner?"

"I wouldn't like it," she whispered with her head bowed, staring into the glass of water in her hand.

"I didn't think you would. Come and walk me to the door."

On bare feet with French manicured toenails, she walked toward me, still holding the glass of water. The scent of hot creamy pussy filled my nostrils as she passed by me. I followed her out of her bedroom and down the hall. I grabbed my leather jacket from the floor as the fresh memory of Mallorie giving me the best blow job I'd ever had appeared in my mind's eye. Thunder woke up and jumped to attention. When we reached the door, she turned around to face me. Our eyes bore into each other's for several hushed seconds.

"I'll call you if that's okay with you."

I nodded before I stepped forward and opened the door. I walked out into the hallway and made my way toward the elevator. Maybe I would reach my crib in time for Genesis' next feeding and diaper change.

Chapter Ten

Pilar

I closed my book *Crisis in Suburban America* and turned off my night-light the moment I heard the front door open and close. I didn't want Ty to know I was clocking his comings and goings, but I was. I always did. After I caught his slick ass cheating on me all those years ago in undergrad, I never trusted him completely again. I forgave him and stayed with him because he was my heart, and he still is. A black woman can't live without her heart. Shit, tell me any human being who can.

I've been asked a million times from many people why I cheated on Ty with Chad if I loved him so much. It's a legitimate question, but the answer ain't all that easy to articulate. A combination of things caused me to do what I did, but there's no justification for my stupidity. Yes, I will be the first to admit that sleeping with Chad was the biggest mistake of my life. I own it because it's the gospel truth. I can't take it back, though. Life just doesn't work that way.

But please allow me to explain why I cheated. Understand and accept it or not, but here is my truth. I didn't feel needed or desired anymore at the time. Ty and I had been together since the tenth grade. We were inseparable back then. He was my first, and I *thought* he'd be my only for life. We were the popular couple at Excel Academy, the small private school we'd attended located in the nice section of Cascade in Atlanta. Everyone, including the teachers and administrators, knew we were an item. Our close relationship was envied by many. Girls were jealous of me because I was the bae of the hottest guy in our school, and guys hated Ty because Excel Academy's baddest cheerleader was hitting splits on only him.

I was secure in the relationship throughout high school. Ty and I spent every second outside of school together. My grandmother and his mama didn't mind because they saw real love and commitment between us even though we were young. They weren't surprised at all when we decided to stay in Atlanta to attend college. I think they liked the fact that Ty had chosen to become a Morehouse man, and I would be right across the way at Spelman. It worked. We were so happy and in love. Together, we had mapped out our future. Ty was going to be the next Johnnie Cochran, and I would change children's lives all over the A by curing their minds and spirits as a sociologist.

My dream crashed when I caught Ty cheating our sophomore year in college. My trust in him was destroyed. By the time he entered Emory, it seemed like we were just coasting along and going through the motions. I felt like I was being taken for granted, but I never complained.

School was Ty's focus, often leaving me out in the cold alone, sad, and neglected. I needed his attention. I wanted him to look at me the way he used to. I longed for the spicy love life we'd once had. But Ty didn't have time for any of those things anymore. He couldn't even spare a few moments for *me*. And because I was young and naïve, I started looking for what I was missing inside my relationship . . . on the outside.

It all began with a weekend trip to Jacksonville, Florida, to visit my father. I went to a Sparks' football game with my cousins, Yalissa and Sherraye. They were on the prowl for any available Arena League football player, and I just happened to have been tagging along.

"Where's the victory party at, handsome?"

"Me and some of my teammates gonna be chillin' in VIP at Metro."

"Oooh," Sherraye squealed, placing her hand on number 85's chest. "Can me and my sister and our cousin roll with y'all?"

He licked his lips and pinned me with his eyes. I felt naked standing in the parking lot because of the way he was gawking at me with lust pooling in his eyes. It reminded me of the way Ty used to stare at me from across the library table when he was supposed to have been studying. Back in those days, he could never get enough of me, and I didn't mind giving him every drop of my body and soul.

"Yeah, y'all can meet us there. Tell me your cousin's name so I can give it to the lead hostess. She'll be looking out for y'all. I'll tell her to have someone bring you ladies straight to my table. What's her name?"

Sherraye turned and frowned at me before she looked at the football player again. He had the body of an African god, but his face was nothing to break a fingernail over. "Oh, that's Pilar. She's our cousin on our daddy's side. She's visiting from the A. She's a good little college girl and shit. And she's got a man too."

"Pilar . . . That's a nice name. I like it 'cause it's odd. What kinda name is that?"

"It's Spanish," Yalissa blurted out as if I weren't standing there capable of speaking for myself. "Her mama is Puerto Rican. Anyway, her last name is Turk just like ours."

"So, she's half Puerto Rican. That's how come she's got that creamy skin and pretty hair. That booty is phatter than JLo's too."

I stood there like an invisible statue unimpressed but somewhat flattered. At least he had noticed my presence, although he had yet to address me directly. I would play his little game all the way to his VIP table at the club where I planned to sip expensive champagne and nibble on some shrimp. Then I would return to my daddy's house and sleep like a baby until morning when I would board my flight back to Atlanta to reunite with my man.

As on schedule, I heard Genesis' soft whimpers floating through the baby monitor around one o'clock, putting a brief pause on my walk down memory lane. It was a good thing that Ty was home. He could take care of her while I pretended to be asleep. I heard him whispering to our daughter and moving around their room, which allowed my mind to drift back to the moment when Sherraye, Yalissa, and I reached the club that night. We were immediately escorted to Chad Morris's table as soon as the maître d' heard my name. My cousins had filled me in on the Jacksonville Sharks' star wide receiver on the drive to the Metro. They'd obviously realized he was feeling me, and they wanted to make sure I knew enough about him to make an impression. *Honey, please!* I wasn't remotely interested in some arrogant football player who was trying to conquer my coochie for the night. I had a man. Ty hadn't given me much attention in those recent months, but I was still very much in love with him, and he was always in place.

Bottles were already popping when we approached the table, and Chad kept my champagne flute filled at all times after he pulled me onto his lap. He also kept his big-ass hand on my thigh. I ain't going to lie. I was flirting with him because he was all into me, and I was having a good time. Chad and I danced a few times while Sherraye and Yalissa looked on with envious eyes. I could feel the jealous energy they were shooting in my direction. It was *thick*. So, when they announced they were tired and ready to leave, it came as no shock to me. If a pair of brothers had been pouring champagne for them and feeding them prawns from their fingertips, they would've stayed at the club until sunrise.

"You ladies go ahead. I'll make sure Pilar gets home safely."

Sherraye glared at me, narrowing her eyes to thin slits. Her false eyelashes seemed to be threatening to stab me in the heart. Yalissa was too damn drunk by this time to care about Chad giving me his undivided attention while ignoring the hell out of her and her sister.

"All right, then," Sherraye grumbled. "We'll pick you up from Uncle Leroy's house in the morning at eleven o'clock sharp to drive you to the airport. Be ready."

"I will. I'll see you two in the morning. Good night."

An hour or so later, Chad and I exited the club and walked hand in hand to his gold pimped-out limit-ed-edition Cadillac Escalade. He helped me inside like a perfect gentleman. I felt like a pampered princess in his presence. It had been a long time since I had been treated so special.

"Do you really want this night to end, or would you like to sip more champagne out on my deck overlooking Jacksonville Beach? I promise I'll have you at your dad's house way before the sun comes up."

My heart told me to take my ass to Leroy Turk's house and go to bed, but my ego and pride were screaming something totally different. I thought about Ty and that nasty-ass majorette back in undergraduate school and all of the rumors I'd heard since then about him sleeping with one chick or another behind my back. I knew he had fucked Marvella Johnson although I could never prove it. Regardless, the lack of attention and affection as of lately was gnawing at me. What would be the harm in me spending time with another man? Nothing was going to happen because no matter how much Ty neglected me, he was still my bae, and I loved him more than anything.

"I would love to see your home," I told Chad after convincing myself that spending time with him would have no impact on my relationship with Ty.

We didn't speak again for the remainder of the drive. The faint sound of smooth jazz floating from the stereo speakers kept my mind occupied. It was a remedy for my anxiety.

"We're here," Chad announced, killing his engine twenty minutes later.

I admired the contemporary town house before me. The beige, two-story stucco structure was surrounded by other ones of the same design in various colors. The small oceanfront community seemed peaceful.

Without another word, Chad exited the SUV and walked around it to open my door. He helped me out and escorted me up the stairs to his front door. Once we were inside, he turned on the light in the hallway and smiled at me. "Let me give you a tour."

He led me from room to room in the spacious home, identifying each area like a real estate agent hoping to make a sale. The entire house had been decorated to perfection with vibrant colors, original art, and to my surprise, lots of green plants.

"You have a very nice home, Chad."

"Thanks, but you ain't seen my most favorite spot of all. Come on. Let me show you what made me want this house more than anything else."

I allowed him to lace his fingers through mine and lead me toward a set of double glass doors. I watched him release the heavy deadbolt lock before he pulled the brass handle. We stepped outside on the deck. The scent of saltwater greeted us as we stood under the bright star-splattered sky. The view of the moon glowing over the waves was like a dream.

"Have a seat," he whispered in my ear, the warmth of his breath causing me to shiver. "I always keep a couple of bottles of Krug on chill for company. I'll grab one and some glasses. Get comfortable."

I had time to change my mind about hanging out with Chad. All I had to do was ask him to take me to my daddy's house. But why would I do that? I was long overdue for a good time with a man. I deserved champagne and a few innocent kisses under the stars while enjoying the sea breeze. I sat on the wicker chaise lounge and watched the moonlit, rippling water. It was a beautiful night. I preferred to be spending romantic moments like this with Ty, but he was an entire state away making love to law books and his laptop.

"Champagne for the lady . . ."

I blinked back tears at the memory as I returned to the present. That was the last thing Chad said as he offered me a flute filled with champagne. He placed the bottle on the wicker table and squeezed his massive body onto the chaise lounge next to me. We sipped the sweet bubbly quietly for a while. Then he took my empty flute and placed it on the table. He was a good kisser. I remember that like it was yesterday. He had fast hands too. It felt good being in his arms. Soon, all thoughts of Ty vanished. The next thing I knew, the skirt of my maxidress was above my thighs. My thong was gone, and my legs were spread far apart, each thrown over an arm of the chair. My pussy was being devoured like it was Chad's last supper for life. His long, wide, drenched tongue was at work, slithering from my clit to my asshole in slow motion like a snake. He flicked and twirled it thoroughly over every inch of my moist flesh from hole to hole while he growled like a wild beast. It felt so damn good that I was purring and humming. Shit, I couldn't deny it. Chad Morris was a professional pussy eater.

The stars started dancing as my climax began to build and burn in the pit of my stomach. I couldn't breathe as tiny waves of ecstasy washed over me. A gush of liquid love streamed from my pussy like a dam had burst. Chad kept licking, sucking, and grazing my clit with the edges of his teeth until I floated back to earth slowly and gracefully like a feather.

Everything after that unfolded in a blur. He did use a condom, though. I clearly recall that because I was surprised that a man of his tall height with such large hands and feet could have such an average-size dick. I watched him roll the condom over those four or five measly inches of length and minimum thickness in pure shock. He was in, out, and *done* in about two minutes tops. It was over before it even began. I wanted to cry because I had just cheated on the love of my life, and it wasn't even worth it.

After I got cleaned up, we exchanged numbers at Chad's request, but I had no intention of ever calling him. I never wanted to see him or hear from him again. He programmed my daddy's address in his GPS and drove me straight to his house on Van Gundy Road. He walked me to the door although I didn't want him to.

***

"I'll call you tomorrow night."

I nodded, searching for my key inside my purse. I was relieved when I found it. I unlocked the door and tried to hurry inside, but Chad grabbed my arm and pulled my body fully against his. His lips latched on to mine in a deep, wet kiss that almost made me vomit. I was beyond disgusted. I pushed against Chad's chest and eased out of his snug embrace. He took a step back and reached inside his pocket. He pulled out a wad of cash and peeled a few bills off.

"Buy yourself something pretty," his whispered, pressing the money into the palm of my hand. "I'll talk to you tomorrow after I get settled in my hotel room in New Orleans." He kissed my cheek before he turned and walked away.

Chapter Eleven

Mallorie

I hung up the phone, totally frustrated that I hadn't been able to reach Tyson since the flop at my condo. I had never been more embarrassed in my life. Finally, fate had granted me the opportunity to fulfill my most desired fantasy. And what did I do? I fucked it up *royally*. I had enjoyed my brief sexual encounter with Tyson to the highest degree, though. It wasn't every day a girl like me could have a man of his caliber alone in her home. I had impressed myself when I invited him to my place on a whim. It had given me the boost of courage I'd needed to tell him what I wanted from him. Slutty, sleazy, and easy—I'm sure all of those adjectives had crossed Tyson's mind at some point between the surprise invitation to my condo and the moment my mouth made contact with his juicy, gigantic dick. I had gladly swallowed him whole after dreaming about the experience thousands of times since Bridgette's bachelorette party. Visions of me tasting that thick, long chocolate bar had threatened my sanity every single night. So, when I ran into him at the courthouse, I knew it was fate. That was exactly why I'd acted on it. And for that same reason, I was trying to reach him again. I wanted to finish what I had started. But this time, there would be no screwups.

I sat back in my chair, contemplating my next move. I wanted to see Tyson. I *needed* to see him so I could explain a few things to him. First of all, I'd only choked while I was sucking him because I was trying to show off. It was *my* fault and not his. I was being greedy by taking on more dick and come than I could handle. His penis is *enormous,* and I'd known that beforehand. I'd rushed into the blow job like a fool because I was so damn horny and overly excited. But that beautiful, delicious cock had exceeded my limit. I would have to practice a few times before I could master my deep-throat skills on Tyson. I was more than willing to put in the work, though. I wanted another chance with him. I craved him like an addictive drug.

I picked up the phone and dialed the DA's office for the third time that day. Twirling a strand of my hair around my index finger, I waited for the receptionist to answer once again.

"Hi, this is Mallorie Whitaker. I know Tyson Maxwell is unavailable right now." I laughed nervously. "I just called a few minutes ago, and you told me so. Anyway, I'd like to leave a message for him so he can call me when he returns. Again, I'm Mallorie Whitaker, and I can be reached at 404 . . ."

"Mother is driving me crazy with this engagement party and the wedding. We should skip both events." I giggled at the thought.

"Your mom means well, babe. All mothers of the bride tend to jump overboard. Just go with the flow."

"I will."

"Neither one of us wants the engagement party, but I'm excited about the wedding. What about you?"

I drew the iPad closer to my face so I could stare into Collin's big blue eyes. They reminded me of the ocean off the coast of Aruba. Gosh, they were so pretty. I wished they had magical powers so he could cast a spell on me to make me fall madly in love with him. Then I *would* be excited about our wedding too, and I wouldn't be masturbating every freaking night while I thought about Tyson.

"Babe?"

"I'm sorry, Collin. I got lost in your baby blues."

He smiled. "I'm glad I still have that effect on you. After April the thirtieth, you'll be lost in these eyes forever. I can't wait."

"Neither can I," I lied.

"Go to bed, babe. I know it's late, but I just wanted to see your gorgeous face. I love you."

"I love you too. Good night."

My heart ached for Collin. He was looking forward to me becoming his wife while all I could think about was fucking Tyson. I felt like the scum of the earth, but I couldn't control my craving. I logged on to Facebook and searched for my fudge fantasy. I was surprised I'd never thought about contacting him this way before. After a quick search, I found him. He and his adorable daughter made up the cutest profile picture ever. Four different pictures of her in snazzy outfits were displayed in a collage for his cover. I searched all of his pictures and posts because his page was public. It appeared that he didn't log on very often, but I decided to send a message to his inbox anyway. I simply left my cell phone number and asked him to contact me. I sent him a friend request too.

My jaw dropped when I saw Tyson sitting in his SUV at the red light. It was him all right. I was close enough to the front window of Starbucks to see him clearly. I wanted to bolt from my chair, run outside, and hop inside his Laredo with him, but Julie would think I had lost my mind. I couldn't control my heart. It was beating at a dangerous speed, like I was on the brink of cardiac arrest. I sat there looking at him with visions of me going down on him flashing through my mind. I crossed my legs against the dampness in my crotch. My clit was buzzing. I exhaled when the light turned green, and he pulled off.

"Who were you staring at? I thought you'd seen a ghost."

I looked at Julie and giggled nervously. "I thought I saw someone from work."

"How *is* work?"

"It's great. I'm learning a lot. I'd prefer working in the DA's office prosecuting criminals over defending them, though."

"You better not ever let your father, uncles, or Godfrey hear you say that. They'd have you tarred and feathered."

"I know. They expect me to join the firm as soon as Collin and I return from our honeymoon."

Julie's green eyes lit up like a pair of sparkling emeralds. "Do you have any idea where you guys are going?"

"No. Collin wants it to be a surprise. He only told me to pack for the tropics and bring lots of bikinis. He's going to announce our destination at the rehearsal dinner."

"Oh my God, I'm so excited for you, Mal. Collin is a great catch. I wish he had a brother."

I smiled. "He only has two sisters, but there's this hot friend of his from high school who I think may be just what the doctor ordered. His name is Matthew. I'll introduce you two at the engagement party."

"You will?"

"Sure. Why not? He's single, and so are you. Maybe you two can make a love connection."

"At this stage in my life, I'll settle for a *lust* connection."

I laughed at Julie's choice of words because I knew *exactly* what she meant. I had a lust connection of the most intense kind, but it wasn't with Collin.

"Did you give him my earlier message?"
"Yes, ma'am. I sure did."
"I see. Well, please ask him to call me again. Thank you." I hung up the phone.

Tyson was ignoring me. It had been over a week since our little episode at my condo. I'd been calling him at the courthouse and messaging him on Facebook every day without a single response. *Girlfriend, you have thrown your pride out the window,* my brain screamed as I watched the busy afternoon traffic zip up and down Andrew Young International Boulevard. I couldn't understand why Tyson was hiding from me. I should've been the one dodging him after the way I'd humiliated myself that night. But I couldn't get the monkey off my back. The more he avoided me, the more determined I became. How sick was that?

I knew very little about the guy, but I was helplessly drawn to him. Our conversation at Connections had allowed me to pick his brain only a little. He exuded confidence, strength, and superintelligence. I wanted to know more about him. Hell, I wanted to know *everything*.

I had been checking his Facebook page constantly, hoping I could catch him online. He had posted a picture of his daughter yesterday around noon. She's the most gorgeous thing. Her angelic face reminds me of a baby doll's face with those chubby cheeks. I wondered who her mother was. There were no pictures of her anywhere on Tyson's Facebook page. Believe me. I'd done a thorough search but found nothing. Tyson had told me that he was a single father, but that was all he'd said. I didn't know if he had been married to the child's mother or if they'd only been friends. Tyson Maxwell was a man of many mysteries, and I wanted to crack every damn one of them.

Chapter Twelve

Tyson

I was any and everything except a fool. That was how come I knew Pilar was up to something the moment I walked into the house. The smell of spicy Buffalo shrimp, sweet potato fries, and cheese corn muffins welcomed me. Pilar was a good cook, and she prepared dinner at least four times a week. But she normally only cooked my favorite meal on special occasions like my birthday or New Year's Eve. The fact that she had whipped it up for dinner on an ordinary Thursday evening fired off a warning shot.

Whatever game she was planning to play would have to wait because I had a surprise for Genesis. Daddy had bought his baby girl a new book about zoo animals, and it made noises. Plus, Agatha, one of the assistant DAs, had given me two tickets to Saturday's matinee at the Center for Puppetry Arts. Genesis didn't need a ticket to see the puppet show because she was less than two years old. So, I was going to invite Pilar to go with us. Family activities were important to me, so I tried to plan them as often as possible.

I set my briefcase on the floor in the hall and walked into the kitchen. My world brightened when I saw my daughter sitting in her highchair. She smiled at me and flapped her little arms like a happy baby bird.

"What's up, princess?" I kissed her nose. "What's going on, Pilar?"

"Nothing. Dinner is almost ready."

"That's good because a cat is starving. You cooked all my favorites. What's the occasion?"

"I had a taste for sweet potato fries," she said, drying her hands with a dishcloth. "Nothing goes better with sweet potato fries than Buffalo shrimp. And, quite naturally, I had to throw in my grandma's cheese corn muffins. You ain't complaining, are you?"

"Nah. I was just curious."

I removed Genesis from the highchair and took her into our room. I placed her in her crib with all of her stuffed animals while I changed from my suit into a pair of sweats, a T-shirt, and sneakers. I was sure Pilar would allow me to enjoy dinner before asking me for some money or announcing that her mama was coming down from the Bronx for a visit. I had no idea what she wanted, but she was buttering me up for something. Unfortunately for her, I wasn't no damn biscuit.

Genesis and I returned to the kitchen just as Pilar placed the last serving dish on the table. The aroma of the fiery shrimp made my mouth water. I put my princess back in the highchair before I took a seat. After Pilar joined us, I blessed the food like my grandma had taught me to do as a child. Then I piled my plate up high with food. We ate in silence with an occasional outburst of babbling from Genesis. I didn't know who the hell Pilar thought she was fooling, but it damn sure wasn't me. Her jittery body language and shifty eyes told me she was about to lay something on me that she knew I wasn't going to like. I braced myself and prayed to God it had nothing to do with a *man*. No, we weren't involved romantically anymore, but I didn't need some dude disrupting my family. Genesis was too young for that shit.

"You know that my dad's health is a little iffy right now," Pilar reminded me out of the blue.

"Yeah, I know."

"Well, he wants to see me. He's been asking to see Genesis too. He hasn't laid eyes on her since she was a month old."

"Spit it out, Pilar. What are you trying to ask me? Just say it."

"Daddy bought me a plane ticket to fly down for a visit. Genesis and I are leaving for Jacksonville tomorrow morning. We'll be back Tuesday afternoon."

"You agreed to visit Leroy with Genesis *before* talking to me?"

"I didn't think you would mind. You know how sick he's been. We'll only be gone a few days."

"It ain't right, Pilar. You *know* it ain't right. Go ahead. I don't care if *you* go. I ain't got no holds on you anymore. But Genesis ain't going nowhere. I have plans for her this weekend."

"My daddy wants to see her, Ty. You can't deny a sick man a visit from his only grandchild."

I felt my pressure shoot straight to the top. "I wouldn't deny you permission to travel with my daughter if the arrangement had been made properly. I'm Genesis' *father!* You were supposed to run the visit by me *before* Leroy purchased the ticket." I pushed back from the table and stood. "The only reason why I'm going to allow you to take her with you is because I have a heart. I don't want your daddy to lose money. But next time, you better check with me on anything concerning my daughter."

I stormed to my room and grabbed my wallet, keys, and cell phone. I slipped on my leather jacket and headed for the front door. I needed some air and lots of space between Pilar and me. I didn't like her very much at the moment.

I made a pit stop in the kitchen to kiss my baby girl's cheek. "Good night, sweetie." I gave Pilar the evil eye. "Make sure you tell *Chad* I said hello when you get to Jacksonville."

I was about to turn around and leave after the third knock when the door finally swung open. I could tell by the twinkle in her eyes that she was happy but surprised to see me. I was relieved she wasn't angry at me for refusing her phone calls and ignoring all of the Facebook messages. She wasn't dumb, so there was no way she hadn't picked up on my dodge game days ago. Yet, there she was, smiling and taking me in with those bright eyes. A few seconds passed before we spoke at the same time, breaking the silence.

"You go first."

"Nah," I said, shaking my head. "You go ahead. Ladies first."

"What're you doing here, Tyson?"

"I was in the neighborhood, so I decided to pay you a visit."

"I'm sure. Well, don't just stand there. Come on in."

Mallorie twirled gracefully and reentered the condo.

I followed her inside and closed the door. We passed by a sitting area to our right on the way down the hall as well as the kitchen. I watched the hem of her red Matt Ryan jersey flap against her thighs with every step she took. *Formalities and small talk be damned,* I silently told myself as she walked into her bedroom with me playing her shadow. She sat on the edge of the big round bed and scooted backward before she collapsed, resting her back on the pink comforter. She obviously wanted me to know she wasn't wearing panties. That's why she spread her legs apart, which caused the jersey to crawl up high enough for me to see her pussy.

"Oh, so, it's like *that,* huh?"

She smiled enticingly as her eyes twinkled with mischief. "Yeah, it's like *that.*"

Thunder was down with the program because he was *up* and pulsating. I removed my wallet from the pocket on my leather jacket and searched it for a Trojan before slipping it back inside. I eased out of my jacket and tossed it to the side. I watched Mallorie closely as she started fingering her clit and thrusting her hips slowly. She started moaning like a dog in heat. The scent of wet pussy invaded the air. My dick swelled and extended a few more inches when Mallorie lifted her hand from her wetness and brought it to her lips. She stuck her fingers in her mouth and tasted herself before she started sliding them in and out of her pussy again. Her hums and purrs intensified. She was getting louder and more feverish by the second. She sounded like Thunder was already up in that pussy. It was so drenched that I could hear her juices sloshing every time she stroked herself. I tore into the condom with my teeth and pulled my sweatpants and underwear down below my knees. I rolled the condom quickly but carefully over Thunder before I approached the bed.

"You want this big black dick, don't you? You've been dreaming about this dick. You want it?"

"Yesss . . . oh yesss . . . mmm . . . yesss . . . please . . ."

"You want Thunder to fuck this pussy?" I asked, grabbing her legs and dragging her ass down the bed closer to where I stood at the edge of it. "Do you want me to murder this pussy?"

"Yesss, Tyson! Yesss! I want it! Give it to me!"

"Turn your ass over."

Mallorie flipped over on all fours like an obedient dog without hesitation. I grabbed hold of Thunder and rubbed him against her wet opening and the tip of her clit, teasing her. Her thin body trembled with need as she whimpered and breathed loudly. I laughed at how horny she was. That shit turned up my heat too. She groaned and squirmed like she was about to lose her damn mind. She wanted me inside of her *already*.

I eased my dick a few inches inside her pussy and paused. It was tight as hell. I figured she'd been saving it for her fiancé while he was away. Her walls hugged Thunder so tightly that it was almost painful. I pushed in deeper, and it sounded like my dick had splashed into a pool of water. The pussy was soaked and dripping. And damn if it wasn't as hot as fire.

"Ah . . . ah . . . ah . . ." Mallorie moaned when I rammed Thunder all the way in to the hilt.

I grabbed her small-ass cheeks and went to work, sliding my dick in and out of her with force. I caught a medium-paced rhythm, stroking her like I owned the pussy and not the dude stacking paper over in Africa. Mallorie snatched two handfuls of the comforter when I smacked her ass.

"Take this dick! Take all of it!" I popped her ass again but harder this time.

"Fuck me, daddy! Fuck me, daddy! Oooh!" She pushed her ass backward into my hips like one of those wild and freaky chicks in a porn flick. She pumped and slammed into me fast and damn near out of control.

Her inner muscles squeezed and clenched my dick, pulling me in deeper. The grip was like a deadlock. I was in a pussy trap. The bucking and rocking grew faster and faster. Mallorie was howling and screaming some unintelligible shit that sounded like gibberish to me. Then all of a sudden, she froze in midmotion and let out a peculiarly high-pitched squeal. Her walls choked the life out of Thunder as her body shook like crazy. Seconds later, my back stiffened as a powerful nut crept up on me. Air got caught in my throat, and I fought to swallow it. I rammed my dick one last time, hitting a spot so far up inside of Mallorie that I swore I had injured her. I collapsed on top of her back, pinning her thin body to her fancy bed. I rolled off of her onto my back and stared at the ceiling, trying to catch my breath.

Chapter Thirteen

Mallorie

I snatched up my landline phone after the first ring and tiptoed toward the bathroom. I knew it was Collin because he was the only person who would call me at this dreadful hour of the night. I zoomed in on Tyson, hoping the phone hadn't disturbed his sleep. Fortunately, he was still knocked out. I had covered his flawless naked body with a blanket as he slept, snoring softly at the foot of my bed. We'd had sex two more times before he finally drifted off to sleep. I was cold and exhausted after our fuck fest, so I'd crawled to the top of the bed and eased underneath the covers before sleep covered me like a rain cloud. Now, I was stumbling in the buff through the darkness trying to get to the bathroom before the phone stopped ringing. I pressed the power button just as I entered the bathroom. I closed the door behind me.

"What took you so long to answer the phone, babe?"

I yawned. "I'm sorry. It was on the other side of the room. I must've left it on the dresser after talking to Mother last night."

"I couldn't stop thinking about you, Mal. Is everything okay?"

"Um . . . sure . . . yeah . . ." I stammered with a guilty tongue. "What could be wrong?"

"I don't know. Some brides experience a lot of pressure during the planning stages of the ceremony and end up melting down. I don't want that to happen to you. It's just a wedding. We could've had a small ceremony at your parents' house as far as I'm concerned."

"God forbid. Mother would've had a major stroke if we'd suggested that. I'm not stressed out at all, Collin. Mother and the bridal consultant have everything under control. I'm just going to show up and smile."

"And you're going to be the most beautiful bride in the world."

The bathroom door opened suddenly, startling me. I nearly shit on myself. I turned around and came face-to-face with Tyson. I didn't know what the hell to do. Collin was still yapping away in my ear, fantasizing about our perfect wedding day. My jaws had literally locked on me, so all I could do was hum my agreement and nod.

Tyson didn't move a muscle. He just stared at me. My eyes fell to his penis. It was erect and pointed in my direction. My mouth watered. I noticed the condom on it, and my pussy instantly creamed. Without warning, Tyson gripped me around my waist and picked me up. He sat me on the bathroom counter and positioned his body between my thighs. He entered me and stood still, panting and pinching my nipples with his fingertips. He was using more pressure than I was used to. It hurt, but if felt so good at the same time.

"I-I . . . I only have a few more hours to sleep," I told Collin. "I'm going back to b-bed now. Good . . . good n-night."

"Good night, babe," he whispered. "I love you."

"Me too."

I made sure I pressed the power button before I spread my legs farther apart. The phone crashed to the black-and-white tile when it slipped from my grasp. I was in a state of delirium, feeling my walls filled with rock-solid chocolate dick. I threw my head back when Tyson rammed himself deeper inside of me. He leaned in and sucked my left nipple with excessive suction. He bit it before he released it, and I cried out in pleasurable pain. His strokes were long, powerful, and speedy. I felt myself climbing the clouds on my way to the stars. Sex with Tyson was a million times better than what I could've ever hoped for. Now, I understood why white people often said once you go black, you'll never go back. Collin wasn't capable of satisfying me to this level of bliss. I now knew what it meant to have my brains fucked out. There wasn't an intelligent thought in my head. My body was floating on air as Tyson pumped in and out of me like a freight train.

"Whose pussy is this?" he asked, yanking a handful of my hair, which caused my head to snap backward. *Damn*, my scalp burned. He yanked harder.

"It's yours, daddy! It's yours!"

"Damn right! *I* own this pussy!"

He leaned down and bit my right nipple with medium pressure. It hurt so fucking good. A fresh stream of my love juice flowed freely. That familiar prickle started in the pit of my stomach and spread all over my body within seconds. Even my toes twitched and curled as my climax crashed down on me, taking my breath away. I opened my mouth to scream Tyson's name, but no sound came out. He had fucked me into a mute. I wrapped my legs around his waist because I wanted to be closer to him. I had to feel his body when it exploded. My wish came true faster than expected. He threw his head back and roared out his release. The sound of sweat-drenched flesh meeting flesh filled the bathroom before his thrusts into my body slowed down and eventually stopped. I gazed into his eyes and thanked my lucky stars for the passionate moment. On impulse, I leaned in to kiss his lips. I wanted to taste his tongue, but he turned his face away.

"I'm hungry. What do you have to eat around here?"

He disconnected our bodies, and I immediately felt a chill replace his masculine heat. He carefully removed the condom and tossed it into the open commode. I watched him take a piss like it was an experience he and I shared every single day. It was kind of weird, though. Collin had never done anything like that in my presence. I couldn't even recall a time I'd ever heard him fart.

"I'm not Martha Stewart or Rachael Ray by any stretch of the imagination," I announced over the sound of the commode flushing. "Cooking is *not* my thing. That's why I eat out a lot. But I could fix you some bacon, eggs, and wheat toast. I keep breakfast food in the refrigerator because that's my favorite meal of the day. I think I have some oatmeal and humus too. I could—"

"Nah, nah, I was thinking of something spicier."

"I have some microwavable Buffalo wings in the freezer. I hope they haven't expired." I laughed like crazy. "I can't even remember when I bought them."

Tyson started scrubbing his hands with soap and steaming hot water like a surgeon preparing for the operating room. "You know what? I passed a Denny's on my way here. I'll stop and order some chicken strips and smother them with hot sauce."

"Please don't do that. Take a shower and relax. I'll go to Denny's and pick up the food for you. I'll be back in twenty minutes."

He looked at me as if I had grown another head for a moment before he said, "Cool."

I walked out of the dressing room with a fake smile plastered on my face. I twirled clumsily, giving my mother and future mother-in-law a full view of the hideous dress they'd selected for me to wear to my engagement party. I felt like June Cleaver in the plain A-line hunter-green dress with a white lace Peter Pan collar. Nothing was appealing about it. It wasn't stylish or flattering to my petite figure at all. Barbara Bush had sexier dresses in her closet.

"You look absolutely stunning, my dear," Mrs. Cartwright drawled out. "Collin will be very pleased."

"And the price is a steal," Mother whispered. "With my Platinum Preferred customer's account, it'll only cost me $1,000."

I bit my tongue to remind myself that prim and proper little rich girls weren't supposed to cross their mothers, especially not in the presence of others. Like the chaste Southern belle Mrs. Cartwright believed I truly was, I smiled politely and returned to the dressing room.

In all honesty, I was a wee bit stressed out over the upcoming engagement party and all the wedding hoopla. And the ugly dress didn't help matters one bit. But the thing that bothered me more than flowers, china patterns, and invitations was Tyson's outright disregard. I hadn't spoken to him since he'd left my house before daybreak Friday morning. It was *Wednesday*, and he hadn't had the decency to pick up a phone and dial my number. I had made it a priority to give him all of my numbers before he left my condo. I even saved my cell phone number to his contact list on his iPhone. He knew how to contact me, so why hadn't he reached out? And why didn't he give me his cell phone number so I could call him before he took off?

I thought I'd shown him a funky good time during his unexpected visit to my place. At least I had tried. I'd done everything I thought would please him. I couldn't remember treating any other man better. And I sure as

hell couldn't recall having better sex in my life. Tyson
was the perfect lover. He had a flawless body and the
most amazing penis in all of creation. And he knew how
to use it too. Every time we fucked, he hit spots that
made my heart skip a few beats. Collin would need a GPS
to find those spots . . . and a longer dick too.

I changed out of the ugly dress and into my navy
business suit with Tyson still fresh on my mind. I wanted
to talk to him, but I didn't want to make the call. Why
couldn't he reach out to me? Maybe he was busy with
work and his daughter. Hopefully, he would pay me
another surprise visit over the weekend. I would keep
my schedule clear and cross my fingers. I smiled, just
thinking about the things I wanted to do to him. I even
thought about us going out to dinner or catching a movie.
It would be risky, though. All hell would break loose if
someone who knew Collin or me were to see me out on
the town with a strange black man. It would be even
worse if we ran into a family member. No, going out
wasn't an option. I would order takeout food from the
restaurant of his choice. Then we would fuck until we
couldn't anymore.

"Any messages for me?" I asked Debbie, the cute little
receptionist.

She smiled. "No."

I walked toward my cubicle disappointed. I plopped
down in my chair and frowned at the stack of case files
on my desk. I was going to be busy for the rest of the
day. I released hot air from my cheeks. Before I could
talk myself out of it, I picked up the phone and dialed the
DA's office. The number was stuck inside my head.

"Fulton County District Attorney's office. How may I
help you?"

"May I speak to Tyson Maxwell, please?"

"Transferring you now. Have a good afternoon, ma'am."

"Thank you," I said, twirling a strand of my hair nervously around my index finger.

"This is Tyson Maxwell."

"Hi. It's me, Mallorie."

Silence.

"Did I catch you at a bad time?"

"Uh . . . nah . . . Not really. What's up?"

"You haven't called me."

"Was I *supposed* to?"

"I was hoping you would. I want to see you. Can you come over and play tonight?"

"Nah. Tonight isn't a good time. I have to pick up Genesis from my mother's house after work."

"Who?"

"Genesis, my daughter . . ."

"I had forgotten her name. It's a very odd name, but it's beautiful just like her."

"Thank you. Look, Mallorie, I'm about to go into a meeting. I—"

"Friday," I blurted out, cutting him off. I refused to let him get off the phone before he agreed to visit me again. "Come to my condo Friday."

"Maybe. I've got to go now."

"Okay. I hope to see you on Friday."

Chapter Fourteen

Tyson

I didn't have no damn meeting to go to. I just didn't feel like talking. I had enough shit messing with my head trying to deal with Pilar and our fucked-up situation. She walked up in the crib yesterday with her lips poked out, pouting like a brat. Maybe she thought I owed her a favor or some money for bringing my daughter back home. She'd had the nerve to call me Sunday night to ask me if they could stay in Jacksonville until Friday. Talking about her daddy was going to pay the penalty fee to have her flight changed. I told her she could stay down there *forever*, but I would be burning rubber down I-75 South to pick up Genesis first thing Tuesday morning. I wasn't down with extended miles between my baby and me for more than a few days, and Pilar knew it. She had played her damn self for even asking me some dumb shit like that. Now, she was walking around the house with an attitude, but I didn't have a single fuck to give.

Nah, there was no room for drama in my life. Although Mallorie seemed safe and easy, I still didn't want to get in too deeply with her. She was a *white girl*. I could never take her home to meet Mama. No way. Also, I detected a little clinginess in her personality. She had stalked this dick until she got it. And when she finally got it, she took it like a pro. The girl could fuck, and she had an insane head game. That first time when she choked on Thunder was definitely a fluke. All four times she sucked my dick between Thursday night and Friday morning, she was on *fire*. The chick didn't gag or spill a drop of come. She damn near sucked Thunder dry. I swear she deserved a crown for giving the best head on the planet.

I wondered if all white girls were like that, or was Mallorie just talented. She was generous in bed without any hang-ups. She was like a little sex slave, willing to do anything to please her master. A lot of women could learn a few tricks from her. She knew how to take care of a cat's sexual needs. That's probably why she had that phat-ass piece of ice on her finger. Her fiancé had fallen victim to the pussy and the good head. I'm sure he loved her too and for other reasons. Sex was not enough to keep a man hanging on. So, Mallorie had to have some other valuable qualities and abilities. She was very attractive with a pleasant personality. Being rich wasn't a bad thing, so I'm sure it had earned her some points too.

No matter what made Mallorie Whitaker a good catch, I wasn't interested. And even if I were, I wasn't emotionally available for a relationship. My life was in serious need of repair.

"Ty! Why didn't you knock on the door? *Damn*."

I smirked and shook my head as Pilar stood in front of me wet and butt-ass naked. She placed a hand over one of her breasts and the other over her vagina. I don't know why the hell she was trying to hide her body from me. I probably knew every inch of it better than she did. I had mercy on her and reached for a towel from the shelf. I tossed it to her, and she wrapped it around her body in a hurry. I laughed out loud, and I could tell it pissed her off to the max.

"You can be an asshole sometimes, Ty. Why are you still in here?"

"Because *I* pay the rent and all of the bills up in here. I can go in any room I want to at *any time,*" I teased, still laughing my ass off.

"Then maybe I need to find me someplace else to live."

"Bye! Mail Genesis and me a postcard so we can send you a house-warming gift."

"Oooh, I *hate* you sometimes! I swear I do!"

"No, you don't, girl. You love me. That's why you're so damn mad. I make you juicy, and you know it." I cracked the hell up.

Pilar power walked past me, punching my shoulder hard in the process. She was furious for no good reason. I had made an honest and innocent mistake by bursting into the bathroom while she was naked. She knew me well enough to know I would never disrespect her by sneaking a peek at her goodies. I wasn't no damn pervert. I opened the cabinet under the sink and grabbed a bar of soap. That was the only reason why I had come into the bathroom in the first place. The master bathroom was fresh out of Dove. I would buy two packs tomorrow from Sam's Club after work.

Later that evening, I walked into the living room and found Pilar rocking Genesis to sleep in the recliner. Kevin Hart was acting a fool on television in *Ride Along* on BET. Pilar wasn't paying him any attention. She was singing a lullaby softly to our baby girl. I picked up the remote control from the coffee table, dropped down on the couch, and turned off the TV. Pilar looked at me like she wanted to stab me in the heart.

"I'm sorry for walking into the bathroom on you earlier today. It was an honest mistake."

"Whatever."

"Damn, girl, I'm trying to be civil. Anyway, I see you lost that pregnancy fat." I went into a laughing fit.

Pilar rolled her eyes and smacked her lips before she jumped up and left the room. I sat staring into space for a little while before I turned the television back on. Thursday night TV sucked. There was nothing worth watching, I noticed, while flipping through the channels. I turned to the music video channel to check out half-naked chicks with big asses. The first video ho I saw was so fine that my dick bricked up on me on sight. Her phat ass was jiggling like Jell-O, and it looked good enough to lick. I was hornier than a priest. I guess I had seen too much female flesh over the past few hours. I removed my cell phone from my pocket and scrolled through my contact list. I found Mallorie's number and dialed it. She picked up after the second ring.

"Wow! To what do I owe this pleasant surprise, handsome?"

"What are you wearing?" I asked, standing up. I left the living room and headed to my bedroom where I closed the door.

"I have on my Matt Ryan jersey. Why?"

"Take it off and lie down on your bed."

"I'm already lying down."

"Did you take off the jersey?"

"Yesss," she hissed in a soft breath.

"Open your legs and play with your clit. Do it real slow."

"Aaaah . . ."

"That's it. Is that pussy wet yet? Is it juicy?"

"Uh-huh . . ."

"Put two fingers inside of Miss Kitty. Think about my dick. Pretend I'm all up in it, hitting your spot over and over again *hard* like you like it. I'm yanking your hair and biting your little pink nipples. They hurt, but you like that rough shit."

"Oooh . . . aaaah . . . mmm . . . Tyson . . ."

Thunder was hot and stiffer than iron. I pulled my sweatpants and boxer briefs down to release him. I sat down on the bed. My dick had already squirted a little bit of precome. I stroked it, imagining Mallorie's lips wrapped around it and licking it with her warm tongue.

"Take your other hand and play with your titties. Squeeze them nipples until they hurt."

"Mmm . . ."

"Keep playing in that pussy. Write my name on it with your fingertip. Mark that shit with my name. Are you writing that shit?"

"Hell, yeah, daddy; I'm writing it."

Thunder had caught a buzz. More precome dripped. "Stick out your tongue. Flick it. Can you taste me? Can you taste my sweet chocolate milk?"

"Yesss . . . yesss . . . ah yesss . . ."

"Swallow it."

"It's so fucking sweet."

"I want that pussy to pop," I growled on the verge of a nut. "Make that juicy, hot pussy pop. Come on! Make it pop for daddy! You better make it pop *right now!*" I yelled and stroked Thunder faster.

"Aaaah! Aaaah! Damn it! Aaaah!"

I busted a mountain-size nut while Mallorie screamed out her climax.

"Yeah, I'll help with the harvest celebration again this year, Mama."

"That's good because we need more men to help this time."

"What about that dude who's sweet on you? Did you ask *him* to help too?"

"How do you know about *Dafiq?*"

"Khadijah told me about him. She said he's a cool brotha, but you're giving him a hard time. You better stop playing games before another one of those sistas at the mosque scoops him up."

"They can have him."

"*Nooo!* You need a man, Mama. It's been a long time since you've had male companionship. You're overdue for a tune-up."

"Tyson James Maxwell Junior, I am your *mother!* Stop talking to me like that."

"I'm just saying," I chuckled. "I mean, you know what happens when you don't wear earrings. The hole closes up."

Mama hung up in my face. I was in shock. I must've really pissed her off. I smiled as I pulled into my parking space. It was Friday, and I was one happy dude. After work, I planned to pick up a six-pack of Amstel Light and order a double pepperoni and sausage pizza from Johnny's. Then I was going to chill with Genesis, watching some kiddie movies. Mallorie would be disappointed, but she would get over it eventually.

I got out of my car and headed inside the building through the employee's entrance. The elevator was already packed when I squeezed inside. It wasn't even nine o'clock yet, but I had already started the countdown to the end of the day as I walked down the corridor. I smiled and nodded good morning to the receptionist and a few coworkers on my way to the office that I shared with two other people. They were standing directly in front of my desk, talking and looking at something. They walked away smiling when I approached them.

There was a gift basket on top of my desk. It was filled with all sorts of gourmet snacks and a bottle of champagne. I snatched the attached envelope off and opened it.

I hope my surprise treat will brighten your day.
I'll see you tonight and give you an even better treat.
  M

There was a picture inside of the envelope too. I pulled it out and immediately stuffed it back inside after I saw it. It was a picture of Mallorie's *vagina*. And her middle finger was stuck inside of it. The girl was a certified sex fiend. I didn't mind her freakiness in bed, but she needed to keep that shit far away from my job.

Chapter Fifteen

Tyson

My phone vibrated a few minutes past midnight, waking me from a sound sleep. Genesis was so close to me that I was afraid it would wake her too. Pilar didn't stir. She was snoring lightly on the other side of the baby. We all had fallen asleep on the living room floor sprawled out on a huge blanket watching movies. I sat up and grabbed the phone from the coffee table.

"Hello?" I whispered hoarsely.

"Are you coming?"

I was surprised to hear Mallorie's voice on the line. I was about to ask her how the hell she'd gotten my cell phone number when I realized I had called her earlier in the week. She'd obviously saved my number in her phone.

"I'm already in bed. I was dog-tired after work. The only thing I had the energy to do was spend time with my daughter."

"I understand, but I wish you had called me to let me know you weren't coming. I ordered Thai food and bought a bottle of Hennessy."

"Yo, don't open that bottle. Save it for me."

"I'll think about it. Let's have phone sex again."

"I can't."

"Okay . . . Why not?"

"I just can't. I'm going back to sleep now. I'll hit you up tomorrow. Good night."

"Who was the bitch that called you last night asking for a booty call?"

I just stared at Pilar from across the table and stuck a forkful of cheese eggs in my mouth. She didn't have a right to ask me any questions about my personal life. What I did and who I did it with was none of her damn business.

"Anyway, I'm going over to my cousin Kayla's house today to do her hair. I want to take Genesis with me if that's okay with you."

"What time will you be leaving and when will you be back?"

"I'll leave here around noon, and I should be back before five. Is that cool, *sir?*"

It was cool because I needed to get ready for a gig. Some doctor chick wanted me to strip at her niece's bachelorette party at a hotel. But I wasn't about to tell Pilar that. She had no idea I was stripping.

"I've got some errands to run, and I'm going to meet a couple of my classmates at a bar downtown tonight. You and the princess can spend the whole day together."

"Thank you. Um . . . Can I have twenty dollars for gas, *please?*"

"Will it be a loan or should I just write it off?"

Pilar took a deep breath and released it in a huff. "I'll pay you back at the end of the month, Ty."

"Cool. My wallet is on my dresser."

"Thank you."

"Yeah yeah yeah . . ."

***

"Hello?"

"I'm parked outside your building. I just finished dancing at a bachelorette party. Can I come up?"

"What time is it?"

"It's almost two. If it's too late or you don't feel like—"

"I'll call the security desk. Pablo will allow you to come up."

"Cool."

I entered the building five minutes later and approached the chunky security guard. True to her word, Mallorie had handled her business. It was quiet in the exclusive highrise. I rode the elevator up to the ninth floor and hopped off when the doors opened. Mallorie was standing in the hallway dressed in her signature bedtime attire, smiling and waving at me.

She hugged me when I got within reach, but I gently pushed her away.

"I'm sweaty. I need to take a shower."

"Okay."

We walked the few feet to her door and went inside the condo. She secured the locks and activated the alarm system.

"Are you hungry? There's plenty of Thai food in the refrigerator. I could fix you a plate and pop it in the microwave."

"Nah, I'm good. I just want a hot shower and a few hours of rest."

"I'll get a washcloth and a towel for you. What else do you need?"

"A glass of that Hennessy would be nice right about now."

"Coming right up."

I threw back two glasses of liquor before I got in the shower. I was feeling light and mellow under the warm and powerful water spray. Mallorie's expensive organic soap with scrub beads felt like heaven against my skin. It smelled good too, but I think it was better suited for women, though.

I couldn't explain how I had ended up at Mallorie's spot, sipping Hennessy, and now, bathing in her fancy crackled-glass shower. I supposed it was because it was late when I finally left my gig with fat pockets, and I knew Genesis was already asleep. Pilar was too, not that I gave a damn about her. Maybe I simply didn't want to be alone. Yeah, more than likely the subconscious desire to be in the presence of another human being was floating somewhere in my psyche.

"What the—" The sound of the shower door sliding open had caught me off guard.

I saw Mallorie's wide and toothy smile before her naked body entered the stall, and she closed the door. Her hand immediately went to work, massaging my pecs and abs. She wiped away the soapy film as the warm spray of water pounded against my flesh. There was no way she could've ignored Thunder at this point. He had awakened from his sleep rigid and at full attention. I felt the surge of warm blood rush down there, filling him and making him stiffer by the second. Mallorie reached down and grabbed him, stroking him with soap lather all over her hand.

"*Shit*," I hissed in response when she went downtown.

The feel of Mallorie's tongue circling the tip of my dick gave me goose bumps. My knees almost buckled like a little weak-ass bitch. She continued to flick and twirl her tongue around the circumference of Thunder's head as she stroked him. Then she went in for the kill, deep throating my dick like only a professional head master could. My back hit the snow-white tile behind me, trapping me at her mercy. The gulping, slurping, and moaning pulled me into a zone so far into lust that I saw bright lights flashing and the sound of bells ringing filled my ears. I didn't know what the girl was doing to me, but I felt like a kid enjoying the most thrilling roller-coaster ride of my life. Babe was squeezing my butt cheeks and pulling on my dick with the perfect amount of suction. Her tongue was doing that snake thing that always guaranteed me a crazy-ass nut. Her face was fully smashed against my pelvis, flattening her nose against my lower belly. I felt the warm air flowing from her nostrils blowing my pubic hairs.

When my body jolted involuntarily under the first spasm, Mallorie moaned and increased her oral grip. Semen filled her mouth, and she gulped it down, swallowing without a single gag. I yanked two fists full of her hair, tangling my fingers through it. The slurping and moaning continued between gulps. When the wave had fully subsided, and I was completely depleted of energy and come, I sighed and fought to regain my composure.

"Damn, girl," I managed to say through pants for air. "I may have to crawl to your bed."

She stood up, giggling. "I aim to please."

"I need another drink. Go get that bottle of Hennessy and meet me in the room."

"Tyson, are you asleep?"

I turned over onto my back. "Nah, I ain't sleepy. I'm just resting. You know I don't do sleepovers. My face has to be the first face Genesis sees when she wakes up in the morning."

"Is she with a sitter now?"

"Look, Mallorie, I'm kind of private. I've been like that since I was a kid. Some things I just don't discuss in detail with certain people. My daughter is one of them."

"What about *family?* Is it safe for me to ask about your parents?"

"My dad left the family when I very young. My mama raised my sister and me alone with his financial support. I have a stepmother who I despise and a half sister. My dad's an attorney, Mama teaches African American studies at Clark Atlanta University, and my sister is a med student at Emory School of Medicine."

"Have you ever been married?"

"Nope."

"Engaged?"

"Uh-uh. Never. Now, let me get all up in *your* business." I sat up and propped my back against a few pillows. "How come you're fucking me when you're on your way down the aisle? The dude obviously loves you, or he wouldn't have proposed and put that iceberg on your finger. And when is your wedding date anyway?"

"My wedding will start promptly at five o'clock in the evening on Saturday, April thirtieth. I'm not sure if you want to hear the answer to your other question."

"Oh, believe me, I want to hear it."

"You were my fantasy."

"Come again."

"I've been obsessed with black men since I was 15. I used to masturbate thinking about Denzel Washington, Usher, Will Smith, and Tyrese. I craved the black sexual experience, but it was always out of my reach."

"Girl, stop playing and tell the truth. A black dude would've tapped that ass a long time ago if you had asked him to. Your mom and pops told you not to bring no *nigga* home. That's the real story."

"That's not true!"

"Yeah, it is. Your parents would disown you and deny you your trust fund if you were to take me home and introduce me as your new boyfriend. Then they'd put in a call to the Ku Klux Klan to come and cut off my dick, stick it in my mouth, and lynch my black ass. Then after taking my last breath while swinging like a piece of fruit from the tree, they'd set my corpse on fire."

"How can you sit there and talk about something so horrible? Things like that make me sad. You shouldn't joke about such barbaric behavior. And for the record, my family would *never* take part in anything so awful."

Mallorie could deny it all she wanted, but I knew in my gut that her family would never accept a black man into the fold, and I was cool with that because my mama wouldn't welcome a white chick into our family either. And as far as Mallorie's fantasy about black men was concerned, she wasn't the only white girl who had dreamed about the chocolate experience. She just happened to be one among the masses who had been bold enough to make it happen. It was foul how she was cheating on her fiancé with me, though. But I owned no guilt. I hadn't pursued Mallorie. She had hunted me down. Yes, I could've denied her request, but I was curious about snow bunnies and what they had to offer.

I'd needed to know what superpowers a white woman had that would make a man leave his beautiful wife and two great children to start a life with her. Mallorie was *everything* in the bedroom, but neither she nor any other woman could take me away from my child. No one could do that. Only death could separate me from Genesis.

I snatched the covers from my naked body. "Blow me one more time before I leave."

Chapter Sixteen

Pilar

"You smell funny." I wrinkled my nose against the stench of Ty's body and leaned back in the recliner.

"Girl, give me my baby and go back to bed. I'll finish feeding her."

"No! You need to go and take a shower before you touch her. Go and wash that stank-pussy scent off."

"Man, whatever."

Ty must've thought I was crazy. Here it was five thirty in the morning, and he was just rolling up in the house smelling like a wet puppy and tuna. He'd been out fucking some nasty-ass ho. I couldn't believe him. He had a big nerve to want to touch my baby with the smell of rank sex all over him. I was *hot!* I won't deny that I was also hurt to know that he was sleeping with other women. He used to be more discreet about his private life, but now, he was as bold as hell. He was entertaining booty calls at all hours of the night and coming home smelling like fishy pussy. He just didn't give a damn about me at all anymore, and it broke my heart.

No, I wasn't his woman, but I was still in love with him. I probably loved him more than I ever had because he'd given me the most precious gift any woman could ever dream of. Genesis was a symbol of the deep love and strong bond we'd once shared. I would never be able to look at her without thinking about Ty. He was a part of her, and I was the other half. The three of us belonged together. We were a family.

That's why when Ty had first suggested that we live together after Genesis was born, I readily agreed. I hoped that our hearts would somehow find their way back to each other. I believed the birth of our daughter would usher in forgiveness and help us to reconcile. But over the past six and a half months, nothing magical has happened. Ty and I are still nothing more than two roommates who happen to be former lovers, living together raising our daughter. It hurt like hell, but that was our reality, and I'd accepted it. However, what I refused to accept was his blatant disrespect for me. If he wanted to screw around with other women, he could. After all, he was a grown-ass man. But he didn't have to rub my nose in his shit. Walking in the house early in the morning smelling like funky sex was not cool. Then he'd had the audacity to touch our daughter. That was foul.

I didn't have a problem with Ty moving on with his life because I needed to do the same thing. I was still young and pretty. And like he'd said, I had lost all my pregnancy weight, plus an additional ten pounds. The cute pharmacist at the Publix near our apartment complex had noticed it too. He had asked me out to dinner a few times because all of this lusciousness was visual therapy for his bedroom eyes.

Men hollered at me all the time when I was out and about even when Genesis was with me. I could get booed up in a heartbeat if I really wanted to, but I wasn't ready to do that yet. I wanted to wait until Genesis was older and less dependent on me. She required a lot of attention, and I was determined to give it to her. Ty helped out a lot, and I was appreciative. I only wished he could see me as more than just his baby mama or the high school sweetheart that had cheated on him. Maybe he would one day, or maybe he wouldn't. Either way, *today* I was still in his life. My status may not have been what I wanted it to be, but as long as we were under the same roof, I still had hope.

"Is she asleep yet?"

I looked up at Ty. He had showered and was standing above me dressed in only a pair of checkered cotton boxers. His exposed pecs and six-pack were still a treat to my eyes, even though I repulsed him. He smelled fresh, and it was making me moist below.

"No, she's fighting it. I guess she was waiting for you. I know she's not hungry because she drained both breasts and burped like a wino. The two ounces of pear juice is for her bowels. It keeps her regular. Her diaper needs to be changed," I told him before I handed Genesis to him.

"I'll take care of it. Go back to bed, Pilar. You're off the clock."

I didn't want to go back to bed. I wanted to ask him where he had been and who he'd had sex with. I didn't have a right to ask him anything, but my curiosity and jealousy were bubbling over. "Where were you tonight? You told me you were going to a bar with some class-mates. You didn't smell like you had just left a bar when you first walked in. You smelled like you'd been having sex."

"I don't feel like arguing right now, Pilar. I just want to hang out with our daughter until she falls asleep. Let it go."

"I'll let it go. But I want you to know something. I'm a good person despite what I did, Ty. I was wrong, and I've never said I wasn't. Don't allow your hate for me to affect our daughter."

"I would never do that."

"You just did tonight."

***

I checked my watch for the hundredth time and realized it was getting late. I knew I should've had my ass
at home helping Ty get Genesis ready for bed, but I had
a point to prove to him. If he could lay up all night with
some stank ho and slither back into the house early in
the morning smelling like chitterlings, fish, and ass, I
could hang out too.

"Are you okay? You seem nervous. And you've checked
your watch more times than I can count."

"I've never been away from my daughter before. She's
always with me. I'm planted at home even when she
ventures out."

"Who did you leave her with?"

"She's with her father."

"Well, don't worry. She's in good hands, isn't she?"

"Yeah, she's a daddy's girl, and he loves her to pieces.
He takes excellent care of her."

"Then relax and enjoy your cup of latte and *me*."

Julian flashed a sexy smile, and I swear I heard the
angels sing. They had to be *black* angels too because
their three-part harmony was rich and soulful in their
rendition of Salt 'N' Pepa and En Vogue's "Whatta Man."
Julian was absolutely spot-on. I *did* need to relax and
allow myself to enjoy a stolen moment in his presence
while he was away from his job. The only time I ever
saw him was behind the pharmacy counter at Publix,
dispensing drugs to his hundreds of customers and
counseling them on how to take their meds. I had driven
to the store on a mission this morning as soon as Ty and
Genesis left for eleven o'clock church service.

I had noticed that Julian worked every other Sunday,
and this particular Sabbath was my lucky day. I entered
the store and walked directly to his counter and gave him

the one thing he'd asked for several times since Genesis was born: my phone number. Sure, he could've gotten it from my customer file or even my daughter's, but he was one of those rare by-the-rule brothas who wanted to hook a chick the old-school way. He told me right away that he would be getting off work at five o'clock and invited me to meet him at Starbucks fifteen minutes later. I went back home giddy as a teenager and waited until five. I wasn't worried about Genesis because I knew she and Ty would be at Aminata's house chillin' and grubbin' like they did most Sundays. But it was almost eight o'clock, Genesis' bath time. Her father usually bathed her most nights, but I would always nurse her before he did. I hated that her last meal before bedtime had been some formula with a few teaspoons of single-grain rice cereal sprinkled inside. Guilt was a motherfucker.

"Pretty lady, I'm going to do you a favor. Go and pick up your daughter from her father and go home. I'll call you later. Is that okay with you?"

I wanted to get to know Julian better, but my situation was so complicated. A nice guy like him didn't deserve to be pulled into my mess. I hadn't told him anything about my home life yet. The only thing he knew was that I had an infant daughter, and her father and I were no longer a couple. What he didn't know was that we all lived together. I couldn't hit him with some heavy shit like that straight out of the gate. He would've taken off running without ever looking back. Eventually, I would have to come clean, though, but not now.

"Thanks for understanding," I said sincerely. "I'll be expecting your call." I stood from the table. "I had a great time, Julian. Good night."

The house was dark and quiet when I arrived. I flipped on the light in the front hall so I could see. I almost had a heart attack when I saw Ty sitting in the recliner in the living room glaring at me like I was a career criminal who had just murdered his mama. I walked past him, refusing to acknowledge his presence. His name wasn't Leroy Turk, so I didn't have to answer to him about anything unless it was directly related to our daughter.

I slammed the door behind me after I entered my room. My cell phone battery was low, so I hooked it up to the charger on top of the dresser. I was looking forward to a call from Julian. I wanted to find out what he was all about. He was fine as hell with caramel skin and copper eyes. His thighs were as muscular as was his chest. He had the body of a Mandingo warrior. I could only imagine what it looked like naked. My breathing staggered as I closed my eyes and envisioned him standing before me raw and aroused. It had been a year and some change since I'd been intimate with a man. My body was hungry and thirsty for some sexual activity of the nastiest kind. Ty was the only man I'd ever given myself to before I lost my mind and cheated on him with Chad. The brother had spoiled me. He used to do any damn thing to please me without limits or complaints. I didn't know if Julian could match or exceed Ty's skills, but I wanted to find out in due time.

Hard knocking at my bedroom door startled me. Instead of opening it to see what Ty wanted, I locked it.

We had nothing to talk about. He had ended our relationship. And he'd also convinced me to live with him for his own selfish reasons. Now that I was trapped in his world, he was slinging his dick everywhere without any regard for my feelings. Two could play that game. I now wanted a taste of the single life too. I didn't know if Julian would be a part of this new phase or not, but I wasn't about to rule him out. I stripped out of my jogging suit and put on a plain white T-shirt all while Ty maintained a steady beat on my door. He could knock and talk shit until his knuckles started to bleed, but I wasn't going to answer my door.

Chapter Seventeen

Tyson

Shit got real after that night Pilar went MIA on Genesis and me. Even now, two weeks later, I still have no idea where she had been or who she'd been with. But I have a strong hunch that she was kicking it with some dude. And she still is. Every Sunday night she returns home by ten o'clock, which is two hours *past* Genesis' bedtime. Only a man could cause a woman to skip bedtime rituals with her baby. Whoever the punk is, he must be whispering a whole bunch of bullshit in Pilar's ear. She has become very cocky and flip at the lip. We argue about every little thing. There was a semblance of peace in the house before she started her secret Sunday outings. I started to skip church and dinner at my mama's house last Sunday just to screw up her plans, but I changed my mind at the last minute. I wasn't about to start playing games with her. I'm a grown-ass man. I didn't have time to play.

But to get even, I started a routine with Mallorie. Most Friday nights, I was at her condo sipping Hennessy and eating gourmet takeout food before our private porn party. I swear the shit that girl does to me needs to be included in an instructional sex videotape for females all over the world. Her pussy ain't special or anything, but there's nothing Mallorie *won't* do in the bed, on the floor, in the shower, in the kitchen, or any damn where.

She has no limits and no shame. So, while Pilar is doing whatever she does with her mystery man on Sundays, I enjoy fantastic freaky Fridays with Mallorie.

"What are your plans for Thanksgiving?"

"We have a big family dinner every year at my grand-mother's house. The day before, I'll be helping my mother and a group of members from her mosque serve food and distribute commodities to the homeless and needy at the Murphy Center in Ridgewood. It'll be my third year in a row working on that particular project."

Mallorie sat straight up in bed and looked down at me. "Did you say *mosque?*"

"Yep."

"Wow! So, your mother is *Muslim?*"

"Yeah. Is something wrong with that, Mallorie? You sound like you're offended or something."

"I'm not offended at all. In fact, I'm actually fascinated. How is it that you and Genesis are Christians, and your mother is Muslim? Don't families usually worship togeth-er? My entire family is Presbyterian—on both sides too."

"It's a long story that I don't feel like getting into."

"All right. Tell me more about the Thanksgiving com-munity project for the needy. I didn't even know Muslims celebrated Thanksgiving."

"They don't. That's why they call it a *harvest celebration.* Members of the mosque give out boxes of food, clothes, and other commodities to the less fortunate. They also serve the attendees with a hot meal and entertain them with motivational speeches, music, dance performances, and literature. It's a cool project that I'm proud to be a part of."

"It sounds cool."

"What do your church and your family do to provide for the poor during the holidays?"

"Sadly, my church doesn't do anything. My parents, my uncles, and their wives attend a silent auction every year right after Thanksgiving. It's sponsored by the Sons and Daughters of the Golden South Historical Society. Some of the proceeds are donated to the Salvation Army."

"Sons and Daughters of the Golden South, huh? That's a code name for the modern-day racists' confederation," I grunted and shook my head. "I would love to be a mouse in a corner at *that* event. I'd be the only *darkie* there besides the servers, cooks, and janitorial staff."

"Why are you so critical of white people, Tyson? Not every European American is racist or bigoted, you know. If that were the case, Obama would never have been elected president the first time, and his reelection would've been impossible. Every black person in the country could've voted for him, but their votes alone wouldn't have been enough. Lots of whites, like me, supported him. Hispanics, Asians, and Native Americans did too."

"I ain't hard on white people, but some of y'all are a trip. If you don't think the organization your family supports exists for the sole purpose of preserving prejudiced principles and expanding the racial divide between African Americans and other minorities and whites, you're delusional."

"You may be right about the Sons and Daughters of the Golden South, but I still say there are *millions* of white people in America who aren't racist. Do you think you would be here in my bed right now or any other time if I were some pathetic racist?"

It was my turn to sit up and stare Mallorie down like she had lost her fucking mind. "Are you serious? *Are you fucking serious?* Don't confuse sex with racial consciousness and harmony, boo. Step away from the craziness. You ain't trying to marry me, and I damn sure don't have any plans to wife your ass. Masters used to fuck their female slaves every morning, noon, and night. But did that divert them from their belief that black people were equivalent to—or even less than—common yard dogs? Did sex upgrade those poor women from being property to human beings?"

"I didn't mean—"

"Shut the hell up. You started this shit, and I'm about to finish it. Do you actually believe that Thomas Jefferson—the primary author of the Declaration of Independence and the third president of this punk-ass, prejudiced country—wasn't racist because he fathered children with his *slave,* Sally Hemings? Get the fuck out of here!" I had to laugh to keep from strangling the clueless snowflake with my bare hands.

With a fully flushed face and terrified eyes, Mallorie just stared at me like a deer caught in the headlights.

"Strom Thurmond, a proud, self-proclaimed segrega-tionist and white supremacist, was a racist bigot down to his bone marrow, but he loved chocolate pussy. He fathered a daughter with one of his family's young maids. He provided for his child financially, but he never ac-knowledged her publicly because he was a *racist,* Mallorie. Get a fucking clue!"

I snatched back the covers and got up from the bed. Damn a shower. I had two bathrooms at my crib. I just wanted to get the hell away from Mallorie fast before I punched her in the face. She had told me I'd fucked her brains out. So, maybe that's why she'd had the boldness to spit that bullshit at me. No one in their rational mind would ever believe that sex was the remedy to cure racial prejudice or white supremacy. I was back in my blue and white jogging suit in less than a minute. I was putting on my shoes when I felt Mallorie leave the bed. She walked around to stand in front of me.

"I didn't mean to upset you. Maybe I got carried away trying to express my thoughts. The main thing I want you to know is that I'm not a racist. I know plenty of white people who aren't either. *That* was the point I wanted to make, but I somehow screwed it up. I apologize."

"I'm good. Come walk me to the door."

Genesis wasn't in her crib. That was the first thing I noticed when I tiptoed into our bedroom. Obviously, she was in bed with Pilar. I stripped and took a long, hot shower with a few thoughts tumbling through my head. I was over that stupid argument I'd just had with Mallorie. Now, I was trying to mentally prepare myself for the annual Thanksgiving brunch slash Christmas-tree-trimming party at my dad's house. Khadijah and I were expected to be there as usual.

Lorna, my dad's wife, was a cold piece of work. Her personality reminded me of cheap liquor. You couldn't take it all in with one long swig. You had to sip it slowly, so you wouldn't get drunk too fast and end up puking your liver out. And you would most definitely have a hangover the next morning. Lorna was extra, and she did the most. She tried way too hard, but it was to no avail. I would *never* like her, nor would I accept her as my stepmother. She wasn't worthy of my respect. That gold-digging whore knew my daddy was married with young children when she was sleeping with him all those years ago. She had met my mama and been in her presence on many occasions. Her home-wrecking ass just didn't give a damn. She didn't care about Khadijah or me. Our family meant nothing to her. All she cared about was money, influence, and, of course, the almighty big black dick.

I threw on a pair of plaid cotton boxers and left my bedroom. Daddy was missing his baby girl. I wanted to hold her and inhale her baby-fresh scent of Johnson's baby powder and lotion. My fist stopped in midair when I heard Pilar giggle softly. Her voice held a breathy and sexy tone like she was horny as she whispered and cooed to someone on the phone. I started to burst into the room without knocking just to piss her off. She had no business having phone sex with some punk while my daughter was in bed with her.

My anger got the best of me. I turned the doorknob, ready to serve her my wrath. My blood started to boil— when I realized the door was locked. I banged on it with my fist. "Open the damn door, Pilar! I want my daughter!"

I counted to ten and exhaled all while clenching and unclenching my fists repeatedly. I could hear her scurrying around the room. She wasn't talking, though. She'd probably hung up on ole dude because she thought I was going to kick the door in. To be honest, I was mad enough to do just that. I was about to knock again when the door swung open. My eyes roamed up and down Pilar's body. She had on one of my old Morehouse College T-shirts and a pair of red flannel pajama bottoms.

"Genesis is asleep, Ty. She had a bad case of gas tonight. While you were out with one of your hoes, I was on the phone with your mother and the pharmacist, getting help for our daughter. So, don't bring your ass up in here with an attitude, okay?"

"Is she all right now?"

"Yes, she's fine now, but no thanks to *you*. Do you realize how humiliating it was for me to have to call your mother? You know she hates me, but she put her feelings aside, and so did I for Genesis."

"Why didn't you call *me*, Pilar? *I'm* her father."

"And what would you have done, huh? You don't know any more than I do about baby gas and colic. Your mother was helpful, and the pharmacist was *excellent*. I rushed to the store and bought the medicine she needed. It worked, and she finally stopped crying and went to sleep. Anyway, I'm tired. Is there something else you care to discuss at one o'clock in the morning, *sir?*"

"Who were you talking to on the phone just now?"

Pilar smiled and folded her arms across her chest. "That ain't your business, Ty. I don't get into your personal life, and I would appreciate if you'd return the favor. Good night."

"Hold up." I stuck my foot in the door before it closed and pushed it with my hand. "Give me the baby."

Without a word, Pilar turned and walked toward the bed. She picked up Genesis, cradling her to her chest, and brought her to me. I took my baby girl and walked down the hall to the sound of Pilar's bedroom door slamming shut.

Chapter Eighteen

Mallorie

"Okay, Mal, just walk in there and spread some love, hope, and cheer. Smile and be polite."

After giving myself a pep talk, I got out of my SUV and walked to the back of it to unload my hatch. I needed help with the boxes, and I was sure I would get it as soon as I entered the center and asked. I grabbed the box filled with new women's clothes with the tags still attached and placed it on the ground. I closed the hatch, grabbed the box, and hurried to the door. I stumbled inside and was stunned at how jam-packed the place was.

"May I help you, ma'am?" a young man dressed impeccably in a dark suit and a rather neat bow tie approached me and asked.

"Yes, you may, if you don't mind. I have three boxes of turkeys and two filled with whole chickens in my SUV. I also have a few boxes of brand-new toys, one packed with children's clothes, and bags filled with toiletries. I can't remember what else I brought. I may have gone overboard. Could you help me bring it all in please?"

He looked around the room and made a few hand gestures. Like magic, a group of men hurried in our direction. "Please help this young lady unload her vehicle. She was nice enough to donate some items for the cause." He removed the box from my hands and smiled at me.

"Lead the brothers to your SUV, ma'am. They'll unload it for you."

I spotted Tyson out of the corner of my eye. We stared at each for a few seconds before he turned his head and walked away. I was taken aback. He didn't even acknowledge me. It was baffling and hurtful. Here I was, doing something good . . . something I was proud of. Why did he seem angry or displeased? I turned and exited the building with three men following me.

"Thanks so much, gentlemen. I don't know how I would've gotten all this stuff inside."

Very quietly, the nice men and I unloaded my hatch, and in two trips, we were done. I stood in the back of the room, unsure of what to do next. A young lady was on the small stage playing a lovely song on a flute while an older gentleman accompanied her on an upright piano. I had never heard the song before, but it was nice. I watched and listened until someone approached me.

"Hello. My name is Khadijah. Thank you for all of the wonderful things you donated. Our guests will appreciate every single item. May I fix you a plate of food?"

"Oh no, I'm not hungry just yet. Actually, I brought my apron and a hairnet because I was hoping to serve."

"*Really?*" Her eyes flashed and repeatedly batted in what appeared to be utter shock.

"Yes. Is that a problem?"

"Of course not. We could use the help. Come with me. What is your name?"

"I'm Mallorie Whitaker."

"It's a pleasure to meet you, Mallorie."

I followed Khadijah into the kitchen. She washed her hands in a large stainless steel sink. I did the same thing after I had secured every strand of my hair under the net and put on my apron. I followed her to the serving line a few feet away from the stage. A gorgeous woman with a gigantic Afro, dressed in what I believed was an African outfit, was sitting on a bar stool behind the microphone reading from a book. Her gold earrings were shaped like the continent of Africa. I was fascinated. The flawlessness of her skin reminded me of creamy milk chocolate just like Tyson's. The poetry about children of color and their contributions to the world was uplifting. I was enthralled by her rich voice and the precise articulation of her words. It sounded like she was singing instead of talking.

"You can help me serve the rolls and string beans," Khadijah told me, forcing my eyes away from the African queen onstage.

"Cool," I said as I accepted a pair of plastic gloves from her. I put them on and immediately got busy with my task.

Khadijah and I worked busily in comfortable silence as the woman continued reading onstage. So many people were crammed in the center. I felt like I had died and gone to heaven by being a part of a project that helped others. My heart smiled. Every now and then, I would catch Tyson staring at me from across the room. He was busy distributing clothes and toiletries to men. His line was endless, curving around the room just like mine.

"*Guilt* is powerful. It can serve as motivation at various points in our lives," the pretty lady onstage said. Her book was now closed, and she had removed the cordless microphone from its stand. "For centuries, people of European descent have committed unmerciful atrocities and cultural rape against every race and ethnicity in the universe that was not their own. They kidnapped Africans from their homeland where they had lived as kings and queens in peace and harmony among their loved ones and native men. Those evil men brought our forefathers here bound in shackles and chains to the land they had stolen and killed the Native Americans for."

"Speak on it, sister! Speak on it!" a man in the back of the room shouted and clapped his hands. A round of thunderous applause from others followed.

"It's the truth! Tell it, Dr. Shahid!"

"Speak, sister, speak!"

"They were lazy, incompetent, and incapable of thoroughly building a nation," she continued. "They were ignorant, unintelligent, and consumed by greed and the desire for power. Europeans wanted to rule the world. But first, they needed to build a new and independent nation. Yes, they wanted to flex their pseudosuperiority by establishing a nation on new land, but they didn't possess the wisdom, knowledge, or physical strength to make it happen. That's why they needed *our* people, the original men—*black men*—to do it for them. Why? Because we had already done it before."

"Speak, Dr. Shahid, speak!" a woman shouted this time, and hand claps filled the room.

"Yeah, we had been there and done that! *We* had founded the very first civilization known to man. Some historians refuse to acknowledge us as the originators of civilized societies in Eastern and South Africa, then known as Azania. They want to give all the credit to the Egyptians and the people of Mesopotamia. Don't believe it. If that were true, why didn't the wicked slave catchers go to Egypt and Mesopotamia to capture men and women there and bring them to this stolen land to develop it for them? Because *we* were the first."

The entire room erupted in boisterous applause. People shouted and cheered their approval of the words being spoken. I was paralyzed with fear. My brain was frozen. I could barely breathe. I had been stupid to come, but my heart was in the right place.

Khadijah must've noticed that I was shaken. She took me by the hand. "If you want to leave, I understand. I could walk you out through the back door. It's in the kitchen."

I couldn't speak over the boulder-size lump in my throat. I blinked a few times as I continued watching the pretty speaker onstage and listening to her harsh words. I had heard it or read it all before. Most of it was true, but it wasn't *my* fault.

"That's right. They stole African men and women from their homes, destroying their families and villages and brought them here to stolen land. The Native Americans' blood cried out from the earth as our men built houses, government buildings, and monuments for the white man on top of it. Our forefathers tended their land, cultivated their crops, and harvested it for them. But their lives were valued less than a barrel of cotton or a bundle of sugar cane. They were the white man's *property!*"

I looked across the room into Tyson's eyes as the audience applauded and cheered once again. I found no sympathy or concern for me in his features. He wasn't the one speaking, but he had to know that I felt horrible listening to a speech that cast a dark shadow over my entire race. My heart was aching, but not only just for me. I sympathized with African Americans for the way that they had been mistreated in the past by some white people in our country and for the continued racism that still existed today.

"Our women were their masters' belly warmers who often gave birth to their half-white children against their will. They raped our women every day without remorse, battering their bodies while destroying their spirits. And on the flip side, wives and daughters of slave masters dreamt about the big, strong bucks on the plantations at night. They wanted our men even way back then, but they were too prudent and proud to admit it. But today, they throw themselves shamelessly at

every black professional athlete, entertainer, and busi-
nessman of wealth. A young black woman doesn't stand
a chance against white women's plots and schemes to
get our men in their beds."

Suddenly, my legs found strength and agility at that
moment to move. I hurried into the kitchen and ran
toward the back door. It was locked, and my hands were
trembling too much to release the bolt. I couldn't see
very well anyway through the tears spilling from my eyes.
I was on the brink of a mental breakdown. I had never
experienced such humiliation.

"Let me help you, Mallorie," Khadijah whispered, rubbing my shoulder. She opened the door and pushed me
gently outside into the cold. "Where is your car?"

I pointed toward the front of the building with a trembling finger. I felt Khadijah's chilly hand take hold of my
wrist before she pulled me along. I was numb from head
to toe. It was almost like I had been shot with a stun gun.

"There it is," I mumbled, lifting my chin in the direction
of my SUV. I pulled my keys from the pocket of my skirt
as we walked closer. "Thanks so much, Khadijah. It was
nice meeting you. I didn't come here to start trouble. I
only wanted to help those in need."

I jumped inside my vehicle, started the engine, and
whipped out of the parking lot as quickly and carefully
as I could. I turned around on impulse and saw Tyson
standing at the entrance of the building watching me
drive away.

Chapter Nineteen

Tyson

"Shut the front door. Let me make sure I've got this straight. You and Mallorie, the white girl I met yesterday, have been fuck buddies for a month? What the hell, Tyson?"

"We're just having sex, Khadijah. It ain't like we're trying to build a life together. You, better than anyone, know my situation with Genesis and Pilar. Plus, Mallorie is engaged."

"*What?* Oh, Allah, be merciful."

"Yeah," I confirmed, shaking my head at how stupid I must've appeared to my sister at the moment. "It's one of those crazy things that sort of just happened. We met at one of my gigs, and the rest is history."

"*Damn!* Is she okay? Mama was in rare form yesterday at the harvest celebration. That poor child ran out of there in hysterics. I thought I was gonna have to call the paramedics."

"I don't know what's up with Mallorie. I called her all last night and a few times this morning, but she won't answer my calls."

"Do you blame her? You didn't exactly run to her rescue, Tyson. Did you even *greet* the girl?"

"Man, I was in shock when she walked into the center. I had no idea she was coming. I had mentioned the event and its location to her, but I didn't think she was crazy enough to come. If she had told me about her plans, I would've discouraged her from bringing her ass up in there."

"But she's your *friend,* Tyson. You're having sex with the girl. You should have been more supportive. You should've been the one to get her out of there. Instead, you allowed the task to fall on me."

"I didn't know what to do. Mama was onstage acting like Farrakhan, and I was busy giving out stuff to the young men. What should I have done, Khadijah?"

"A real friend would've greeted her and made her feel comfortable. You ignored that white chick in a community center full of Muslims and Negroes, forcing her to fend for herself. I did the best I could as a courtesy, but your mama traumatized the girl. She showed her ass!"

"Mallorie shouldn't have been there—*period.* But after she did show up, I guess I could've acknowledged her and spared her from the emotional assault from Mama. I'll fix it. I'm sure she needs a few days to regroup. I'll give her the time she needs before I reach out to her again."

"Yeah, you need to handle your business."

"I will."

Moments later, I pulled up to the guard shack at the entrance of my daddy's exclusive gated community. The houses were insanely huge and separated by acres and acres of land. There were only ten mansions in the entire upscale neighborhood.

"I'm Tyson Maxwell Junior. My sister, Khadijah Maxwell Shahid, is with me. We're here to visit our father."

"He and Mrs. Maxwell are expecting you two. Can I see your IDs?"

I wanted to cuss that tubby bastard out. He was sitting there looking like a black, greasy Uncle Tom. Dude had seen my sister and me many times before. Khadijah handed me her license, and I removed mine from my wallet that I'd stuck in the glove compartment. I handed them over and watched the fat Negro check both thoroughly before he handed them back to me.

He opened the brick and wrought iron gate. "Go right ahead, Mr. Maxwell. Happy Thanksgiving to both of you."

I gunned my engine and sped away without giving his fat ass a response. My mind didn't need to toil with him. I was a few seconds away from visiting the wicked white witch of Roswell and my henpecked daddy. The only person I was looking forward to spending time with was my little stepsister, Bailey. She was innocent and had absolutely nothing to do with how her parents had come together. She bore no responsibility for her home-wrecking mother's past behavior or our father's infidelity during his marriage to my mama.

I pulled into the last available spot in the circular driveway at the very end. Lorna's parents and some of her other family members were in town from New England. They were a classic clan of Caucasians, pretentious as hell. They didn't give a damn about my daddy. They were just fond of the fortune he had accumulated and bestowed upon Lorna. She was the family's rock star because she had snagged herself a rich, dumb nigga to take care of her and loan them money whenever they needed it. My daddy was stupid if he thought for one minute that his wife would've pursued him if he hadn't been an up-and-coming attorney with potential and a promising future. Had he been a paralegal like she was when they first met, he would've been just another good-looking black man to her. She probably would've let him tap that ass on the down low, but she wouldn't have married him. Ain't no damn way.

I exited my whip and rounded it to open Khadijah's door with that thought in mind. I helped my beautiful sister out and wrapped my arm around her shoulders. I was very overly protective of her because she was fine as wine, intelligent, and she dressed like a fashion model. When men looked at her five-foot-six, size-eight body all decked out in designer clothes, they could smell, taste, and see money. I wasn't about to have some slick moocher trying to push up on my sister for a free ride to sexual bliss and financial freedom. He would have to kill me first. Khadijah had that video girl's body with a tight round ass and a pretty chocolate face just like our mama's. She had started rocking dreadlocks two years before I gave them a try. Hers had grown down her back. The girl was a natural mocha beauty. And whereas I didn't take expensive guilt gifts or money from our daddy, Khadijah did. She zipped around the A in an ice-cold black BMW convertible he'd bought her with cash.

We reached the front door and looked into each other's eyes briefly before Khadijah rang the bell. It chimed a cute little classical piano tune. I braced myself for Lorna's big, fake, over-the-top greeting. The façade was just seconds away. Every year she went overboard trying to convince her folks that she was a perfect stepmother and Daddy was the world's greatest father. I didn't know why she wanted them to believe we were a great big happy family when we were anything but.

The door finally opened. "My goodness! Aren't you two a sight for sore eyes." Lorna grabbed Khadijah in a bear hug and kissed her cheek before she reached up and wrapped her arms around my neck and puckered her pastel pink-glossed lips against my cheek. When I was a little boy, I used to wipe her kisses off in her face. Hell, I wanted to do it right then. "Come on in."

Khadijah and I followed her into the house. "What's up, Lorna?" I asked in the form of a greeting.

"I'm well. How are you?"

"I'm cool."

"Where is Genna?"

"*Genesis* is with her mother until this afternoon."

"You should bring her over one day soon. Her grandpa and grammie would love to spend some time with her."

My sister's eyes bucked wide like an alien from the *Men in Black* movie in response to Lorna's reference to being my daughter's grandmother. Khadijah cleared her throat. "How are you, Lorna?" she asked, following her across the marble foyer toward the great room.

"I'm fine. I'm still working out three days a week and power walking every day. How is medical school, darling?"

"It's great."

"TJ, the kids are here, honey!" she yelled like a hillbilly to my father before she walked away.

Daddy appeared grinning, dressed in a pair of navy, green, and yellow plaid golf pants and a white Polo shirt. He was the whitest black man I knew. Clarence Thomas, Ben Carson, and Larry Elder didn't have shit on Tyson Maxwell Senior's Uncle Tom ass. They would look like members of the Black Panthers standing next to this cornball.

"Son, baby girl, how are you two?"

"Fine," we answered in unison.

He extended his hand to me for a weak-ass shake and pecked Khadijah on the forehead. "Well, come with me. Everyone is in the great room trimming the Christmas tree and sipping mimosas or cranberry-peach Bellinis. Brunch will be served soon. The catering staff is putting the final touches on the food as we speak."

We followed him into the great room where we met a sea of whiteness.

"Good morning," I said behind a fake grin.

"Hello, everyone," Khadijah greeted.

The smiles and greetings we received in return seemed
sincere, but I wasn't about to dance a jig. But my heart
did a happy dance at the sight of my 15-year-old stepsister, Bailey, as she rushed toward us.

"Hey, big brother and sister!"

We formed a group hug. It felt good to hold Bailey
and Khadijah. I was the one man on earth who would
die for *both* of them. My daddy wouldn't even take a
bullet for Khadijah. Bailey Louise and I weren't as close
as Khadijah and me because Lorna wouldn't allow us to
bond as deeply as we wanted to. I often had to beg her
and my daddy to let her visit me or to take her out on
a brother-sister date. And because Khadijah lived with
Malcolm Shabazz incarnate, Bailey couldn't step her
pinky toe inside *that* house. So, I was the one who had to
arrange all of the sibling outings, but *stepmonster* made
it hard for me because she didn't want us to corrupt our
little sister with too much blackness.

"Bailey, you get prettier every time I see you, buttercup."

"If that's true, why don't I have a *boyfriend,* Tyson?"

"Boyfriends are highly overrated, honey," Khadijah
explained. "Your big sister doesn't have one either, but
it's all good. I'm living my life like it's golden, and you
should be doing the same thing."

My little stepsister looked at me and smiled with a
bright gleam in her bluish grey eyes. She was drop-dead
gorgeous with sandy, curly hair down to her black-girl
booty that Lorna despised. Her honey-peach complexion
was even and unblemished. And I was happy that she
didn't have those thin white-girl lips like her mother.
Bailey's lips were plump, just like mine.

"I want to see my niece. When are you going to let me
babysit her?"

"I'll make something happen real soon, buttercup. I
promise. Genesis has gotten so big since the last time you

saw her. She's got a diva personality with lots of attitude too."

"I can't wait to hold her. I love that baby."

"Brunch is served," Lorna announced from the entrance of the great room.

I positioned myself between my sisters, grabbed a hand from each, and escorted them from the room. We followed the white people into the dining room to break bread. Lorna had outdone herself this year. The spacious room looked like a five-star restaurant because of the opulent décor and the uniformed service staff of three. The expensive place settings consisted of crystal stemware, sterling silver flatware, and fine bone china. I was impressed with the entire platinum and ivory setup, but I refused to pay my daddy's fake-ass wife a compliment for her effort.

After everyone took a seat around the massive oval-shaped table covered with platinum linen, my daddy began to thank God for the feast we were about to partake of. For a man who seldom attended the Lutheran church he'd joined at the insistence of his wife before their lavish wedding, he always offered long and eloquent prayers over the holiday meal. God probably didn't even know his name.

I opened my eyes during the bogus prayer and scanned the faces around the table after Daddy caught his second wind. Each head was bowed, and every eye closed. There were only two vacant seats out of the twelve scroll-back chairs around the table. Lorna's brother, Robert, and his wife were missing. They'd opted to vacation in the Netherlands for the holidays.

Shit! Bailey's eyes popped wide open, and she caught me staring at our daddy like he had a booger hanging out of his nose. She smiled and made a silly face at me. I winked and grinned. My little buttercup loved our daddy, but she knew he wasn't worth two dead flies. I guess I loved him too in my own way, but my respect for him was at a minimum.

"Amen," Daddy finally said.

Lorna clapped her hands twice, and the serving staff got busy attending to our nutritional needs.

Chapter Twenty

Khadijah

The two Tysons may have been blessed with the brilliant legal minds in the family and could scrutinize details with accuracy even in their sleep, but *I* had street smarts. My sharp eyes didn't miss much, and my hearing game was always on point. And, honey chile, I could read people, especially *men*. Their eyes, facial expressions, and mannerisms spoke louder to me than to the average person. That's why as soon as my daddy's cell phone vibrated in the middle of brunch, I studied him closely before I cast my vision on Lorna. Her face cracked like shattered glass behind all of that Lancôme makeup and her most recent Botox injections.

I thought she was going to stroke out when Daddy grabbed the phone from the table, checked the ID screen, and rushed out of the dining room. His rude ass didn't even properly excuse himself from the table. But I did, though, a few minutes later after I faked a coughing fit. I headed in the direction of the bathroom before I made a clever detour in the direction of my daddy's voice coming from his home office. I tiptoed to the door, and luckily for me, it wasn't completely closed.

"I can't wait to see you either," Daddy whispered sexily as I listened through the small crack in the door. "I'll be there as soon as we finish eating and I hang out with my kids for a while." He sighed, seemingly in frustration.

"Bailey is the only reason why I'm still in this miserable marriage. I love my daughter, and I don't want to make the same mistake of leaving her like I did Tyson Junior and Khadijah. I'll never forgive myself for abandoning them or their mother for Lorna's needy ass."

Daddy kept talking, but I couldn't hear his words over the pounding inside my head. My heart was beating a million times per second. Karma was a *bitch*. Pops was creeping on Lorna. I didn't know why I was so surprised. Creepers always got crept on. Life was just one big boomerang. Lorna had stolen my daddy from my mama, wrecking our home, and now, some other white woman was about to do the same thing to *her* sleazy ass.

"Yeah, I bought it a size too small on purpose. I like you in tight lingerie. When I see that form-fitting, red lace squeezing all that junk in your trunk, it turns Big Daddy on, Kwanza."

Kwanza? I almost choked on my saliva. I took off running down the hall toward the bathroom. I needed to go in there for real this time before I passed out in the middle of the floor. Not only was my daddy cheating on his wife, but he was also laying that pipe on a *sista*. I couldn't wait to tell Tyson. He was going to bug all the way out. I heard footsteps coming in my direction seconds before I dipped inside the bathroom and closed the door. My breathing was labored, and my palms were moist with sweat. I cracked the door and stuck my head outside after I heard the person pass by the bathroom. I saw Lorna storming toward Daddy's home office like she was about to bust up in there and kick his black ass. I ducked back into the bathroom to potty.

"Shut the fuck up!"

"I ain't lying, Tyson. May Allah be my witness," I said, placing my hand over my heart. "Your daddy is cheating on his precious snow queen with some black chick named Kwanza. He's about to go over there and tear that ass up *right now*. And she's on ready too, baby. He bought her a red, one-size-too-small lingerie ensemble to squeeze 'all that junk in her trunk.' I heard him say that with my own two nosy ears. And check this out. He told ole girl that leaving Mama and us for Lorna was a mistake that he'd never forgive himself for."

Tyson's SUV swerved slightly when he hit the steering wheel and screamed, "Shut the fuck up!"

"And he sounded like a *real* black man when he was spitting his game on that side piece. His voice had dropped all the way down to the bottom like Barry White, and it was dripping with swagger like a dude from around the way. I wish you could've heard him. *Big Daddy* was smoother than a pimp, man."

"Shut the fuck up!"

I looked at my brother's profile. "Is that *all* you have to say, Negro?"

"Hell, I don't know what else to say, girl. All these years since Daddy left us for Lorna, I assumed he was happy living on the plantation. He's never given me a reason to believe he had regrets. I guess the grass ain't always greener on the other side."

"It ain't?" I asked, cocking my head to the side with a smirk on my face.

Tyson's eyes left the road briefly to shoot me a puzzled look. "What?"

"The grass—"

"What *grass*, Khadijah?"

"I'm talking about black women versus white women from a brotha's perspective. Is vanilla better than chocolate? You should know now that you're kicking it with that snow bunny."

I watched my brother shift uncomfortably in his seat as we cruised down the interstate en route to his apartment to pick up Genesis from her mother. For years, Tyson had criticized our daddy for cheating on Mama with a white woman and eventually divorcing her to start a new life in another world. Now, *he* was sleeping with a white chick, and I wanted the answer to the trillion-dollar question that had been nagging every sista on earth, in paradise, and in between since brothas had mustered the audacity to take a walk in the *snow*. Was there something magical at the apex of white women's thighs that Allah had withheld from His African queens? Did their vaginas have mystical powers that would eventually rob sistas everywhere of the love of black men? Khadijah Imani Maxwell Shahid needed to know, so I tapped Tyson's thigh and asked, "Do white women do something special in bed that black women don't?"

He shook his head. "Nope. I mean, not really. At least, Mallorie doesn't. It's basically the same except she has no limits or hang-ups when it comes to sex at all. She'll do any damn thing to satisfy me, no matter what. And she doesn't nag or complain like most sistas do. I don't have to call every day or spend all my free time with her. I go to her crib whenever I feel like fucking, and she lets me do anything I want to do to her body. And she does whatever I tell her to do to me without hesitation."

"What else do y'all do besides screw each other's brains out?"

"Not a damn thing."

"*What?* Y'all ain't ever chilled and watched a movie or prepared a meal together? Do you even know how old the girl is?"

"Nope, nope, and nope. I know all I need to know about Mallorie. And other than my name and a few more insignificant facts, I'm a mystery to her. I like it that way. We ain't trying to get married, Khadijah."

"Then what made you become sexually involved with her?"

"Honestly, she had this whack-ass fantasy about fucking a black man, and I guess I was curious about the snow."

I sighed, trying to understand where my brother was coming from, but his explanation didn't make sense to me. "So, after your first encounter with her, what made you go back? How did it turn into an affair?"

"It ain't no affair. When two people are involved in an affair, they have some kind of feelings for each other. That's not the case with Mallorie and me. Like I told you, she's engaged. And you know damn well I ain't about to catch feelings for a white chick. We'll fuck each other until we decide to stop. And believe me, that will be soon. Her wedding is in April, but I'll be done with her way before then."

I sat in Tyson's SUV while he ran inside to get Genesis from her mother. I didn't have a personal problem with Pilar. My ill feelings toward her had nothing to do with anything she'd done to me, per se. I felt some type of way about her because she had cheated on my brother. Other than her past infidelity, I was cool with her. She was an exceptional mother. No one could deny that. And when she and Tyson were a couple, she was totally devoted to him. There was absolutely nothing she wouldn't do for that Negro back in the day. He was her world.

In my opinion, they had gotten too serious way sooner than they should have. Pilar was a young, naïve virgin back then, and so was Tyson. Neither of them had ever experienced the affections of another lover. The luxury of variety had been absent. That's why Tyson had nailed that majorette from Morris Brown and all of those other sluts after her while he and Pilar were together. And I believe deep down in my heart that Pilar had crept on my brother with that football player because she was too young to be strapped down with one man. The adventurous call of nature had swept her up, and she had been too weak, unprepared, and inexperienced to dodge it.

I smiled when Tyson walked outside with my beautiful niece in his arms. The Coach diaper bag I had bought for her was hanging from his shoulder. I could tell she was babbling from the smile on her face and the way her tiny arms were flailing in the cool autumn air.

"Where is Pilar going for Thanksgiving dinner?" I asked when Tyson opened the back door to secure Genesis in her car seat.

"She's probably going over to her cousin, Kayla's, house. Why?"

"I'm just curious."

Chapter Twenty-one

Pilar

I rushed to my bedroom as soon as Ty and Genesis left. I wanted to take my time preparing for my date with Julian. Mami had to look *hot* on her first visit to his home. He had invited a couple of his buddies over for Thanksgiving dinner. An older woman who worked in the deli at Publix had prepared the feast because she'd felt sorry for Julian because he wasn't able to go home to Cincinnati for the holiday due to his work schedule. He was the most recently hired pharmacist at his job, so he had to work on Thanksgiving until five o'clock. He expected me at his house by five thirty to help him warm the food and prepare to receive his guests.

I had decided to wear a bright orange sweater dress that gripped my curves. I was going to rock my brown suede, wedge-heel boots, and accessorize with gold jewelry. And that included the gold hoops *Ty* had bought me a few years ago. My hair was on fleek because Kayla had hooked it up the day before by setting it neatly on jumbo magnetic rollers. It was all shiny and curly with lots of body. With a little bit of pressed powder, bronze lipstick, and an application of mascara to my long lashes, I would be in full diva mode.

I hurried to the bathroom to take a shower with my strawberry-kiwi scented body care products. The last time Julian and I had met at Starbucks, he told me how delicious I smelled because of that fragrance. He even bit my neck playfully after he kissed me into oblivion. I was thinking about letting him do more than just hug and kiss me tonight. Dr. Moye might get lucky enough to slide up in this sweet butterscotch pussy.

I had just turned on Julian's street when my phone rang. I glanced at the ID screen. "What the hell does *he* want?" I snapped, annoyed before I activated my Bluetooth. "What's up, Ty?"

"Would you like me to bring you a plate home? Grandma and Auntie Darlene cooked too much damn food."

"No, but thanks for asking."

"You must be going to Kayla's house for dinner."

"No."

He paused on his reply like he'd been punched in the stomach. "So, what're you going to eat then?"

"I'll have turkey, dressing, and all the trimmings just like you." My GPS announced that I was approaching my destination. Julian's house was beautiful. "Look, Ty, I'll see you at home later on tonight. I've got to go now."

"Oh . . . um . . . all right then."

I ended the call, killed my engine, and stared at Julian's front door for a moment. I wondered why Ty had called me acting so thoughtful out of the blue. It was almost like he'd sensed I was up to something. But I wasn't doing anything wrong. I was about to share a meal with my new friend. For some strange reason, I felt guilty all of a sudden, though. Damn, Ty.

Julian's front door opened without warning, and he stepped out on his stoop looking as yummy as a caramel sundae. His jeans and simple black V-neck sweater were hugging his muscles to perfection. I tried to blink my lust away, but it wasn't going anywhere. I almost drooled when he started walking toward my car with a sexy smile on his face.

He opened the passenger's door and got inside the car. He smelled good, and I became aroused instantly. Without a word, he leaned over and pulled me into his arms. He kissed my lips ever so softly, and my body melted.

"Let's go inside. I want a few more kisses before my boys arrive."

Julian walked up behind me as I stood at the sink washing dishes. He wrapped his arms around my waist and kissed the side of my neck. I shuddered under his touch. It felt good to be in his arms. His dick got hard against my ass. I was impressed. It felt like dude had an anaconda down there. Good Lawd!

"Rick and Tommy said you're too fine to be with an ugly guy like me."

I turned around to face Julian and got lost in his sexy, coppery eyes. "You ain't hardly ugly, baby. They're just jealous." I pecked his lips.

"Girl, don't start something you won't be able to finish."

"Are you daring me?" I kissed him again.

"You're going to make me put my friends out in the middle of the football game, so I can have my way with you."

"What do you want to do to me?"

"I'd rather show you than tell you. Wait until the fellas leave. I'm going to have you climbing the wall."

A few hours later, around ten o'clock, I stood beside Julian on his stoop waving goodbye to his friends. I was happy they were leaving, but I was nervous too. Julian and I would be alone in his home. All the other times we'd been together we were in public places. Tonight, we would have *privacy* without distractions. The sexual tension between us was thick, and the chemistry we shared was dangerous. We were bound to set his house on fire.

"Come on, baby. Let's go back inside and open a bottle of wine," he said, lacing his fingers through mine.

I allowed him to lead me into his home, and he closed the front door on the rest of the world. We walked into his kitchen, hand in hand. He went to the refrigerator and removed a bottle of Moscato. I watched him uncork it before he grabbed two wineglasses from a nearby cabinet. He turned and winked at me and tilted his head toward the den. That was my cue to follow him.

"Your friends are nice," I told him once we got settled on the sofa.

"Yeah, they're cool. We all went to pharmacy school together at the University of Georgia. Rick is divorced, and Tommy is a serious dog."

"And what about *Julian?*"

He poured wine into one of the glasses and handed it to me. "I, sweetheart, am a gentleman looking for a special lady to settle down with." He poured wine into the other glass as I digested his words.

I believed I was special, but my life was so screwed up. Julian was a good guy. I didn't want to drag him into my madness. But I didn't want to lose the special friendship we had either. He made me smile no matter how gloomy I felt some days. He knew just what to say to brighten my often-dark world. And his kisses sent shock waves all over my body.

He snapped his fingers directly in front of my face. "Hey, where did you go, girl? You checked out for a moment. What's up?"

"I'm sorry." I willed myself away from my worries so I could enjoy his company. "I was thinking about Genesis," I lied.

"She's with her father, I assume."

"Yeah, she's with him and his family. I only have a few relatives in Atlanta, and they all went to New York for Thanksgiving. I didn't go because Genesis' father and I split all the major holidays. I spent time with her earlier today, so the evening belongs to him."

Julian drained his wineglass and removed mine from my hand. He placed them both on the coffee table before he pulled me onto his lap. "Well, I'm happy to have you here with me."

The first kiss was so warm and wet with plenty of tongue action. It blew my mind. I moaned in Julian's mouth when he squeezed my ass. His big hands were gentle, but his touch was fiery. The pressure of his bulging erection underneath my thighs caused my heart to pound like a bass drum in my chest. I wanted Julian. I wanted him *badly*. He grabbed a handful of the orange fabric of my dress and pulled it slowly up to my thighs. When his palm caressed my bare flesh, my clit got stiff, and I felt instant dampness in my crotch. My pussy was moist and sizzling.

On raw, feminine instinct, my legs parted as Julian maneuvered two fingers inside the crotch of my thong. He started strumming my hard and juicy clit with his fingertips, and I thought I was going to lose my damn mind. My pussy was saturated with liquid desire, and it was tingling. Julian was working his magic down there, and I was cooing like a baby and bucking my hips. It had been so long since a man had touched me intimately. It hadn't even been a minute yet, but I felt the wave coming. My eyes were fluttering, and I was moaning so freaking loud that I was disturbing my damn self. I was seconds away from coming when my phone rang. It was sitting on the bar across the room. I ignored it because I was on my way to that familiar happy place, baby. I needed an orgasm. Shit, I *deserved* one.

Julian leaned in and licked my ear, and that did it. I fell apart on his lap. The sweetest sensation kissed my entire body from my curly mane down to my pedicured toenails. I almost jerked off of Julian's lap. But through all of my orgasmic bliss, my phone never stopped ringing. I took deep breaths as I came down from the stratosphere. I felt like a new creature, but I wanted *more*. I wanted Julian to fuck me into a damn coma and back to consciousness again.

"Let's go to bed, baby," he whispered in my ear. His warm breath caused my body to quiver with pure lust. "But answer your phone first."

I stood from his lap and hurried over to the bar. I cringed when I saw Ty's face and telephone number flashing on the ID screen *again*. "Hello?"

"Where are you?"

"What's up, Ty?" I asked as calmly as I could. He didn't need to know my whereabouts.

"Genesis is having problems with gas again."

I peeped at Julian with my peripheral vision. He was staring me down. He had removed his sweater, and his pecs were inviting me to come and suck his nipples. I had to be careful not to say anything that would shed light on my housing situation, but the sight of his chest was messing with my head. "Um . . . she . . . She has some Mylicon for that in my medicine cabinet," I whispered.

"Yeah, I know. I found it and gave it to her, but it's not working. She's still crying and fussing. I don't know what to do."

Damn it! "I'm on my way." I ended the call and looked at Julian who was looking right back at me. His dick was still saluting me. I could see that big anaconda pressing against his jeans' zipper. "Genesis is gassy again. Her daddy said the medicine isn't working. I'm sorry, but I've got to go, Julian. Please forgive me."

"Go and take care of your daughter, baby. She's more important. We can pick up where we left off Sunday evening, okay?"

"Of course."

Chapter Twenty-two

Tyson

I pulled back the curtain when I saw headlights coming toward the building. It was Pilar. I was shocked when she got out of the car all dolled up. She must've been out with ole dude. She was wearing the hell out of an orange dress. Damn! Thunder's disloyal ass betrayed me. I stepped away from the window and walked over to Genesis. She was sitting in her bouncy chair looking pitiful, but at least she wasn't crying anymore.

"Where is she?" Pilar rushed in the door in a panic.

I pointed to our daughter. She walked over and released the restraints on the bouncy chair and lifted the baby into her arms. Genesis gave her mom a half smile before she lay her head on her bosom.

"She just stopped crying about ten minutes ago right after she farted a couple of times like a fat man who'd been eating pig's feet. Her gas smelled rotten too. Daddy almost had to run outside for some fresh air," I laughed.

Pilar didn't respond. She just stood there bouncing Genesis in her arms and rubbing her back. She loved our little girl. I could never refute that. Whoever she had been with and whatever they'd been doing hadn't kept her from coming to see about her child.

"What did she eat for dinner, Ty?"

"Mama gave her some mashed potatoes with gravy, dressing, cranberry sauce, and small pieces of the turkey's thigh."

"She ate some good food. Maybe she ate too much of it, though."

"Maybe. Did her *mama* eat some good food today too?"

"I sure did. Did you?"

I nodded.

Pilar sat down in the recliner and started humming a lullaby to the baby as she rocked her in her arms. I took a seat on the couch. I looked at the mother of my child and wondered how different our situation would be if she hadn't been unfaithful to me. We'd probably be married and raising our daughter in a *real* family. I was sure we would be happy too.

"This is Mallorie Whitaker."

"What's up, stranger?"

She hit me with the silent treatment, so I figured she was still in her feelings over how things went down at the harvest celebration. Maybe I should've given her ass a few more days to snap back before I reached out. But it had been a week since Mama had wounded her with words. It wasn't like she had laid hands on her, though.

"Oh, so you don't want to talk to me no more? Cool. Have a nice life. Peace."

"Wait a minute, Tyson! Don't hang up. *Please*."

"Why didn't you tell you were coming to the harvest celebration?"

"I wanted to surprise you. It never crossed my mind that my presence would cause a problem for anyone. Who was that woman anyway? And why was she so mean to me?"

"Dr. Shahid wasn't being mean. She was speaking her truth, expressing her beliefs. You just got hit in her line of fire."

"Her beliefs sounded like *hatred* to me."

"You're entitled to your opinion."

"I wouldn't have felt as bad if you had done something or even said one sentence to me, Tyson. You never parted your lips to defend or comfort me. You didn't even say *hello*."

"What the hell did you expect for me to do? Did you want me to jump onstage and tackle the woman for speaking or snatch out a gun and start shooting up the place because you got your feelings hurt? I was shocked when you walked into the center. I wasn't prepared to babysit you. You saw how busy I was, Mallorie. And everything happened so fast. I didn't know what to do."

"I'm not sure what you should've done, but you could've done *something*."

"You know what, Mallorie? I'm not going to have this conversation with you. I called to check in and make sure you were okay and to apologize. I'm sorry for whatever I did or didn't do to defend you at the harvest celebration. I hope you're all right now. Anyway, I need to get to court now."

"Knock, knock," Pilar called out, opening my bedroom door. She poked her head inside. "Aren't you guys going to church this morning?"

I sat up and wiped the crust from my eyes. "Nah, we're tired. Genesis woke up in the middle of the night whimpering. I think her little tummy was hurting again."

I could tell Pilar was disappointed that our daughter and I would be at the crib all day long. We were about to ruin her special secret Sunday. She wouldn't dare leave the house knowing Genesis was feeling less than 100 percent. She wasn't that kind of a mother.

"I guess I'll go to the grocery store to buy something to cook for dinner then. What do you have a taste for?"

"I could eat your smothered pork chops in brown mushroom gravy with some whipped potatoes. And if it's not asking too much, please, fry some cabbage."

"I can make that happen."

"Thank you. Get my Wells Fargo debit card out of my wallet. It's on the kitchen counter."

It had been two weeks since that awkward conversation with Mallorie. She'd called several times after that, but I hadn't picked up my phone. And I had schooled the receptionist at work about my little situation with her, so she had been blocking all calls from Mallorie Whitaker like a telephone bouncer. I would never admit this out loud, but I missed hanging out with her. Yeah, she and I were only fuck buddies, but she was cool, and she took care of my manly needs. I was no longer dealing with other females sexually or otherwise because I didn't have time. Between my internship, studying for the bar exam, and being the best father possible to Genesis, I had very few spare moments. And I was working every Saturday with the lawn service now to bring in extra cash for Christmas. The day was quickly drawing near, and I wanted to make sure my daughter's first Christmas in the world would be a special one.

I had a gig coming up Friday night at a mansion in Alpharetta. Rich, white women didn't mind making it rain for sex or the fantasy of it. I was going to make $500 for one hour of entertainment, plus tips. The only catch was the bride wanted a private dance. Hell, I guess she wanted to go out with a bang. I wasn't about to get busy with her, though, and I had specified that she had restrictions on her hands. I was a dancer and not a male prostitute.

I pushed my buggy filled with groceries over to the pharmacy counter. I had promised my sweet, elderly neighbor, Mrs. Watkins, I would pick up her prescriptions and deliver them to her. I was going to ask the pharmacist to recommend a medicine to help with Genesis' problems with gas and indigestion too.

"How may I help you, sir?"

I didn't know why the bucktooth pharmacy technician was batting her eyes at me. I wasn't checking for her. "I'm here to pick up prescriptions for Cora Watkins. I need to speak with the pharmacist too."

Bucky, the beaver, went to the back and retrieved Mrs. Watkins's five prepaid prescriptions, and I signed for them before I placed them in my buggy. A few seconds later, a tall, exotic-looking brotha came from the back smiling.

"I'm Dr. Moye," he informed me, offering his hand in a friendly and firm shake. "How may I help you, sir?"

"My 8-month-old daughter has been suffering from severe gas periodically over the past few weeks. Her mother and I've been giving her Mylicon drops as recommended by a pharmacist. It helps, but I was hoping you could suggest something stronger or maybe a medicine that could prevent the onsets."

The guy looked at me like *he* had a bad case of gas. It was kind of strange. Then he folded his arms across his chest and said, "Gas is one of those things some babies suffer with, sir. Different foods and formulas are the main causes. Is the child on solid food yet?"

"Yeah, Genesis has been eating table food since she was 4 months old. Her mom is still nursing her to supplement her formula too, though. I guess Mommy and child are going to have to pay closer attention to what they eat from now on."

"That'll be a great start. In fact, make a food log even to record your daughter's reactions to whatever she eats or drinks, Mr. um . . ."

"My bad. I'm Tyson Maxwell."

"Make sure you and your wife list the foods your daughter can tolerate and eliminate the ones that seem to cause her discomfort, Mr. Maxwell. Keep giving her the Mylicon drops as well. If her symptoms become more frequent and unable to be relieved, make an appointment for her to see her pediatrician."

"We'll do just that. Thanks, man."

I flexed my muscles a few times and exhaled as the intro to Donna Summer's "Hot Stuff" blasted in the next room. I was about to stack some paper. I burst into the party on cue and went to work. I was doing my thing, giving my private audience of rich and rowdy white women exactly what they wanted when my eyes collided with Mallorie's. She froze in midmotion with her hand high in the air, clutching a stack of crisp green singles. I almost lost my groove at the sight of her, but Christmas was coming, and the goose was getting fat. Daddy had to make it do what it do. I kept dancing as sweat poured down my glistening muscles, saturating my flesh. Some women approached me to get their feel on as they stuffed money in my red silk boxer briefs. I showed my appreciation with deep pelvic thrusts and continuous smiles.

I kept a side eye on Mallorie the entire time I wiggled and stirred the women into a state of horniness. She watched me with keen eyes like she'd never seen me before or even knew my name. I couldn't read minds, but I damn sure could read *eyes*. Mallorie's steel-grey ones were filled with lust for me. She was fighting hard, attempting to suppress visions of the many steamy nights I'd taken her body to a sexual utopia. But she was clearly losing the fight. Her fidgety body language and heavy breathing were telling signs. Her pussy was overflowing like a river after a torrential rainfall, and her clit was painfully stiff and sensitive between its hairy lips. I couldn't see it or feel it, but I would bet every green dollar at my feet and stuffed in my drawers on it.

The moment I exposed Thunder, causing the room to erupt in emotional chaos was Mallorie's breaking point. She whispered something to a thick, tanned chick with a short hairstyle and tugged her arm. The girl looked at me with fire in her dark eyes and smiled. In response, I pumped my hips, causing Thunder to swing back and forth. The shameless come-and-get-it smile the girl flashed shocked me. Mallorie frowned and yanked the chick's arm and forced her out of the room.

Chapter Twenty-three

Mallorie

"Look! There he is! Go talk to him. I'll wait here. Go on, Mal. I want to meet him."

I hesitated as I watched Tyson weave in and out of the two dozen or so cars parked outside the house. I wasn't sure if it was a good idea to approach him or not. It sounded cool when Camden first suggested it, but now, I was having second and third thoughts about it. I hadn't spoken to Tyson in two weeks, and our last conversation hadn't exactly been a pleasant one. I'd been missing him like crazy, but I had been busy preparing for Collin's visit, our engagement party, and Christmas. Those preparations had preoccupied my mind during the daytime, along with my internship. But at night, especially *Friday* nights, my body went into full sexual withdrawals. No man, not even Collin, could do anything to feed my need like Tyson could. He was no longer my fantasy; he was my *addiction*.

"Mal, hurry up! He's about to get in the SUV," Camden screeched, reminding me of what I was supposed to have been doing.

Without another thought, I hopped out of my SUV and ran toward him just as his hand reached for the door handle. "Tyson!" I waved my hand and increased my pace.

He turned and stared at me. Then he stuffed his hands in the pockets of his leather jacket.

"How have you been?" I asked timidly.

"Busy. What about you?"

"I've been tied up as well. I had no idea you would be dancing here tonight."

"I could tell. You looked at me like I was a zombie or something."

"I was caught off guard." I looked toward my SUV. "My friend, Camden, came to town to help me get ready for the engagement party. We've been friends since we were kids." I laughed nervously. "Why don't you come over and hang out with us? She wants to meet you. I'm not sure why, but she just does. Can you come over for a little while to chill? I've got a bottle of Hennessey. I could order some food if you're hungry."

"Is your fiancé back in the States yet?"

"No, he hasn't arrived yet. He'll be here the day after tomorrow."

He nodded. "Order me a medium well rib-eye steak and a loaded baked potato from Stan's Steakhouse. I'll get there as soon as I can. I have a stop to make first."

"OMG! He is a *dream*, Mal. And he's so raw and rugged. He's like hot sex wrapped inside a package. I can't blame you for carrying on with him. But how're you ever going to let him go? You're going to have to wean yourself slowly from that chocolate hunk."

"Ssshhh . . . Lower your voice, Cam. He might hear you. He's probably out of the shower by now, but I can't tell."

"I'll go and check." She stood up from the sofa, but I snatched her back down. "What's wrong with you?" she asked, laughing. "I'm going in there to see if he needs anything."

"He's fine."

"Hey, are you being *possessive* of your fudge fuck fellow?"

"Stop it, Cam. I don't think you should be flirting with him."

She smiled tauntingly. "And why not? He's not your *man,* Mal. You're engaged to *Collin.* Remember? You and Mr. Chocolate are only sexing each other up."

I opened my mouth to respond, but Tyson entered the den wearing only a pair of blue and white flannel pajama bottoms. His well-toned pectoral muscles and washboard abs robbed me of words and air. I loved it whenever he allowed his dreadlocks to hang loose.

I jumped up and hurried to the kitchen to get his food and a glass of Hennessey. As soon as I opened the oven, I realized I shouldn't have left Tyson alone with Cam. She was an unabashed sexaholic, and she went both ways. The girl had slept with as many women as men. I admired her for her liberal and uninhibited approach to human sexuality, but I didn't want her to make any advances toward Tyson. He and I were in a sexual relationship, and regardless of the absence of an emotional connection, I didn't want Cam to lay a finger on him.

I cringed when I heard her flirty laughter after a mumbled statement from Tyson. Was I jealous? Of course, I was, although I had no right to be. I made sure the steak and potato were warm enough and hurried to the cabinet to get a glass. I tucked the bottle of Hennessey under my arm and left the kitchen, carefully balancing everything else in my hands. "What's so funny, Cam?" I asked the moment I entered the den.

"This gorgeous hunk of a man was just telling me how he got into the private erotic dancing business."

A bolt of anger suddenly struck me. I had never heard that story before. Maybe it was because I had never asked. Leave it to Cam to dig into Tyson's personal life after only knowing him five minutes. There were certain things I wanted to know about him too, but I'd never been bold enough to pry. I ignored my feelings over Cam's nosiness and walked over to serve Tyson his food. I poured a generous portion of the liquor into the glass and placed it on the end table next to the love seat within his reach.

"Thanks. Can I get a couple of ice cubes in the Henny, please?"

"Sure."

I left the room again to get ice. I grabbed a red plastic cup and filled it with cubes from the automatic icemaker. When I returned to the den, Cam was sitting next to Tyson on the love seat. I narrowed my eyes at her and retook my seat on the sofa opposite them.

"Tyson told me he's in his last year of law school at Emory, Mal. Isn't that the law school Godfrey and your dad went to?"

"Yeah, they both went to Emory, and so did my grandfather and all of my uncles."

For the next twenty minutes, I sat quietly watching Tyson devour his steak and loaded potato and sip Hennessey all while listening to Cam talk about her world travels. I felt like an outsider in my own home. I was seething because I felt my friend was purposely manipulating the situation to maintain the spotlight on herself. Tyson was *my* friend. Cam was acting inappropriately by flirting with him openly and ignoring me.

And he seemed to be enjoying every minute of it. I thought Tyson's preoccupation with Cam had everything to do with her big bubble butt. Ever since we were in middle school and the early stages of puberty, her *black-girl* figure, including her phat ass, had been a conversation piece. She'd also been blessed with a set of hefty, perfectly round D-cup breasts to go along with her voluptuous curves. Guys of every race and ethnicity used to rave over her. My body looked like it belonged to a little boy compared to hers.

"You're hilarious, Tyson," Cam sang seductively and squeezed his thigh.

I had missed whatever he'd said that she found so funny. In all of the weeks I'd been spending time with Tyson, I couldn't recall a single moment I would've mistaken him for a comedian. I wondered what the hell he had said to make Cam burst into a fit of uncontrollable laughter. I was pretty certain it was all an act. Yes, she was putting it on thick to impress him or to simply stroke his ego. Either way, I was sick of her shenanigans, and for the first time, I wanted Tyson to leave my condo without us having sex.

"It's getting late, Tyson. Don't you want to get back home to Genesis in time for her midnight feeding and diaper change?"

"Nah," he said after a long swig of Hennessey. "She's with her mother. Everything is under control."

I got up and stormed into the kitchen. I needed a strong drink to relax. Otherwise, I was going to strangle Cam and kick Tyson's ass out of my house. I sat down at the dinette for a few moments to take a couple of cooling-down breaths. I very seldom allowed my emotions to get the best of me, but Cam was pushing all of the wrong buttons on my mental meter. And Tyson's reaction to her wasn't helping the situation. Instead of me preparing and looking forward to celebrating my engagement to a wonderful guy who loved me, I was having a meltdown over my secret sex partner in my kitchen. Tyson had no feelings for me whatsoever. And if he did, he had a bizarre way of showing it. My knees started shaking, knocking against each other when I realized I could have feelings for him. How had I allowed something so ridiculously stupid to happen?

Pull yourself together, Mal! You're not in love with Tyson Maxwell. It's not possible. He's just a man you're sleeping with. The green-eyed monster has only visited you because Cam is flirting with him. It'll be over as soon as he leaves.

I needed that drink more than ever now. Only the strongest thing available would do the trick. I grabbed the tequila bottle from the pantry, opened it, and threw it back. I gulped and gulped, trying like hell to drown my childish jealousy and every foolish thought in my brain. My engagement party was only four days away, and Collin would be home the day after tomorrow. I didn't have time for emotional mix-ups or meltdowns. What Tyson and I had shouldn't have any bearing on my *real life,* the one that included a fiancé, future babies, and a promising career in my family's law firm. I had made the awful mistake of almost allowing my two worlds to merge, but after tonight, my life would be back on its normal track.

I returned to my den just in time to hear Tyson ask Cam in awe, "So, you're *bisexual?*"

Chapter Twenty-four

Tyson

"Actually, I'm *trysexual*. I've tried it all, and I'm open to anything new."

"Get the fuck out of here!"

"Don't tell me Mal never mentioned that her oldest and dearest friend in the world is a *freak*." Camden doubled over and cracked the hell up.

I sat there next to her aroused and curious to the max. She had the hots for me. From the moment I looked into her eyes during my performance at the bachelorette party, I realized she wanted to make me her sex slave. And Mallorie was aware of it too. That's why she had a funky-ass attitude. I hadn't crashed their BFF night out slash sleepover. I was at her crib hanging out by invitation. I could've easily gone home, showered, drunk a few Amstel Lights, and cuddled up with my daughter. But since I was here with them, I felt wild and adventurous.

"Mallorie and I don't discuss our friends. So, no, she's never mentioned you." I looked across the room and held Mallorie prisoner with my eyes. "How come you never told me about Camden? She's cool."

"Like you said, we don't discuss other people when we're together."

"Have you ever been with a woman before, Mallorie?"

She shook her head in the negative and glared at me.

"Why not?" I asked, pushing her out of her comfort zone despite the fact she was pissed.

"Mal has a reserved side when it comes to certain things. It's cool to fuck a black stud behind her fiancé's back, but God forbid if she would ever free herself to explore sex with a woman." Camden removed the half-filled glass of Hennessey from my hand and took it straight to the head.

"Is that true, Mallorie? You would never consider having sex with a woman?" I asked, genuinely curious.

"To be honest, I've never thought about it. I appreciate the beauty of women, but I've never been sexually attracted to one."

"Come here."

"Why?"

"Just come over here with Camden and me," I dared.

Her eyes narrowed, and the flaring of her nostrils displayed her anger over being challenged by me. But she rose to her feet and walked slowly across the room. I reached out and pulled her onto my lap. "Kiss Camden."

"I don't have time for kiddie games, Tyson," she snapped and tried to get up.

I held her in place on my lap with strength she was no match for. I lifted her sweater to tease her nipples with the pads of my thumbs through the lacy fabric of her bra. I whispered in her ear. "Kiss her the way you would kiss me."

Camden took the lead. She pulled Mallorie's face to hers and licked her lips until they parted. Then she stuck her tongue inside Mallorie's mouth and yanked a handful of her hair.

I undid the single front clasp on her bra, releasing her breasts into my palms. I caressed them as I watched her and Camden feast on each other's tongues. My erection was mountainous. I couldn't remember being more aroused in my life. I pinched Mallorie's nipples and rolled them between my middle fingers and thumbs.

Camden pulled away suddenly and stood up. Within seconds, she was as naked as the day she was born. Her thickness caught my eye, and my pulse quickened. I preferred that a woman have hair on her pussy, but something about her smooth, hairless one intrigued me. There was a tattoo of the sun on her right breast, and a half moon adorned the other. A heart encased her navel. I reached out and traced it with my fingertip.

"Take off your clothes," I told Mallorie, still pinching her left nipple.

Compliant as always, she stood from my lap and removed her blue pinstriped slacks and red cashmere twinset. Camden and I watched her as she kicked out of her navy spectator pumps before she pulled her tights and panties down her legs and over her feet. She eased her bra straps down her arms and allowed the lacy fabric to fall to the floor.

"We need a blanket, Mal. Where can I find one?"

"Look on the shelf in the guestroom closet."

Camden hurried down the hall with her ass and thighs jiggling. She was a thick-ass white girl. She returned to the scene in no time. She pushed the coffee table out of the way and spread the cream chenille blanket on the floor. I damn near had a heart attack when she lay down on it and opened her legs wide to reveal a gold stud earring pierced though her clitoris. Thunder was jumping like a raging bull trying to break free from its stall.

"Get down there with her, Mallorie. Daddy wants to see a show. Give daddy something nasty to watch. Make daddy happy."

Mallorie stood and walked over to the blanket. Camden reached up and pulled her down on top of her. She quickly reversed their positions and started kissing her hungrily. She eased down Mallorie's body a few inches and sucked one breast while she kneaded the other one. I was sure I would soon get in on the action, but I couldn't move just yet. I wanted to watch. Camden dipped her head lower to lick Mallorie's naval. I swallowed hard when she eased farther down and kissed the lips of her vagina. Then she separated the two, wet, and hairy lips with her thumbs and exposed her swollen, saturated clit. The pungent scent of hot, creamy pussy made my dick even harder.

Camden started flicking the tip of Mallorie's clit slowly with her tongue. Then she sucked it until Mallorie squirmed and moaned out her pleasure. Camden stuck her middle finger inside of Mallorie's wetness and then out again repeatedly. She maintained a steady rhythm on both tasks simultaneously like a seasoned lover. Mallorie's eyes were clamped shut tightly as she grinded her pussy against Camden's face. She was humming and bucking wildly. I was amazed at how much Mallorie was enjoying having her pussy licked by another woman. But I was also fascinated. It was time to join them. I couldn't hold out another minute. I pulled down my pajama bottoms and boxers to free Thunder. Camden must've heard my sudden movements because she rose and turned her head to stare at my rock-solid dick.

She crawled the few feet over to me and pushed me to sit again on the love seat. Without a second to spare, she swallowed Thunder whole like he was an old familiar friend. My meat swelled even larger in her throat as she pulled, slurped, and moaned. Her tongue action was on the money, running up and down the length of me. My balls were being caressed like they were a pair of priceless jewels. Camden was sucking me off into a sleepy high. It felt so damn good that I wanted it to last forever.

I didn't know why the hell I looked at Mallorie in the heat of the moment, but I regretted it immediately. She was watching me get my dick devoured like she wanted to kill me. I closed my eyes to shut her out. I didn't have a problem when Camden was licking her to the clouds. Hell, I *enjoyed* it. That shit had turned my heat all the way up. There was no room for jealousy in a threesome because everybody could get their rocks off.

Camden raised her head, and I wanted to cuss. I was so close to filling her mouth with my seed. I looked down in her face and pushed the top of her head down again, hoping she would take the hint to finish what she had started. But she ducked away.

"Fuck me."

I just stared at Camden because I felt Mallorie's eyes on us. It was like she was sending me a silent message *not* fuck her friend in her presence. The tension in the room was thick.

"I know you've got a condom. Put it on and fuck me until your heart's content. Come on," she said before she lowered her head and licked precome from the tip of my dick. She stroked me and moaned. "Please fuck me. I'll give it to you like you've never had it before."

I glanced at Mallorie for a few seconds. She was on her knees watching me, no doubt, wondering if I was going to give Camden what she was begging for. I ain't going to lie. I wanted to fuck her, but I felt some type of way about the scenario I had created. It was hard to think with Camden licking and stroking Thunder.

I finally pushed her away and left the room to get a condom from my wallet. I ripped it open, rolled it on my dick, and rejoined my threesome mates. "Lie down on your back, Mallorie." I saw some reluctance in her eyes.

"*Lie down.*" After she followed my order, I looked down at Camden. "Eat her pussy good until she comes."

She crawled back on the blanket and started chowing down on Mallorie's kitty cat like a ravenous animal. I got down on the blanket and positioned myself behind her thick ass. I jammed my middle finger in her pussy from the back. It was juicy and dripping down her thighs. I touched the gold stud with my dick, rubbing it up and down her stiff clit a few times. Pussy juice was cascading down like a waterfall.

"Fuck me now, Tyson! *Now!*"

I entered Camden with one deep and forceful push. She cried out and arched her back. I sensed she was a rough and rambunctious type of broad, so I grabbed hold of her jiggling butt cheeks and started riding her hard and wild. The rougher I got, the more her pussy dripped and clenched around me. I didn't know who was moaning louder, Camden or Mallorie. All three of us were getting our worlds rocked at the same damn time. I was as far up in Camden as I could go, and she was licking Mallorie's coochie dry. The sounds of sweaty flesh pounding against flesh mixed with grunts and groans filled the den. It reminded me of a brothel. We were taking kinkiness to a brand-new level.

Mallorie came first, and she cussed up a blue streak in the process. Then her girl's inner muscles gripped Thunder so tightly that it made my heart do a flip. My nut came in slow motion, as I rammed into Camden with all of my might one last time. My toes curled and twitched as hot, rushing sperm filled the condom. I threw my head back and roared loud enough to wake every fucking resident in the building.

Seconds later, Camden whimpered and bucked back into my hips like she had lost complete control of her body. She banged both fists on the floor and convulsed. "Damn it, Tyson! Shit! Shit! Shit!"

The sound of drops of liquid hitting the blanket in a rushing downpour yanked me from my sexual high. I pulled out of Camden and looked down. My eyes crossed at the repulsive sight of her pissing on the blanket as her body convulsed violently.

Chapter Twenty-five

Mallorie

"How is the food?"

"It's fine. When did you learn how to cook something other than breakfast?"

I smiled at Collin, genuinely happy to have him home. "I've been experimenting with a few recipes in preparation of becoming Mrs. Collin Cartwright. A good wife has to feed her husband."

"Well, I'm impressed."

"Thank you, sweetie. Claudette, one of the female janitors at work, gave me the salmon recipe. I found the one for the corn pudding online, and I stumbled on the bacon-wrapped asparagus spears in a cookbook at the spa. I'm glad you're enjoying everything. Would you like another glass of wine?" I reached across the table for his wineglass.

He held up his hand and shook his head. "I'm fine, babe. I just want to finish off this delicious food on my plate and take a long, hot shower. Then I want to make love to my fiancée until I drop dead."

Making love was nothing compared to hardcore *fucking*. I would prefer the latter on any given day, but Collin was not that type of man. He was a reserved Southern gentleman, and I was his precious princess. There would be no vulgarities or roughness or exciting physical challenges in his arms in my bed tonight. My body and mind would have to readjust to the slower and gentler form of sex while Collin was in town. I had already begun counting down the days until his departure for Africa so he could complete his assignment, and I could transform back into the *real* Mallorie Whitaker, even if it would be only temporarily. I just hoped I would survive my forced hiatus, and Tyson would be willing and available to relieve me once Collin was gone.

For the past two months, I had indulged in raw and unrestrained sexual activities of the raunchiest kind. I had never experienced such freedom since I'd lost my virginity in the back of that car. Now that Collin was home, I would have to crawl back into my little pristine box and pretend to be the young lady everyone believed I was.

The taste of my vagina on Collin's lips and tongue while he kissed me was something I had missed. Tyson and I had never shared a kiss, and he'd made no attempts to take the party *downtown* either. Camden had been the last person to eat me out, and I hated to admit it, but she could teach Collin a thing or two about oral sex.

"I love you, Mal," Collin whispered softly, looking into my eyes as he entered me.

I smiled. "I love you more."

I looked out my window at the stars as the slow and methodic ride began. Collin's lovemaking was always so predictable. I met his gentle strokes with lazy thrusts in a moderate rhythm. I squeezed my inner vaginal muscles as tightly around him as I could. My body had to adjust to a much thinner and shorter penis. I prayed that Collin couldn't detect that my walls had been stretched.

Hopefully, the two weeks and four days without pene-
tration along with my daily Kegel exercises had caused
things to tighten up down there. The minimum flow
of feminine moisture was working in my favor as well.
Collin couldn't get my juices flowing like Tyson always
did. There would be a sloppy wet mess in my bed if his
big black dick were pumping in and out of my cunt right
now. And I would be screaming and howling with a full
voice as he talked nasty and growled in my ear.

Just the thought of being with Tyson swept me away.
A clear vision of his exquisite, naked body spread across
the starlit sky. I felt blood rush to my clit. I increased the
pace of my hips and rotated them like I did whenever I
fucked Tyson. In my mind, I was with him and not Collin.
My inner muscles clenched around him and released him
again.

"Oh God, Mal! Babe, I love you!" Collin's words were
heartfelt and tender to my ear, but he wasn't there. *Tyson*
was.

I squeezed and released him again and again and
again, all while bucking my hips upward with force.
He kissed me deeply and with so much passion as he
eased in and out of me. His body was saturated with
perspiration, and he was quivering. It wouldn't be long
before his release.

"Aaargh! Oh God! I missed you!"

I felt the surge of warm semen enter my womb the
instant Collin ejaculated. It was something else I'd
missed. We had discontinued using condoms the night
he proposed and relied totally on my birth control pills,
which I took religiously. There was no latex barrier
between us like Tyson and me.

Collin stopped moving and took in several gulps of air.
He looked at me and smiled brightly before he kissed my
lips. "Did you come?"

"Of course, I did," I told him untruthfully.

"God, I love you."

"I love you too."

"Ah, you're perfect, Collin. Don't move a muscle, my dear," Mother instructed before she frowned at me. "Oh, dear God, Mallorie Elizabeth, please relax that toothy smile. You remind me of a caricature."

I did as I'd been told and relaxed my smile a little, displaying only my top teeth. The photographer snapped a few pictures before he directed Collin and me into another pose. We were in the middle of an impromptu photo shoot at our engagement party. Mother and Mrs. Cartwright had ushered Collin and me into my father's study away from all of our guests so we could take pictures for the wedding announcement. It would appear on the society page of the *Atlanta Journal-Constitution* and in every elite publication in the city six weeks before the wedding.

"I think we have enough shots to choose from," the photographer announced. "I'll email you the edited images in a few days. Merry Christmas."

Collin and I thanked the young man before we left the room while our mothers remained behind discussing the seating arrangement for the reception. With his hand in the small of my back, my handsome fiancé guided me through the house as we smiled at our family members, friends, and associates who had gathered to celebrate our engagement. My father, under my mother's overbearing insistence, had spared no expense for the posh private party. There was plenty of delicious gourmet food, and cocktails of every brand and preference were in abundance. The seven-piece jazz ensemble that had been hired for the evening was absolutely amazing. I wouldn't mind having them at the reception, but it wasn't up to me. Every minute detail of the wedding had to meet Mother's approval regardless of what Collin or I wanted.

"This is a great party, Mal. Congrats."

I smiled at Kiyomi, my longtime friend from middle school to the present. "Thank you. I'm so glad you could make it."

"You guys picked the perfect time to throw this fancy shindig. Everyone comes home for Christmas. Your engagement to your beau gave me another reason to celebrate," Kiyomi said with a sassy smile. She was talking to me, but her slanted eyes were glued to Collin.

"Allow me to introduce you to the man of the hour." I wrapped a possessive arm around Collin's waist. "Babe, this is Kiyomi Winston. We've been friends since the seventh grade. We were cocaptains of our cheerleading squad in high school. And she'll be one of my eight bridesmaids in our wedding."

"It's a pleasure to meet you, Kiyomi." He reached for her hand and shook it.

"Oh, we've met before. It's so nice to see you again," she purred, still holding Collin's hand.

Is she flirting with my man?

"Are you sure? I don't recall ever meeting you. Please remind me where we met."

Kiyomi threw her head back and laughed with her hand resting on her round and perky breasts. "It was at little Porter Davenport's christening luncheon. You know . . . Carter and Ivy Davenport's adorable son. They hosted this huge over-the-top party outside under a white tent after the ceremony. Remember? You and Mal were there. We danced together a few times because my friend here had a migraine."

I vaguely remembered that party two years ago. And from the confused look on Collin's face, he didn't seem to remember it at all. Recalling insignificant past events wasn't on my list of priorities. I was more concerned with the *present*, more specifically, the lustful way Kiyomi was eyeing Collin. Every woman knew how to execute the I-want-you look. Therefore, we were able to detect it in the eyes of another woman as well. The subtle touch she made to my man's arm while she smiled flirtatiously and batted her slanted dark eyes at him wasn't lost on me. I was pissed enough to blow a gasket. If Kiyomi didn't withdraw her claws, I was going to kick her butt all the way to her mother's homeland of Japan. I refused to tolerate her disrespect.

Collin must've smelled the lust Kiyomi had for him rising from the pores of her smooth golden skin. He took a backward step and tightened his arm around my waist. "If you said it happened, I believe you. I just can't remember that day clearly. Anyway, you'll have to excuse this gorgeous woman and me. We're making our rounds to greet as many guests as we can. I'm sure you understand."

We walked away, and the first person to step into our path was Camden. She and I had only spoken over the phone since *that night,* but even then, neither of us had mentioned what had happened. I would be grateful to the heavens if we'd both forget about the entire incident and never discuss it *ever*. As expected, Cam had performed all of the duties she'd been assigned to help with the engagement party, and I was thankful. Seeing her now with Collin by my side made me very uncomfortable. Technically, I had cheated on him with Cam. And she knew all about my fling with Tyson. In the twinkling of an eye and without any justification at all, she could ruin my entire life. My body trembled involuntarily at the mere thought of the power the threesome had given my childhood friend over me.

"I'm so happy for you," she whispered in my ear as she hugged me. She released me and turned to Collin. "You're one lucky guy. Be good to her, or you'll have to answer to *me*."

"It's hard to be unkind to a lovely angel. And that's exactly what God has blessed me with, Camden. Don't worry. I'll treat Mallorie like royalty for the rest of her life."

Chapter Twenty-six

Tyson

"Merry Christmas!"

I couldn't respond right away. The phone had awakened me a few minutes past midnight on Christmas morning to a slight beer buzz before Mallorie's cheerful voice rang in my ear. This wasn't supposed to be happening because she was *officially* engaged now, and her wedding countdown was on.

"Are you there?"

"Yeah, I'm here. Merry Christmas to you too. Aren't you supposed to be with your man? I figured your engagement party would be lit about now."

"Oh no, it's over. After dinner and the formalities, lots of guests danced and got sloppy drunk. It was hilarious. I'm on my way home now."

"Where's *he?*"

She giggled. "He got wasted too. I left him droopy-eyed and slurring with his buddies. They're going to a bar in Midtown that doesn't close until three o'clock. More alcohol is exactly what they need for sure." She fell silent for a moment as if she'd run out of words to say. Then in a voice dripping with longing, she whispered, "I miss you. I wish you could meet me somewhere right now, but I'm sure you can't . . . Can you?"

"Nah, I ain't going anywhere. Christmas is all about my baby girl. After dinner, I gave her a warm bubble bath and read her a Christmas story. She crashed shortly afterward. Then I arranged all of her toys in a cute little display in the living room, popped a few beers, and fell asleep. You woke me up."

"I'm sorry. I didn't mean to."

"It's cool," I said, sitting up on the sofa. "Genesis' little eyes will pop open around one o'clock, so I needed to wake up anyway. Now that she's older, that's the *one* time she wakes up during the night. She'll want her diaper changed and an eight-ounce bottle of warm breast milk mixed with formula and sprinkled with a few tablespoons of rice cereal. I'm about to mix it now."

"Where will you get the breast milk from?"

"What did I tell you about being nosy, Ms. Whitaker?" I sighed and shook my head at her sly attempt at cracking the privacy code between us. "It ain't cool to pry when you've been asked not to. But to satisfy your curiosity, the breast milk is in my frig. It's amazing what a Medela electric breast pump can do."

"There's no need for sarcasm, Tyson. I get it. Genesis' mother expresses the milk and gives it to you to store in the refrigerator at your home. Cool."

"What are you and your fiancé going to do to celebrate the holiday?"

"Fortunately, we'll spend most of the day with his family up in Smyrna since last night's event was held at my parents' estate. The Cartwrights are such sweet and down-to-earth people. They're not rich snobs like my family. I always enjoy myself at their holiday gatherings."

"Well, I'll have Genesis all day long because she'll be leaving in the morning heading to New York with her mama. They're going to visit her other grandma until after the New Year. I'm going to miss my little princess. I'll be lost without her."

"What're you and the baby going to do later today?"

"I imagine she'll spend the morning playing with all these damn toys my sister and I bought for her. We kind of went overboard." I grinned as my eyes swept over all of the baby dolls, stuffed animals, and other toys piled high in a shiny red push wagon. There was also a stack of books, a few musical instruments, and building blocks off to the side.

"Once she gets tired of playing, I'll take her to see my mama since she doesn't hang out with the rest of the family on Christmas because she's Muslim. She'll be the only family member absent from my aunt Darlene's house. My sister is also a follower of Islam, but she'll be right there at the dinner table with us feasting on everything except for the ham and my cousin Gertrude's famous chitterlings."

"It sounds like you guys will have lots of fun over a delicious Southern meal."

"We will."

"Well, enjoy the holiday with your family, Tyson."

"You do the same with yours and your future hubby."

"Um . . . He's leaving in three days, and um . . . I . . . um . . . hope we can hook up soon."

"Maybe."

"Okay. Merry Christmas."

"Merry Christmas."

What the hell is taking Mama so long to answer the damn door? I wondered before I pressed the lighted button, ringing the doorbell again repeatedly. I knew she was in there. Where else would she be at one o'clock in the afternoon on Christmas Day? I shifted Genesis to my other hip. She smiled at me, and it made my heart dance. "Where is your nana, little girl? Where is she, huh? Where is that militant woman?" I asked, nuzzling the side of her face with my cold nose.

The door opened slowly, and my mama appeared wearing a short white bathrobe splattered with red roses. I believed it was silk. She looked straight through me with an unreadable expression on her face that I had never seen before.

"May we come in?"

Without a word, she waved her hand and took a step backward to give us entry space. She followed us inside into the foyer, and instantly, I sensed something was off. Smooth jazz music was playing softly in the back of the house. My instincts told me it was coming from her *bedroom*. Usually, my mama would grab Genesis from my arms and make a fuss over her, but not today. She stood before us barefoot and seemingly nervous, tugging at the belt on her sexy bathrobe. Her body was in great shape for a woman in her mid-50s, but her boobs weren't firm enough for her to be running around braless. But I guess she could get a pass in her own home.

"We stopped by to say hello. You know my munchkin and her mom are flying out to New York tomorrow morning. They're going to spend the rest of the year and a few days afterward with Consuela and the Puerto Rican posse up in the Bronx."

Finally, Mama reached out and removed Genesis from my arms and kissed her chubby cheek. "Nana is going to miss her ladybug."

"She'll miss you too." I unzipped the diaper bag hanging on my shoulder. "That's why she brought you this present," I announced, pulling out a small gift box wrapped in bright green paper and topped with a white bow.

"You know I don't celebrate Christmas, boy."

"That's why it's a *New Year's* gift. Genesis wants you to have it early since she'll be in New York January the first."

"Thank you, sweetie pie. Nana loves you. Please—"

"Baby, where are you?" Some tall, bald, light-skinned dude with a neat salt-and-pepper mustache and beard strolled into the room.

For a man of his mature age, he was kind of buff. It was easy to see since he was wearing only a black towel wrapped around his lower body. Everything else was on display for my unappreciative eyes. He needed to thank Allah that Genesis was just a baby and didn't know the difference in what he was or wasn't wearing. Otherwise, I would've had words for his ass.

"I'm sorry, Aminata. I didn't know you had company, sweetheart. I must've missed the doorbell over the water running in the shower."

My mama looked so embarrassed, like she wanted to cry or crawl inside a hole and die. But I didn't feel sorry for her. I was her son, but I was also an *adult*. Once she and ole dude started kicking it and having relations or whatnot, she should've had enough respect for me to tell me. Then I would've known better than to show up for an unannounced visit with my daughter. I wasn't mad about the guy tapping that ass because I wanted *somebody* to clear out the cobwebs down there. I just didn't appreciate finding out about it *this* way. I felt like I'd been sucker punched in my stomach.

Mama handed Genesis back to me and turned to the high yellow stud draped in a towel. "Dafiq, this is my son, Tyson, and his daughter, Genesis."

"As-salaam alaikum," he had the nerve to say, taking quick giant steps toward me with his hand extended.

I wanted to pimp slap that big grin off his face instead of shaking his hand. That same hand had been all over my mama's body, and it was probably about to explore her curves again as soon as my princess and I left. I felt my mama's eyes penetrating through my core. She had taught me to be respectful to my elders a long time ago, and she wouldn't tolerate any rudeness from me, even though I was a grown-ass man now. So, I stepped out of my feelings, tossed her gift on the display table, and accepted Dafiq's hand in a goodwill gesture. "Wa-Alaikum-salaam."

"I apologize for this awkward meeting, Tyson. I have nothing but love, admiration, and respect for your mother and her family. This is not the ideal situation for me to meet Aminata's firstborn. Please forgive me. I take full responsibility for everything."

The ice around my heart melted a little when Dafiq walked back over to my mama and embraced her. He kissed her temple lovingly before he apologized to her. There was a glimmer in the older cat's hazel eyes that told me he was sincere and he truly cared about her. I watched them whisper to each other before he disappeared down the hallway.

I was *almost* impressed. Khadijah had described the guy as the real deal and the ultimate gentleman. Maybe she was right. Even the strongest and most influential male Muslims fell from grace sometimes. History notes that The Honorable Elijah Muhammad couldn't control his penis back in the day. Dude's dick stayed all up in some outside pussy. He had a flock of bastard children running around to prove it too.

"Mama—"

"Tyson—"

We spoke at the same time.

I nodded and smiled. "Go ahead, Mama."

"I'm so sorry, son," she said softly as she approached me with her arms outstretched.

I wrapped my free arm around her. "You don't owe me an apology. You're an adult, and whatever you do in your home with whomever you choose to do it with is your business. I have no right to be upset. I should've called before we came over." I smiled at Genesis when she stuck her finger in my mouth before I looked at Mama again. "How come you didn't tell me you and Brother Dafiq were an item?"

I couldn't believe the fierce and feisty Aminata Shahid had suddenly become shy and meek. She smiled at me bashfully and lowered her eyelids like an innocent virgin who'd just heard a nasty joke. I didn't know what Dafiq had been doing to my mama, but he must've been doing it right. The cat had her blushing and squirming.

"I wanted to make sure it would stick first. And I didn't feel like hearing all of your jokes and teasing. Your sister was cool when I told her. She ain't silly like you."

"So, you and Khadijah are keeping secrets from me? I'm very deeply hurt."

"Don't be upset with your sister now. I swore her to secrecy. We confide in each other all the time. Some things are just better off between us girls."

"I heard that. Where is Khadijah anyway?" I asked, looking around like she would suddenly appear.

"She went to take little Miss Bailey the Christmas presents y'all bought for her. Why didn't you go to the plantation with her?"

"I ain't trying to see Daddy or Lorna anytime soon. I called Bailey early this morning to wish her a Merry Christmas. She understands the deal. Hell, she's living in the drama."

"What *drama*, Tyson?" Mama asked, cocking her head to the side.

Wow! She doesn't know, I silently concluded. I couldn't believe Khadijah hadn't told her about our daddy's black mistress and his confession of regret for leaving us for Lorna. But it was clear to me by Mama's relaxed countenance that she was really clueless.

"*What drama?*"

"Ask Khadijah. It looks like she's keeping secrets both ways."

"Maybe she forgot to tell me. But if *you* know something about Hoke and Miss Daisy over there on the plantation, pour the tea, Negro."

"Nah," I said, backpedaling toward the door and laughing. "Ask your secret-keeping daughter what she discovered Thanksgiving and ask her how come *she* didn't pour the tea. Being out of the loop ain't no fun, is it, Mama?"

"Touché. Okay, I'll get the scoop on Lorna and her field hand from your sister." She walked over and hugged me and kissed Genesis' cheek. "Tell my mother and Auntie Darlene I'll call them later. I love you two."

"We love you too." I opened the door, stepped outside, and turned to face my mama again. "And we're glad you're wearing *earrings* again."

That little joke earned me the evil eye before the door slammed shut in my face.

Chapter Twenty-seven

Julian and Pilar

"So, you're at home all alone on *Christmas?*"

"Yeah. I thought it was only fair to let Genesis hang out with her father all day since she and I are leaving for New York in the morning."

"I know, baby," I said, touching my growing erection as I pictured Pilar on my lap Thanksgiving. Her pussy was beyond wet that night, and she was ready for me to commit a homicide on that thing. "I just figured you'd hang out with your cousin and her family today since I'm up here with my folks."

"Kayla and the kids are in Houston with her hubby and his family for Christmas and New Year's because they were in the Bronx for Thanksgiving. There ain't no telling where her brother, Juan, is today. He and I aren't that close anyway."

"Well, I still hate that you're alone today. If I were there with you right now, you'd be butt naked, stretched out, and wide open. And I would be so far up inside of you that my dick and your uterus would be on a first-name basis. They'd be giving each other high fives. Your bed would be *rocking,* baby."

"Is that right, sir?" she asked, purring like the legendary femme fatale, Eartha Kitt, the *original* black Catwoman. "Is that how we'd be spending Christmas?"

My dick stood up and nodded its head in the affirma-
tive. "Damn right," I whispered, wishing I was between
them thick thighs this very moment.

"We'll have some private time together as soon as we
can get our schedules in sync."

"Yeah, we've been playing tag, but we keep missing
each other. I *hate* it, but I had planned months ago to
be up here the week before Christmas and return the
day afterward. And just as I'm about to head back south,
you're on your way to the Boogie Down."

"I'm sorry. I'll make it up to you. Let's make a pact right
now."

"I'm listening."

"By any means necessary, you and I will spend the
entire night together at your place January the fifth."

"That's a plan, baby. But what about your daughter?
You've got to make arrangements for her."

"Trust me, her father won't let her out of his sight for
the first few days after we return from New York. I may
not see my baby for a week."

I nodded, believing every word Pilar had just said. I
had met Mr. Tyson Maxwell. He loved himself some
Genesis. I admired the brother, though. He was no
deadbeat. I was looking forward to him taking care of
his daughter January the fifth because I damn sure was
going to take care of her mommy. "I can't wait. Get ready
for the time of your life, baby."

Whew! Dr. Julian Moye had me sweating. That deep
and gravelly voice telling me how much he wanted me
caused my pubic hairs to bristle. I had a little porcupine
in my panties, and it was leaking because I was about
to come just replaying his words in my head. I had
never wanted a man the way I wanted him. Well, that

is, except for *Ty*. But his ass didn't count right now. He was nowhere on my radar. Did I still love him? Yeah. But could I move on without him? *Hell, yeah!* This new thing with Julian was slowly drawing me out of my fear of living my life without Ty being a focal part of it. For the first time since our breakup, I could finally see a glimpse of a rainbow after the storm. Yes, I had caused all of the turmoil, but I was ready to move past the guilt and pain so I could start afresh. From day one, I'd taken responsibility for my actions, but until this point, I had never forgiven myself for cheating on Ty and causing our separation. Sometimes, I felt like I deserved a life sentence of unhappiness without the possibility of ever finding love again.

Julian had changed all of that, though. His kindness, patience, and understanding had whetted my appetite for love, passion, and romance again. My feelings for him and the desire to spend time in his presence couldn't be compared to the temporary insanity that had caused me to become involved with Chad. I was an entirely different person back then. I was a young, naïve little girl, seeking attention. Also, I was vulnerable, needy, and desperate. And Chad had sensed it, and he'd used that knowledge to his advantage.

I remember the second time he and I ended up together. It wasn't because I was falling in love with the Negro. I wasn't even in *lust*. I guess I had agreed to hook up with Chad again because he was available. He had showered me with gifts, flowers, and phone calls after our first encounter, and I had appreciated the attention. It had helped ease the sting of being ignored by Ty. So, when Chad called and offered to fly me out to Arizona for his game, I didn't hesitate. I had just gotten over a sinus infection, and I had a few more antibiotics to take to complete my treatment. I felt fine, though. I figured a trip to Arizona would make me feel even better.

I sent Ty a text message while I was sitting on the plane in first class waiting for takeoff. Basically, I lied and told him Sherraye had won a free gambling trip for four to Biloxi, and Yalissa, their friend, Shay, and I were going with her. He hit me back, telling me to have fun with my cousins. Moments later, I was off to Phoenix to watch Chad play. His team, the Sharks, won, and he had played an outstanding game.

"I saw your fine ass up in the stands cheering for a nigga." He snaked an arm around my waist and drew my body to his. His lips covered mine in a sloppy, wet kiss that I could've lived without.

I pulled away subtly and smiled, hoping not to offend him. "You were a beast out there. That last pass you caught was ridiculous. How did you catch that ball over your shoulder like that with one hand?"

"I've got big, skillful hands, and I'm fast, baby. A nigga's been blessed with good coordination too. You know that." He licked his lips and winked at me. *"Let's get out of here. I want to show you off with your sexy self. We have a late reservation at Oceana's. I'm gonna wine and dine you before I take you to the hotel and make you my dessert."*

And that's exactly how the evening went down. Looking back on it, I thoroughly enjoy a delicious meal of steak and lobster with amazing side dishes. And Chad had kept the champagne flowing throughout dinner. He wanted me to fly out to Las Vegas two weeks later for their last game of the regular season. I didn't know if I wanted to see him again or not, but I liked the idea of possibly visiting Sin City because I'd never been there before.

After dinner, we went straight to Chad's luxurious suite at the Royal Palms Hotel and Spa, and sure enough, my luggage had been delivered and placed inside the sitting area in plain view. Dude had handled every detail of my trip to a tee. We sat out on the terrace for an hour or so sipping more champagne while we chitchatted about nothing important under a beautiful, full moon. I was comfortable, but I wasn't looking forward to sleeping with Chad again. But what was I going to do? The guy had flown me out in first class to watch him play. I'd enjoyed the action from one of the best seats in the arena with bottle service and some of the tastiest hors d'oeuvres to ever pamper my palate. And there I was in a posh suite that was big enough to swallow the entire two-bedroom apartment I shared with my cousin, Kayla, back home in Riverdale. Also, the man had announced that we were going shopping and sightseeing the next morning before lunch at the renowned Wrigley Mansion.

No man in his rational mind would do all of that for a woman he barely knew without expecting some ass at some point during the visit. And I couldn't lie. Mami hadn't seen Ty's dick in almost week because he was too damn busy studying for final exams even to sniff my pussy. So, I decided after my last glass of champagne that I would give Chad what he wanted, and my body would receive the tune-up it needed.

"Damn, boo, your pussy is sweeter than red Kool-Aid. I could eat you out every fucking day."

I squirmed and released a long, deep breath as Chad's tongue traveled from my hard wet clit and over the bridge of flesh to my asshole. That Negro was licking and sucking me from hole to hole while finger fucking me with his middle and ring fingers like he was digging for gold. My pussy was so hungry for some dick that even a small one like his was going to do the trick tonight. But first, I wanted to come from the tongue massage his pussy-eating ass was putting on my clit. Chad's tongue was wide and long. It could cover lots of my sensitive genitalia at one time. He was lapping up my juices like it was giving him life, damn near sucking my pussy dry. The mofo had a Ph.D. in oral sex for real.

"Ah, shit! I'm about to come! Oooh . . . I-I . . . I-I'm coming!" I screamed and squeezed Chad's big head between my trembling thighs.

His tongue and fingers kept working their magic on my kitty cat even as I bucked and cursed through an orgasm so strong that my heartbeat raced off the chart. I continued thrusting and grinding my hot, juicy pussy into Chad's face, and he flicked his tongue over my clit repeatedly, catching all of my sweetness until the last drop.

"I'm about to brand this pussy, baby," he told me in a low and hoarse voice, rising on his knees.

The spot on the satin sheet underneath my ass was soaking wet. I scooted over a few inches out of the mess we'd made and watched Chad roll a condom over his stubby dick. It was stiff and aimed at my hot spot, but it wasn't about to do much damage. My imagination would have to help me get where I wanted to go. But I was about to put it on Chad because that's how Pilar Amelia Turk rolled.

"Turn over, boo. I want to hit it from the back and grip that phat ass."

I assumed the position, and the ride began. His meat was inside my pussy, and I was squeezing it as tightly as I could with my inner muscles. Each of his huge hands was palming an ass cheek like a pair of footballs he'd caught on the gridiron. I'd give it to Chad. The guy was putting some serious work in. He was grunting and singing praises to my good pussy while he rode me like a jockey at the Kentucky Derby. Each time he pushed into my wetness, I backed into his hips in a circular motion. He reached around and started strumming my clit with his right middle finger.

"Gawddamn! This here is the best pussy I ever had! I swear! I'm 'bout to have a heart attack, baby!"

I smiled, loving the way he was enjoying my goodies. I wanted him to want me. Every girl wanted to be desired. I sped up my hip rolls on his ass and slammed harder into his crotch on my backstrokes. Then I hit a Kegel move on him, pulling his dick in deeper. "On my back," I mumbled, tired and bored.

Chad pulled out of me and allowed me to roll over onto my back. He kissed my pussy and stuck his tongue inside the hole and twirled it a few times before he rammed his dick back inside of me. He started sliding in and out of my walls fast and forceful. He thought he was hitting my spot, but he wasn't. His dick wasn't long enough to reach my secret place, but I had to give him an A for effort.

"Uuughhh! Shit! My dick's 'bout to explode! Gawddamn, Pilar!"

I kept bucking, clenching, and releasing his dick with my coochie muscles as he filled the condom with sperm. I instantly became extra moist down there for some strange reason. I swear my pussy was drenched, but I hadn't even come during actual intercourse. Our eyes met for a split second before Chad hopped up all of a sudden.

"Fuck!"

"What's wrong?" I asked.

He looked down at his dick. "The fucking condom broke."

I swallowed hard and sat straight up in a panic. "Oh shit!" I took a few deep breaths to calm my nerves. "I'm on the pill. I take them every day. I never miss. But . . . um . . . What about your status? I ain't stupid enough to believe I'm the only female you're dealing with. This is only our second time together."

"I'm clean, Pilar. I swear. I do my thing, but I never go in without protection. I ain't no fool. I love life. I ain't trying to die. That's why I get tested every six months. I'm straight. Don't worry, baby."

"Do you have oral sex with all of the other women you sleep with? You went down on me the first night we met."

"Hell nah! I don't put my mouth on them hoes. I ate your pussy because I knew you were special. Your cousins told me you were a college girl with a man. I figured you weren't out there like that. And their brother, Brock, is my boy. Any chick related to him gotta be cool."

I had a thorough exam and got tested for every sexually transmitted disease identified by medical science as soon as I returned home. Everything checked out well. I thanked God for His grace and mercy. But several weeks later when I started feeling nauseated and lethargic, I got scared. I wondered if the doctor had overlooked something. So, I went back for a follow-up. That's when I discovered I was pregnant. It was a big shock because I had taken my birth control pills consistently for four years. But the doctor explained that the antibiotics I'd been prescribed for the sinus infection had compromised the potency of my birth control.

After I got over the shock, I was kind of happy because I thought a baby would bring Ty and me closer together. But there was a sinking feeling in my gut. I didn't want to deal with it, but I couldn't ignore the possibility either.

Dr. Vinson had said I was seven to eight weeks along in my pregnancy. That meant that Ty or *Chad* could've been the father of my baby because I had slept with both of them during the time that I was fertile for conception. The only difference was Ty hadn't used a condom. He never did with me because I was his girl, and I was on the pill.

I told Ty about my pregnancy first, hoping it was *his* baby. He was surprised but somewhat thrilled. It didn't take him long to embrace the idea of becoming a father. But my conscience kicked my ass over the next seventy-two hours even as we made love continuously and planned our future as a young couple preparing to raise a child together. I couldn't live with the guilt. I owed Ty the truth. The night I broke the news to him was the moment my life changed—for the worst.

Chapter Twenty-eight

Tyson

"What're you doing?"

I smiled when I heard Mallorie's voice on the other end of the line. A brief chat with her would be a good way to take a break. "Studying."

"Have you eaten anything?"

"Yeah. I stopped by my mama's house and ate with her, her new boyfriend, and my sister. I'm full as a blood-sucking tick. Why did you ask?"

"I just dropped Collin off at the airport, and I was hoping you'd come over. I'll stop at the liquor store and buy a big bottle of Hennessy. I'm starving, so I'll pick up a gyro to snack on."

"I'm in my pj's. I don't feel like putting on clothes or driving. I'm good."

"I'll come to you then. What's your address?"

"Nah, that's not a good idea, Mallorie."

"Why not? Genesis is in New York with her mother, and you're there all alone. And it's been weeks since we've fucked. I'm overdue for that dick. I can't stop dreaming about it. I'm having chocolate withdrawals."

"I'll have to give you a rain check. I've got to knock the bar exam out of the park. I'm using the holidays to get a jump start. You should be doing the same thing."

"Tyson, I think you just fed me a spoonful of bullshit."

"Say what?"

"You're smart. You'll pass the damn bar no matter what. It won't kill you to spend a couple of hours with me before you resume studying. I think you're having one of your famous privacy-issue moments. You don't want me to know where you live. Isn't that the truth?"

"You're absolutely correct. The location of my residence is private. I don't entertain company at my crib. This is Genesis' and my classified domain. Whenever we want to see someone, we go and visit them."

"You're selfish and very unfair, Tyson."

"I've heard that before. Tell me something new."

"You act as though it's a compliment, but it's *not*."

"I'm about to let you go, girl. I'm studying. I don't have time for your temper tantrums. I'll catch up with you after the New Year."

I ended the call. Mallorie was into her feelings, and I didn't have time or tolerance for her emotional outburst. I was missing my baby, and Pilar was acting a fool. She knew damn well she was supposed to check in with me twice a day so I could know how my daughter was doing up there in New York. She had agreed to our little deal before they left. She didn't call at all yesterday, and by the time I called her, Genesis was already asleep. Nope, my princess couldn't talk, but I wanted to hear her babble and coo in my ear. As her father, it was my right to know what was going on with my child. I wasn't some lame-ass absentee sperm donor. I was an active, hands-on, 100-percent, *real* father. Nothing or no one came before Genesis.

Pilar was pissing me off by not holding up her end of the contact deal. Next time, she would travel to New York solo. She had only called earlier today after totally ignoring me yesterday because she needed me to wire her ass some money. She *claimed* that Genesis was running low on diapers, and that special formula we often mixed with her breast milk was double the price up there as it was in Atlanta. Whatever. When it came to my daughter, I never hesitated to shell out money, and Pilar knew that. I honestly believed she used my soft heart for Genesis against me sometimes. But I couldn't take the chance of withholding money from my daughter regardless of whether she truly needed it. My daddy may have been an asshole, but he did do right by Khadijah and me financially, and I was determined to do the same for my baby girl until I took my last breath.

The hefty trust fund my daddy had set aside for me when I was a little boy, which had matured and drawn interest over the years, made it possible for me to take care of Genesis and Pilar. When I first learned about the money at the age of 14, I swore I would never touch one red cent of it. I was going to allow it to get fatter and fatter over the years and will it to my kids. But shit happens. The day I found out Pilar was expecting, I decided to hire a financial advisor to invest the money and set up a monthly disbursement plan. I wanted to live off of the interest, leaving the principle intact while I continued law school.

I was living like a pauper back then with only the barest essentials because it was just me. But my baby wasn't going to do without. Oh, hell nah! So, my daddy's money has been covering my dysfunctional family ever since my princess entered the world. I didn't waste it either. It was only used for our most vital daily needs like rent, utilities, food, my car note, gas, and health insurance.

I placed my laptop on the coffee table and padded into the kitchen barefoot to get a beer. I returned to the living room, plopped down on the sofa, and screwed the top off of my brew. I took a long swig before I picked up my cell phone and hit the number one on my memory dial. It was

Pilar's phone number, but Genesis' name and picture appeared on the screen when the phone began to ring.

"Hello?" I heard my daughter screaming the moment Pilar answered the phone, sounding frustrated as hell.

"What the fuck is wrong with her?"

"She's fine, Ty. Her tummy is acting up again. She had gas, but she was also constipated. I just finished bathing her after she *finally* dropped a stinky load."

"You can't be up there eating all of that spicy shit and then nurse her, Pilar. She can't tolerate it."

"Why are you tripping, Ty? You know I stopped eating spicy food even before Abuela died. *I* can't even tolerate it anymore, so you know I'd never pass it along or feed it to my baby."

"How long has she been crying?"

"It's been close to an hour now. But she's calming down now that she's had a BM."

"Did you buy the diapers and formula?"

"I did. I bought some fresh mangos, guavas, and bananas too. Mami made mixed-fruit custard for her."

"Cool, but I want my daughter home with *me*."

"She'll be there soon, Ty."

"Well, it won't be soon enough. I'm going to take her to the doctor as soon as she gets here. She's been having way too many episodes with gas."

"I know."

"Anyway, take care of my child, Pilar. And pick up the damn phone and call me the next time she's sick. I have a right to know what's going on with her."

"Okay, Ty, I will. Bye."

"So, Mom was crying and throwing things across the room at Dad. I just stood there watching her. I didn't know what to say or do. I've never heard Dad curse like that before. He was really pissed. Neither one of them even noticed me standing in the doorway. It was pretty intense."

"What were they arguing about, buttercup? Tell me exactly what Lorna said to Pops."

Bailey looked at Khadijah and me like she wasn't sure if she could trust us or not. I wasn't a fool. The child had been told repeatedly over the years to be careful about what she discussed with her *step siblings*. Lorna didn't want plantation secrets to be disclosed. Nobody was stupid enough to believe that all was peaches and cream at the Maxwell estate. God didn't bless *mess*. A marriage comprised of a cheating ex-husband and his conniving mistress was doomed even before the wedding bells rang or the vows were exchanged. It may have taken close to eighteen years before their perfect world started to crumble, but it finally had. Karma was a sneaky little bitch, and she always took her own sweet time to circle back around to bite you in the ass.

I hated that Bailey was now suffering for the sins of our father like Khadijah and I had. Looking at her from across the small booth inside her favorite pizzeria made me sad. Baby girl was nervous, and her eyes were shifty and distant. She didn't deserve all the stress and uncertainty her parents were putting her through because of their bullshit. Ain't no telling what kind of nonsense my little sister had been dealing with. Our daddy was a ho dog, and her mama was a ratchet piece of gold-digging, home-wrecking, fake-ass, white *trash*—what a parenting combination. With a genetic makeup like that, only intense psychotherapy and medication could save my buttercup.

"Bailey, it's okay for you to tell Tyson and me what's going on. We want to help you, sweetie. What were Daddy and your mom arguing about?" Khadijah asked.

"It's *crazy!*" Bailey screeched, placing her half-eaten slice of pizza on her plate. "It has something to do with *Kwanza*. Apparently, Dad decided to celebrate it this year, and Mom wasn't pleased. I don't know much about the whole African American tradition, but I don't think white people are welcome to observe it. Anyway, since Christmas up until this morning, Dad has been doing the whole Kwanza thing. He's been leaving the house every evening, and he doesn't come home before sunrise." Bailey leaned in and lowered her voice. "I think he's trying to get more in tune with his *blackness*. No offense, y'all, because I'm proud of my African American heritage. Just like Obama, I'm biracial or mixed, but when people look at me, they see a black girl. But like I said, the Kwanza thing was a little too black for Mom, but Dad dove into it headfirst."

Poor baby, my broken heart whispered. I wanted to cry over Bailey's ignorance. She didn't have a clue. Our daddy damn sure was knee-deep into Kwanza all right, but it wasn't what my little sister thought it was. Khadijah and I looked at each other, and an unspoken message passed between us. Daddy was getting his freak on with his young black dime piece, and Lorna knew all about it. But there wasn't a damn thing she could do to stop him. Now, she knew *exactly* how my mama felt when *she* was sleeping with my daddy all those years ago while he was married with two wonderful children. You could say it however you wanted to, but I liked to say it like this: Every bitch has her day.

"Don't worry about Daddy and Lorna, buttercup. Their issues aren't your concern. They'll work everything out, and before you know it, all will be normal again in your world."

Bailey wiped her mouth with a napkin. "I don't know, big brother. Mom was hysterical. She told Dad to get out.

Then she told him she was going to file for divorce and milk him for every penny he's worth, and then some. *And* she threatened to fight him for sole custody of me. She said he'd never see me again. I don't want to live without Dad, Tyson. I love him. He may not be perfect, but he's still my father."

"Lorna was mad when she made those threats, Bailey. She and Daddy are probably at home now making up. Let's go to Tyson's apartment and have a sibling sleepover. It's New Year's Day. I can't think of any two other people I'd rather spend it with than my big brother and little sister."

Bailey smiled for the first time all afternoon, and it gave me life. I didn't know what the future held for my daddy and Lorna, but Khadijah and I weren't going to allow them to destroy our sweet and innocent little sister. We would protect her at any cost. Maybe I would even try to talk to Daddy.

Maybe.

Chapter Twenty-nine

Mallorie

I was enjoying hot nasty sex with Tyson as usual, but something didn't feel quite right. Oh, he was hitting my spot and pushing all of my buttons just fine, but even as the onset of my climax gradually approached, I realized something was missing. I'd been craving his dick, his touch, and his scent for weeks, but now that he was pounding my cunt like he had an attitude with it, I felt cheated. Maybe it was because the holidays had passed and the communication between us had been little to none. We hadn't spoken since the evening I called and invited myself to his place. Lover boy didn't send me a Happy New Year's text message or even a freaking email to let me know he was yet among the living. But an hour after I'd finally fallen asleep on the first night of the New Year, he called me to say he was parked outside my building.

A fucking booty call . . . That's exactly what I'd told myself as I stood in the hallway outside my condo waiting for the elevator doors to open. And as surely as roosters crowed, that's why Tyson had emerged from the shadows to grace my presence. He wanted to *fuck*.

I wasn't good enough to meet his daughter or even visit his home in her absence, but I was expected to be available and compliant to spread my legs whenever he decided I was worthy of his attention. Regretfully, Tyson's mind-set regarding me was unequivocally correct. I would fuck him butt naked in an Alaskan blizzard on a whim. That's why ten inches of rigid fudge cock was ramming in and out of me. It was painful but enjoyable at the same time. It had been awhile since I had been fucked, so my walls were kind of tight. What I'd done with Collin the few days he was home had been child's play compared to the slaying my pussy was taking now. And I was taking in a whole lot more sex muscle both length and width-wise.

"I missed this here pussy," Tyson growled as his thumb slid up and down my clit each time he smashed into my body unmercifully. "Your man's got your heart, but *I* own the pussy. Say it, damn it!"

"You own this pussy, daddy."

I didn't know what overtook Tyson at the moment, but he leaned down and bit my neck and sucked it like a vampire as his hips bucked out of control in rapid succession into my body. I wanted to cry out in pain, but my body betrayed me when it succumbed to an explosive orgasm that caused me to see stars bursting throughout my bedroom. The air circulating around us seemed too thin. I felt like I was suffocating on a cloud of sexual bliss.

I loved the way Tyson made my body feel each time we fucked, but I loathed the way he treated me all other times. I hated to admit it, and I didn't know why it had taken me so long to realize the truth, but I was nothing more to him than his *fuck toy*. I couldn't even honestly call him my friend because friends talked, shared secrets, and had genuine feelings for one another. Although I cared for Tyson, he didn't give a flying fuck about me.

My thoughts about our *relationship*—for the lack of a better word—caused me to cringe after he rolled off of me and landed on his back. My legs dropped to rest on the bed. I stared at the ceiling as he panted for air. There was so much I wanted to say to him, but I didn't want to disturb the peace. And I sure as hell didn't want to make him mad enough to be a ghost again for the next few weeks. I suppressed my thoughts and swallowed my words because I had created the situation. My fantasy had landed me here. I had only meant to live out my dream and be done with him. Never in a million years would I have guessed that I'd become a slave to my own desires. I had badly fooled myself. Somehow, I needed to end the messy situation I had created—and *soon*. But I didn't know how.

Three months from now, I would become Mrs. Collin Cartwright. This thing I was doing with Tyson had to end way before then. Maybe *he* would bow out as my wedding day approached. That would be easier for me. I'd always had a hard time saying goodbye. Every guy I've ever dated had called it quits for one reason or the other. Most of them had grown tired of my casual approach to love, romance, and relationships. I just wasn't serious enough about settling down. I was more interested in the sexual part of the relationship. My attitude shifted slightly when Collin came along. I didn't fall head over heels in love with him, but he earned my respect and enough of my affection to cause me to hang in there with him emotionally.

"I've got to get out of here," Tyson announced as he sat up. "My sisters are spending the night with me. I was supposed to have been doing a snack run. I don't know how I ended up over here."

"Maybe you missed me."

"Maybe."

"Or maybe you were just horny."

."That could've been it too." He stood and searched for his clothes. "My sisters felt sorry for me because I was lonely without my daughter."

"You should be deeply touched that they care."

"I am. It feels good to be loved."

I nodded in agreement. "Who do *you* love, Tyson?"

He pulled up his pants and stared at me for a few seconds. "What type of love are we talking about here?"

"You love Genesis, your parents, and your sisters, of course. But I want to know who else has a place in your heart. Is there someone *special* in your life?"

"Nah. I don't have space in my head or my heart for a serious relationship at this point in my life. Being a good father and finishing law school are my main priorities right now. I ain't got time or energy to invest in anyone outside of my family. Once I land a good job and purchase a home, *maybe* I'll be ready to open my heart to love again."

"How long has it been since your last *serious* relationship?"

"Genesis' mama and I broke up when she was two months pregnant. I haven't dated anyone since. What's up with all of the questions, Mallorie? You know I ain't cool with that."

"I'm sorry. I got bitten by the nosy bug, and I went too far. But can I ask you one more question, *please?*"

He released a deep breath. "Shoot. But if it's something heavy, you won't get an answer."

"Did you love the mother of your child?"

"Yeah, I loved her with all my heart."

"Then why did you two break—"

"You said *one* question," he interrupted me with a reminder. "I answered it. Now, come walk me to the door." He slipped into his leather jacket and flung his deadlocks over his collar before he headed to my bedroom door and opened it.

I followed him in my birthday suit. "I'll call you," I told him at the front door.

"Cool."

"Mallorie Elizabeth, what's that hideous mark on your neck?" Mother wrinkled her nose like she smelled a foul odor.

I rolled my eyes at Godfrey for snickering like a stupid idiot. He was so immature. "I'm not sure," I finally answered my mother. "I only noticed the mark the morning Collin was preparing to return to Africa. Maybe he *sucked* me too hard the night before."

Mother tossed her napkin on the table in obvious disgust. "Dear God, Mallorie! Must you be so uncouth? I raised you to be a lady and not some foul-mouthed sex kitten. None of us care to hear about your sexual activities. We all had enough of your recklessness when you were 15, for heaven's sake."

I smirked as every eye at the dinner table zoomed in on me. I thought Katie, my perfect sister-in-law, was going to faint from the shock of my bluntness. She was as pale as a corpse. I was sure she was totally repulsed, but I couldn't have cared less. My mother had had no right whatsoever to ask me about the hickey on my neck at the dinner table. An inquiry about something so personal should've been done *privately*. But since she'd chosen to put me on the spot in front of the entire family, including my 3-year-old nephew, Garrett, I decided to fire back.

I would sell my soul to the devil for a penny if I could tell her the true story behind my little love bite. She would go into cardiac arrest if she knew that a tall, handsome, *black* stud had sunk his teeth into my flesh as he fucked me senseless. My father and Godfrey would pitch feverish fits if they knew too.

I looked at the family patriarch as he sat quietly cutting into the tender prime rib on his plate. I didn't expect any comments from Father. Over the years, he'd mastered the knack of ignoring my mother and me as a feuding duo and as individual pains in his ass. He and I were far from chummy, but at least he didn't constantly nag or provoke me. We managed to stay clear of each other unless it was absolutely necessary for us to interact. I often wished that my mother would take a hint from the wise, old man and leave me the hell alone. She should've been elated and enjoying life now that my wedding was only three months away. Her dream for me would soon come to fruition. Why had a simple passion mark upset her so?

Godfrey cleared his throat to speak, and I fought the urge to yank my hair out. "Honestly, Mal, you should save something for the honeymoon. And for the record, sometimes too much information is actually *too much information.*"

"That's an odd assessment coming from you, brother, dear. Tell me, just how much did *you* and my beloved sister-in-law save for *your* honeymoon?"

My eyes held Godfrey captive for several seconds while I waited for his response. His jaws were miraculously locked. I smiled as I took delight in watching him squirm in silence. He of all people did *not* want to go there with me. Godfrey and Katie had been married for three years, and Garrett was 3 years old. His birth had preceded his parents' first wedding anniversary by four and a half months, and he was a full-term baby. I've done the math, but apparently, Mother hadn't. Or maybe she'd crunched the numbers too, but she had decided to feign ignorance on the issue for the rest of her life. Either way, a bun in the oven too soon was worse than a simple hickey any day of the week.

Case dismissed.

Chapter Thirty

Julian

My girl was back in town, and she'd been resting up and regrouping for two days after her trip. As planned, we were going to spend our first night together at my place. I was more excited than a kid on Christmas Eve. I had prepared my famous marinara sauce that morning before I left for work so the herbs and seasonings could marinate all day. My cheesy sausage manicotti was going to blow Pilar's mind. Women appreciated a man who knew his way around the kitchen as well as the bedroom. Tonight, I was going to show off my expertise in both domains.

As I sat in the late-afternoon traffic, I mentally went over my list of things to do. I had just left the barbershop where my man, Figaro, had hooked me up with a fresh cut, line, and shave. I didn't consider myself cocky, but I was looking all kinds of sexy. Once I arrived home, I would boil my pasta, drain it, and set it aside to cool while I browned the Italian sausage in olive oil with onions and fresh garlic. Then I would add the marinara sauce. Stuffing the floppy noodles with ricotta cheese would be challenging as usual, but I had plenty of time. My professional pastry bag and tip would do the trick. I would be done in enough time to shower, dress, and put the final touches on my bedroom.

I wanted everything to be perfect for Pilar on our first night together. I was a romantic fella. I'd bought aromatic candles, flowers, and a big bag of red rose petals. Yeah, I was going all the way in for my girl with champagne, chocolates, and nonstop Luther Vandross on cue. No woman could resist a man with Luther crooning in the background. Pilar was hours away from being officially seduced.

I turned into my subdivision and sped down the main street in anticipation of tonight's events. Sure, I wanted to make love to Pilar, but I also wanted to show her a fantastic and memorable time. She deserved to be pampered, spoiled, and romanced because she hadn't dated another man since she and her ex had parted ways. I didn't know what kind of man could break up with a woman while she was pregnant with his child. I didn't want to judge Tyson Maxwell, but something about him disturbed me. He seemed like a cool dude when he came to the store seeking my professional advice for his daughter's problem with gas, but there was another side to him. Maybe in time, Pilar would share more details with me about their relationship and breakup.

I grabbed my bags and hopped out of my SUV. As soon as I entered the house, I heard a trickling noise like running water. It sounded like it was coming from the kitchen, so I hurried in that direction. I wasn't prepared for what I saw.

"Ah, shit! What the fuck?"

I dropped the bags on the counter and almost slipped and busted my ass when I rushed toward the kitchen sink. Water was every damn where. I bent down and opened the cabinet below the sink. A huge waterspout was shooting from the pipe. I turned the knob to disable the valve. I stood up straight and looked around the kitchen. My shoes and the bottom of my pants were submerged in water. I waded through the tiny flood and made my way out the back door. Removing my shoes and socks, I tried to figure out what the hell had happened. A pipe had burst. I didn't need to be a plumber to realize that, but I wondered how and why.

I reentered the kitchen and closed the back door. The fight to remain calm was fierce. I had plans that did *not* include a busted water pipe. I raised my pants legs and waded through the water again and headed to the den. I needed to go online to find a plumber right away. I was willing to pay any amount of money to someone to make my problem disappear.

"Hello?"

Damn! Pilar sounded so bubbly when she answered the phone. "Hey, baby."

"What's up, sexy? Are you ready for me tonight?"

"Yeah, I'm ready for you, but we've got to switch it up a bit."

"What's going on, Julian?"

"I've got major plumbing problems, and every plumber I've called said he couldn't come to repair it until tomorrow morning. So, I was hoping we could do everything at your spot."

"*My spot?*"

"Yeah. The plumber told me to turn off the main water feed to my house. I can't cook, shower, or wash dishes. I'm going to pack an overnight bag and box up the food and the rest of the stuff. I'll finish cooking over there. Everything will go according to our original plans except we'll be at your place instead of mine."

"No. We can't do that."

I frowned. "Why not?"

"Um . . . y-you know I just got back in town, and um . . . I-I haven't unpacked or anything. My apartment is a *wreck*. I didn't even make my bed this morning."

"You have time to make everything decent. I have to pack and put the food in containers. It's going to take me a minute. Go ahead and tidy up your place, baby. By the time I finish here, your apartment should be spotless."

"I don't think so. It's pretty bad, Julian. Why don't you put the food in the frig for another day? I'll treat you to dinner, and we can check into a hotel for the night."

"Why would we check into a *hotel?* What's really going on, Pilar? It sounds like you don't want me to come to your house. What's up with that?"

"Oh no, Julian, it's not that. My apartment is a mess. I would be so embarrassed for you to see it. Let's go to a hotel, baby. We can split the cost."

My instincts told me Pilar was playing games. She didn't want me to come to her house, and I couldn't understand why. We had been kicking it since mid-November, and I thought everything was cool between us. I was feeling her, and I could tell she was into me. So, what was the deal with her resistance to me spending the evening at her place? She was breaking the pact that *she'd* initiated. We had promised each other we'd spend a full, uninterrupted night together by any means necessary on January the fifth. And I was trying my damnedest to make it happen. The plumbing was all jacked up at my house, so it was *necessary* to change the location of our date to her apartment. But she wanted to go out to dinner and spend the night at a hotel instead. The entire idea and her attitude were fishy as hell to me.

"*Hello?* Julian, are you still there? Where should I meet you? It'll only take me a few minutes to throw an outfit, my toiletries, and some *lingerie* in my overnight bag."

"Nah, baby, I'm good. We'll postpone the evening to some other time. I'll chill here tonight. The plumber will be here bright and early. I'll be right here waiting for him."

"*Nooo, baby!* I've been dreaming about this night. I want to be with you."

"I want to be with you too, but it's not going to happen tonight. I'll call you tomorrow."

"Julian, wait, I—"

I hung up on Pilar because she was bugging. I was more disappointed than angry. And I was confused as hell. If her apartment was that nasty, then maybe she wasn't the right woman for me. I wasn't a neat freak, but I kept a tidy house. I knew some women could be slobs, but I couldn't imagine Pilar raising her daughter in filth. Her personal hygiene and her appearance were always a perfect ten. There had to be more to the situation than what she'd told me. Maybe she lived in a rough neighborhood, and she'd been too ashamed to tell me. I could understand that. It wasn't uncommon for a single mother in graduate school to live in subsidized housing or even in the projects. If that were the case with Pilar, I would totally understand. How could I hold her circumstances against her?

I took a few relaxing breaths and released them slowly before I opened the door.

"Hello." Pilar smiled and placed a soft kiss on my lips. "You look handsome as always," she said as she walked past me to enter the house.

That booty was looking scrumptious in a pair of white Spelman College sweatpants, and the matching hoodie fit snuggly over her firm C-cup breasts. Why the hell did she have to smell so good on this particular day? It was going to be hard for me to concentrate on the important conversation we were about to dive into, but pertinent issues need to be addressed. I prayed that what I had read in her customer file, Genesis', and her ex's at my job was a mistake.

"Can I offer you anything to drink?" I asked as I sat on the love seat across the room. I didn't want to sit next to Pilar on the couch. The temptation to touch her was too great. We needed to indulge in major dialogue, and I didn't need any distractions.

"A glass of wine would be nice."

"I think I'll have one too," I said, making my way toward the kitchen. A half bottle of chardonnay was chilling in the refrigerator, so I quickly poured two wineglasses three-quarters from the brims and returned to the den. I gave Pilar a glass and took a sip from mine before I retook my seat on the opposite side of the room.

"You sounded anxious to see me. What's up, Dr. Moye?"

"Why didn't you tell me that you and your daughter live with your *ex?*"

The look of shock on her face and her failure to immediately reply saddened *and* angered me equally. I stared her down as I waited for her to answer my damn question.

"I wanted to tell you, Julian, but—"

"But *what,* Pilar? Did you want to have your happy little family life in Camp Creek *and* your side man too? What kind of woman are you?"

Chapter Thirty-one

Pilar

I couldn't stop the teardrops from falling from my eyes, and my hands shook uncontrollably. That was what having the covers snatched from over your sneakiness and secrecy could do to you. I had been caught in my shit, and I was speechless and afraid. I placed my wineglass on the coffee table.

"It's not what you think, Julian. I swear to you that nothing is going on between Ty and me. We're just a pair of exes who're living together to raise our daughter. We sleep in separate rooms, and he has a full stable of women. We aren't romantically or sexually involved."

"If the setup is so simple and platonic as you just described, why didn't you tell me about it, Pilar? I wouldn't have liked it, but I would have tried to understand. You played me, and I don't appreciate it. I should've found out about your living arrangement from *you* and no one else."

"How *did* you find out? Who told you?" I sniffed and wiped my eyes with the back of my hand.

He frowned and shook his head. The sadness I saw in his usually bright copper eyes squeezed my heart painfully. "That's not important. The truth is the only thing that counts. You and your daughter share an apartment with your ex. By all points and purposes, the three of you are a *family*. There's no place in the equation for me. I'm an outsider; a misfit. I can't be a part of what you guys have going on."

I crossed the room to sit next to him. I covered his hand with mine and searched his eyes. His feelings for me were clear as day. "Can't we at least try, Julian? Now that you're aware of my circumstances, can't we figure out a way to navigate around the obstacles? Ty already knows I'm seeing someone. He just doesn't know who you are. We can keep it that way. What we share is our business and no one else's."

"I'm a *man*, Pilar. I ain't about to sneak around, ducking and dodging in a secret affair with the woman I'm trying my best to get to know. If you and Tyson Maxwell are over and you're nothing but roommates, why can't you tell him you're seeing me?"

"He'll go off! He doesn't want any other men around Genesis."

"I didn't *ask* to meet Genesis. I'm interested in her *mother*. But if we were to remain connected, eventually, I would want to get to know her too. I would never try to take her father's place, but I'd treat her well because she's a part of you. Tell your ex you've moved on."

"I can't right now. Give me some time to prepare because it won't be easy. Ty can be difficult to deal with at times."

Julian snatched his hand from my grasp and stood abruptly. "You know what? I can't do this. You're obviously not ready to write the next chapter in your life's book. You and Mr. Maxwell have some unfinished business. Give me a call when you're ready to emerge from the shadows of your past. *If* I'm available, we'll pick up where we left off. If I'm not . . ." His voice trailed off as he shrugged his shoulders.

I picked up my purse and stood with tears streaming down my face. There was nothing more for me to say.

Good men were hard to find, but I had found one against the odds. It was a damn shame I couldn't be the woman he deserved because of the complicated life I had created for myself. Julian was special, and I cared too much about him to ruin his heart for the next woman with my fucked-up circumstances.

I drove around for two hours in a funk after I left Julian's house. I couldn't go home and face Ty with bloodshot eyes and a broken heart. But it was getting close to Genesis' bedtime, and I wanted to nurse her and hold her so she could comfort her mommy before she went to bed. Life was so unfair sometimes, but I couldn't change it. All I could do was roll with it.

I pulled into my parking space in front of our apartment building and turned off the engine. I checked my face in the lighted mirror on my sun visor. I'd had much better days. I exited the car and dragged my body to the front door with the weight of pain and hopelessness on my shoulders. As soon as I entered the apartment, I heard Ty's deep voice singing off-key. I walked slowly toward his bedroom and peeped in the master bathroom. He was bathing Genesis and singing "The Itsy Bitsy Spider" to her. He sounded awful, but I smiled in spite of it because my baby was enjoying it. Her tiny hands were busy clapping to the music, and the smile on her face was priceless.

"Good evening," I whispered.

Ty turned around and gave me a brief once-over. "What's up, Pilar?"

"I was out running errands. What did she eat for dinner?"

"We stopped by Mickey D's when we left Mama's house and ate chicken nuggets and French fries. We bought you a double cheeseburger with no onions and extra pickles. It's in the microwave."

"Thanks. I'll eat it tomorrow. I'm not hungry. I'll be in my room. You can bring her to me so I can nurse her before she goes to bed."

"Cool."

"Have you decided what you're going to have yet?"

I peeped at Ty over the top of my menu and shook my head. I wanted to try the veal shank, but the stuffed flounder was calling my name. I looked at baby girl. She was smacking on a mozzarella stick her daddy had fed her. It amazed me how well she could chop with five tiny teeth. She was 10 months old now, so she was too busy most of the time to crawl onto my lap to be nursed. Her Minnie Mouse sippy cup was her new best friend now. And she was taking steps too.

"I'm going to have the New York strip and curry shrimp. I'll order the shepherd's pie for the baby. What do you think?"

"That's fine. She hasn't had any problems with her tummy since we were in New York. The shepherd's pie sounds cool." I closed my menu and placed it on the table. "The flounder is my choice. German potato salad and the three-pea soup will be my sides."

I looked around the restaurant filled with couples celebrating Valentine's Day. They all appeared to be happy and in love. That wasn't the case with Ty and me, but at least we were civil enough toward each other so we could enjoy a meal together with our daughter. I had planned to stay home and drown my sorrows in a bottle of green apple Crown Royal, but two days ago, Ty called from work and told me he had made a reservation for us at Nova Bella's. I was surprised but in a good way. I knew his gesture wasn't a romantic one, but at least I wasn't home alone singing the blues with a bottle of booze.

The server returned to the table to take our entrée choices. Ty ordered a glass of wine for us. He used to order my food and beverages for me all the time when we were a couple. I had never dined at fine upscale restaurants before he and I started dating. I used to think I was balling if I went to Red Lobster with my cousin until Ty came along and introduced me to a whole new world.

"What do you want to do for Genesis' birthday, Pilar?"

"She won't know the difference if we were to grill hot dogs on the patio at the apartment or go to Chuck E. Cheese's. Why don't you decide? I'll help you plan it."

"I want to go all out for my princess's first birthday. Hopefully, she'll be walking well by then. Maybe I'll rent a pony and hire a clown. We can have it in Mama's backyard. We'll invite some of her friends from the nursery at church. Kayla's kids are welcome to come too."

I took a sip of wine as soon as the server placed it before me and stared at my daughter's father. "A pony and a clown, Ty? Don't you think that's a bit much for a 1-year-old little girl? She won't remember it. Hell, she may even be scared of the damn pony and the clown too."

"I'll ask Khadijah to video it so when Genesis gets older, she'll see what her daddy did to celebrate her first year in the world."

"Okay. We can do whatever you want to do."

I had to do a double take when Ty walked past me on his way to the front door. He had changed out of his slacks and turtleneck sweater into a black-and-white jogging suit. I left the kitchen and followed him. He was unlocking the door when I approached him.

"Where are you going?"

"I ain't sleepy, so I'm about to go have a drink with a couple of guys from school. I won't be out too late. I turned the baby monitor on."

I looked him up and down a few times. Ty actually thought I was a damn fool. He was about to go on an ass mission with some slut who was mad that he hadn't spent Valentine's Day with her. So, to make it up to the tramp, he was about to go to her place and apologize with his dick. Some women were so stupid and desperate until it was sickening. Without a single word, I did a swift about-face and walked straight to my room.

Chapter Thirty-two

Tyson and Mallorie

A blow job was better than nothing on a night when a guy was experiencing a high level of sexual frustration. Some relief trumped the blue balls even if it wasn't what you really wanted and you weren't with the person you desired. My situation was kind of like having a craving for filet mignon from Bones on Piedmont but having to settle for a bologna sandwich from your grandma's house. I was hungry, and I had to eat whatever was available. So, Mallorie was doing the only thing she could do for me on Valentine's night because she was on her period. Unfortunately for her, she was being *used* in the worst way. I'd needed some of that sexual healing my man, the late, great Marvin Gaye, used to sing about back in the 1980s when the living was supposedly much easier than what we were dealing with today.

Last Valentine's Day, I was so bitter and heartbroken that I didn't give a fuck about love or romance. I was only existing and not living back then in a jacked-up world that was dark, cold, and confusing. Pilar was pregnant with a baby whose paternity was questionable, and my struggle to pass my constitutional law class and other courses was *real*. In my current situation with my dick sliding in and out of Mallorie's throat as she sucked me closer and closer to a nut, I realized I was *still* a fucked-up individual. Something was seriously wrong with me. On the outside, I appeared to be a normal and healthy black man who had his shit together. My intelligence, good looks, and ripped physique had created a bonus package for me that I often used to my advantage.

In a few months, I would be finished with law school, which I'd considered my ultimate educational goal. I would secure a good job, so I wasn't worried about money. My daughter was going to have an even greater life the moment I stepped on the law scene. All of the stars in the sky were lined up in my favor, but I still felt like something was missing.

"Ah shit," I growled through clenched teeth when I nutted in Mallorie's mouth. "Damn, girl, you're trying to kill me."

She didn't show me any mercy. Her lips and throat kept pulling Thunder in as she fondled my balls. She moaned and slurped, swallowing every drop of semen I had released. And she wasn't gagging either. Her head popped up after I stopped twitching through my orgasm. I relaxed on the sofa, and my toes uncurled. Mallorie looked at me and smiled. She seemed proud of her skills and the pleasure she'd brought me. I genuinely liked the girl. She was a good person.

"So, who was your valentine, Tyson?" she asked, rising from her knees. She sat next to me on the sofa.

"Genesis."

She nodded and raked her fingers through her hair. "Of course, she was. Did you buy her chocolates and take her out for a daddy-daughter date?"

"I bought her a big stuffed animal, a pink bunny rabbit to be exact. We went to dinner at Nova Bella's."

"I love that place. Their lamb chops are the best."

"I had surf and turf. She gobbled down half a dish of shepherd's pie, and—" I stopped myself before I mentioned what Pilar had eaten at dinner. I couldn't believe I'd almost told Mallorie I had spent the evening with my ex. I stood and pulled up my drawers and pants. Then I grabbed my jacket from the arm of the sofa. "I've got to run. I made a nine o'clock appointment to speak with my academic advisor in the morning. Call me later."

"Okay, I'll do that. My brother wants me to do some research on a case he just took on, so I'll be at the family's law firm most of the morning. Later, I have a bar study session with some classmates. You're welcome to join us."

"Nah. I study better alone. The group thing doesn't work for me." I put my jacket on and left the room, headed for the front door with Mallorie following me.

"You know I hate brown mustard, Mal." Godfrey slapped the top slice of bread over the turkey, provolone cheese, and veggies, and glared at me.

"That's all they use. I figured brown mustard would be better than no mustard at all."

"Well, you were *wrong*."

"I'm sorry."

"How is the research coming along?"

"It's slow because the case is so messy. There're too many parties involved, but I think our client has a clear advantage in that she was the deceased's first wife, and he was married to her longer than he was to his other three wives. The children from wife number two have a lot of ground to stand on too. The stepson from the widowed fourth wife needs to take a hike."

"He's a greedy son of a bitch."

"I think so too."

I picked up my corned beef sandwich and took a huge bite. I was famished. I'd been working so hard on the case for Godfrey, trying to make a good impression, that I'd completely forgotten to eat. It was almost two o'clock, and I hadn't eaten a morsel of food since the bagel and coffee I'd had for breakfast. My sandwich was delicious, and my tummy was appreciative. Godfrey continued working while I munched away.

My brother and I had never been close. We were four years apart in age, and our personalities were so drastically different. I was pretty sure the only things we had in common were our last name and DNA. We didn't even look like brother and sister. Godfrey's black hair and brown eyes did not connect us as siblings. When we were children, he told me I was adopted because of my dark brown hair and grey eyes. He was such a cruel kid. And he hadn't improved very much as an adult. I couldn't remember a time when he'd actually been nice to me or protected me like Tyson did for his sisters. He didn't talk about his siblings often. In fact, I didn't even know their names. But I loved the twinkle in his eyes and the smile on his face whenever he mentioned either one of them. The only things Godfrey ever had offered me were frowns and sarcasm. He needed lessons on brotherly love from Tyson.

"Mallorie."

"Yes, Tyson?"

"Who the hell is *Tyson?*" Godfrey barked with fire in his eyes.

"Oh God, did I say *Tyson?*"

"Damn right you did. Who the hell is he, Mal?"

"Stop being so dramatic, brother dear," I managed to say smoothly over my nervousness. "I was up late last night watching some movie on Starz. The main character was a guy named Tyson."

"What was the name of the movie?" He leaned back in his chair with a smirk on his face and stabbed me with his eyes.

"I don't know for heaven's sake! I was flipping through channels because I couldn't sleep, and I stumbled on the movie toward the end. The guy was cute, and he was a good actor."

"I hope you're telling me the truth. The last thing the family needs from you is another scandal. You're engaged to Collin, Mal. He's a great guy. Don't do anything to screw up his life. Mother will die a thousand deaths if this wedding doesn't take place. She and Dad would be humiliated and out of a mountain of cash if you get caught with your legs in the air humping some secret lover named *Tyson*."

"I'm telling you the truth, Godfrey. There is no other man in my life besides my fiancé. Tyson is a movie character. Now, drop it, will you?"

I hung up the phone and shook my head as I tried to process the conversation I'd just had. Mallorie's friends wanted me to dance at her bachelorette party. I didn't give Bridgette, the female who'd actually called me, an answer. I wanted to run it past Mallorie first. It was only fair. A situation like that may be too heavy for her. I would be cool with it, though. As long as the event was going to be a private and controlled joint and the money was green, I wouldn't have a problem performing. I scrolled through my contact list and found her number and dialed it.

"What's up, handsome?"

"Yo, your girl, Bridgette, just called me."

"Really? What did she say?"

"She wants me to dance at your bachelorette party."

"Absolutely not."

Damn, she didn't waste any time weighing it out. "Why not? She agreed to my fee plus tips. How come you don't want me to take the gig?"

"Tyson, you don't think it would be awkward for me? I'm about to get married, but the day before the wedding, my secret lover is going to dance and strip in front of my wild and crazy girlfriends? That'll be way too weird. Call Bridgette back and tell her no."

"Wait a minute. You want me to pass on $700 because *you've* got some kind of hang-up over our situation?"

"Exactly."

"We're not an item, Mallorie. Don't confuse what's between us for a relationship. We're *bedfellows*. You knew the deal right out of the gate, and so did I. You're some other cat's fiancée, and I'm single like a dollar bill."

"So, you're going to take the gig, even though I'm asking you not to?"

"Yeah, I think I will."

"Then I guess there'll be no bachelorette party for me. I didn't want one in the first place. I was only going to go along with it for my friends and my bridesmaids. They were looking for a reason to get drunk and watch a naked man dance for them. It's a shame they won't get what they were hoping for after all."

"You're acting like a selfish brat, Mallorie. You're blocking me for no reason. I ain't *Collin*, girl!"

"You sure aren't! He would *never* take off his clothes for a bunch of strange, horny women!"

"Yeah, he's too good to be a stripper, right? Well, unlike him, *I'm* too good to marry a chick who met a man taking off his clothes for a bunch of strange, horny women and ended up fucking him for the next several months, all while wearing her fiancé's engagement ring! Ask *Collin* what he thinks about that!"

I hung up on that silly-ass chick. Mallorie had allowed herself to catch some kind of feelings for me over the months we'd been sexing. I thought she was smarter than that. She had fooled me into thinking she could handle a physical relationship without getting it twisted. Apparently, she'd fallen in too deep. Well, I was going to do her a favor. We were officially done.

Chapter Thirty-three

Pilar and Tyson

It was hard seeing Julian at his job whenever I went grocery shopping. I had seriously thought about driving two exits north to shop at Kroger a couple of times just to avoid the man I still felt connected to. The mystery and the possibility of what could've been would haunt me for a while. I would never know what our friendship would've blossomed into, but if his kisses and touches had been any indication, I would've become *addicted* to his fine ass after our first round of bumping and grinding under the sheets. His hands were gifted. I could only imagine what he could do with that anaconda between his thighs. I could shoot myself for screwing up things between us before I got a chance to ride that pole.

It had almost been two years now since I'd been fucked or licked. Masturbating wasn't doing the trick anymore. I wanted to be held, kissed, and talked to after an orgasm. A vibrator couldn't do that. It couldn't suck my breasts or squeeze my ass either. I was long overdue for a sexual tune-up. I was so horny one night last week that I felt like busting in Ty's room and giving him my last twenty-dollar bill for some dick. I know that sounds pathetic, but I had needs that hadn't been met since I was seven or eight weeks pregnant with Genesis. She was two weeks shy of a year old now. This shit wasn't funny or fair.

I walked in the direction of the feminine hygiene aisle to get a box of tampons. It was close to the pharmacy, so I was going to sneak a peek at Julian too. The sight of him would make my coochie thump and cream, but I didn't care. If that was the only sexual activity I could have in my panties during my dry season, then I'd gladly take it. Maybe I would take a *long* look at him, buy some batteries for my vibrator, and then go home and fuck myself while I thought about him.

I grabbed a big box of Kotex before I stole a glance at Julian. I nearly pissed in my sweatpants when I caught him staring at me. I was so embarrassed. He lowered his head quickly, but I couldn't take my eyes off of him. All of that caramel was making me drool. He was too damn sexy for words. I wished I could roll back time to the evening of our first meeting at Starbuck's. I would tell him about my crazy setup with Ty and our daughter and allow him to work with me or walk away. Now, I would never know how things would've played out.

"Look at Nana's ladybug riding that pony," my mama screamed and clapped her hands. "She hated the clown, but she loves that stinking pony."

I looked at my princess on top of the pretty brown pony. She was an image of beauty in her denim jumpsuit and matching headband. Pilar was on one side of her holding her around the waist while the trainer was on the other side guiding the pony by a rein. I snapped a picture with my cell phone camera.

"She looks like you, Mama."

"She looks like *us* because you're the spitting image of me. When you were first born, your ugly daddy used to tell people you looked like him. He wanted you to have light skin and curly hair like him. But as soon as I saw your ears, I knew you were going to be chocolate like me. It tickled me to death when you started coming into your color."

"Well, I passed the chocolate along to my daughter. Pilar's genes didn't stand a chance against mine. Genesis is all me." I checked my watch. I was expecting my daddy and Bailey any minute. "Are you sure you're going to be cool when Daddy arrives?"

"Ain't nobody thinking about his low-life cheating ass. Yeah, your sister told me everything about him and his new whore."

"Did she tell you about his regrets over how he treated you?"

Mama smacked her lips and waved her hand dismissively in the air. "Yeah, Khadijah told me what that fool said. It didn't move me, though. I actually felt like vomiting. He ought to be miserable, and Miss Daisy is getting exactly what she deserves with her trifling ass. I don't mind Tyson Senior coming to my house for his granddaughter's birthday party. Just keep him the hell away from me. I would hate for Dafiq to have to kick his Oreo ass." She turned to look at her man across the yard flipping hamburgers and hot dogs on a big barrel grill. "He's a good man, son. I'm glad I allowed him into my heart. Mama likes him, so he *must* be a keeper."

"What? Mamie Lee Brooks gave you and Dafiq her blessing?"

"She sure did. My mama is in love with my sweetie pie. He fixed her refrigerator and prepared her income taxes. And when she called and told him she wanted some catfish nuggets, he did his thing. He went and bought five pounds, took them to her house, and fried them in some canola oil while she sat on her ass and watched him. That sealed the deal for Mama. She calls him her *son* now."

"Whoa! That's *deep*."

"Yes, it is."

Movement at the gate's entrance drew my attention. I looked up in time to see my buttercup's perfect smile. She was carrying a great big colorful gift bag. It was stuffed to full capacity too. She hurried in my direction with Daddy dragging behind her. His face was sour like he'd been sucking a lemon. "Be good, Mama. Here comes your ex-hubby and my little sister right now."

"I'm as cool as an ice cube, honey," she assured me, turning around to face Daddy and Bailey.

My sister hugged my mama with her free arm before she even looked at me. "Good afternoon, Dr. Shahid. Thanks for allowing me to come. You look gorgeous as usual."

"I'm glad you could make it, Bailey." She actually pecked my sister's cheek, and I thought Jesus was about to crack the sky in His Second Coming. "You look pretty, sweetheart."

Damn! Dafiq should've started popping that coochie a long time ago.

"What's up, buttercup?" I kissed her temple.

"Hey, my big brother! How are you?"

"I'm cool."

Daddy finally made it over to where the three of us were standing. "Good afternoon, son."

"What's up, Daddy? I'm glad you came." I shook his hand.

His eyes roamed over my mama from her single Afro puff at the crown of her head down to her red Roman sandals. "It's good to see you, Sharon. You look damn amazing."

"Who the hell are you talking to, Tyson? You know damn well I haven't answered to that name in almost twenty years. You will call me Aminata or Dr. Shahid or nothing at all!"

I grabbed Bailey by the hand and guided her across the backyard to the gift table. I was sure she was hungry because of the aroma of good food wafting in the spring air. I wanted to find Khadijah so the three of us could grab plates of food and eat together. I looked over my shoulder at my parents. They were conversing *almost* civilly, it appeared. Maybe Mama wouldn't kill my daddy after all.

One glance at Dafiq as he observed his bae and her ex told me a million things. For starters, he loved Aminata Shahid with a serious passion. Secondly, he trusted her. He kept manning that grill as he watched her roll her neck and point her finger in Daddy's face. Dafiq exuded confidence like he wasn't worried about a damn thing. He knew he had Mama's heart, and he realized she was capable of taking care of herself. If my pops were to step out of line, I believed Brother Dafiq would lay hands on him.

Ty sat straight up in bed when I entered his bedroom without knocking.

"Oh, I'm sorry. I didn't know you were in bed already. I thought you were in the living room watching TV."

"Yeah, I left the television on by mistake when I came in here to check on the baby. I was only supposed to take a power nap before I started studying again, but I fell into a deep sleep, I guess."

"It was a long day. Genesis enjoyed her party. Thanks for everything."

"There ain't no need to thank me. You know I'll do anything for our daughter. This time next year, she'll be sleeping in her own room every night in our brand-new house in the 'burbs."

I turned my head and smiled as I watched my little angel sleep. I didn't know how to respond to Ty's statement. He was building a future for himself and Genesis, but where would I fit in the grand scheme of things? He couldn't erase me like I was an ugly picture he'd drawn on a canvas. And he damn sure wasn't about to take my baby away from me as if I were an unfit mother. I didn't know his plans, but I wanted to be wherever Genesis would be.

Maybe it was time for me to follow Kayla's advice. She'd been lecturing me about finding my own place so I could be independent and free of Tyson. I was a single mother and grad student. There wasn't anything wrong with me living in subsidized housing and receiving assistance from the government to help me care for my daughter. Ty would have to pay child support and maintain medical insurance on her or I would be forced to apply for Medicaid. I just needed to branch out on my own because Ty and I could not live together forever. Our little arrangement had already caused me to lose a good man. I refused to lose my dignity and self-worth too. It was time for me to bust a few moves to make sure I wouldn't be left out in the cold once Ty started his career. I wasn't worried about Genesis because he would take care of her until death. I wasn't foolish enough to think I would be a part of the package, though.

"I don't think she's going to wake up," I finally said. "I'm tired, so I'm going back to bed. Good night."

Chapter Thirty-four

Mallorie

"I don't understand why you didn't just move into the house with Collin. You'll be his wife in less than two weeks."

"It's bad luck, Julie. We'll have the rest of our lives together. I can wait ten days to move in."

"It's not like the man didn't taste the milk before he put a down payment on the cow, honey."

"Shut up, Julie, and go over the letters H, I, and J on the guest seating chart for the reception."

I checked the guest list for the high tables one more time to make sure that none of my feuding relatives would be sitting anywhere near each other. I didn't want a fight to break out at my reception.

"When will Camden, Alyssa, and Kiyomi arrive in town, Mal?"

"Kiyomi is already here. She came early to spend time with her parents. Camden will fly in Wednesday afternoon, but Alyssa can't make it until Friday morning just in time for the bridesmaids' brunch."

"Has Kiyomi been over to help you do anything?"

"Yes, she has. We met at Phipps Plaza the other day to shop for gifts for the flower girls and reception hostesses. We went to Collin's new office afterward, and he took us to lunch."

Julie's green eyes flashed like lightning before she rolled them to the ceiling.

"What was that about? You still don't like her, do you?"

"I don't *trust* her, Mal. She's a spoiled little Asian slut."

"I'll admit Kiyomi is a little bit flirty, but that doesn't make her a slut."

"*Flirty?*" Julie screeched. "I wouldn't call sleeping with her friend's boyfriend flirty, Mal! What Kiyomi did to Twila was unforgivable. They were *sorority sisters*, for crying out loud!"

"I know, but that's all in the past. She has matured and slowed down since then. And she's always been a great friend to me."

"If you say so. Just keep her far away from Collin. I don't like the way she looks at him. Hell, I don't like the way that tramp looks at *my dad!*"

Julie and I laughed hysterically, but I sent myself a mental memo to follow her advice even as we did.

I couldn't explain why, but I had been thinking about Tyson a lot lately as the countdown to my wedding ticked off. I know it sounds ridiculously pathetic, but I missed him. Things had ended between us like I knew they would, and I'd been spared the task of calling it quits. After we argued about my bachelorette party, he cut me off for good. I never wanted us to part ways on a sour note. I always thought we would hook up for our final fuck, wish each other well, and ride off our separate ways into the sunset to pursue the lives the Creator had designed specifically for us. I often questioned if I was supposed to be Collin's wife. But my conscious resolution was always the same: he was the best man I knew, and I should've been grateful to have him.

So, in a few days, I would take the ultimate walk down the aisle to secure my fate in holy matrimony to a wonderful man who would love me until death do us part. It was what every little girl dreamed of after her introduction to the fairy tales of Cinderella, Sleeping Beauty, and Snow White. We all wanted to be rescued by a handsome man who would slay dragons and the entire world for our honor . . . Didn't we? Sure, we did because it was expected of us, and all females were creatures of tradition.

I was somewhat happy, I supposed, but not the way I should've been. I had accepted what was to be awhile ago, but that didn't mean I was ready to take the leap just yet. I needed closure from the last phase of my life. I had to see Tyson and talk to him before I moved on. If we ended up having a fuck fest finale, I would be cool with that. But more than anything, I needed to lay my eyes on him one last time and tell him what our coming together had meant to me. So, I cast everything else to the side, picked up my phone, and dialed his number. I hadn't tried to reach him since our fallout, but the ten digits were inscribed in my memory bank.

I closed my eyes and held my breath as the phone rang. I really needed him to answer my call because my sanity depended on it.

"What's up, Mallorie?"

"I need to see you," I rushed to say, relieved he'd answered his phone.

"I don't think that's a good idea. Your wedding is in three days. I saw you smiling pretty with your beau in the AJC on your wedding announcement. Keep smiling, Mrs. Cartwright, and don't look back."

"Things didn't end right between us."

"They didn't start right either. We never should've gotten involved. The whole damn thing was fucked up as hell."

"That's true, but we *did* get involved, and it changed my life."

"Yeah, you got to live out your fantasy, and now, you can move on with your *real* life with your husband."

"Of course, I will, but I need to see you one last time before I do. Can you come over tonight?"

"No can do. I refuse to cross the line with you three days before you get hitched. It's over, Mallorie. We both knew the deal. Go and marry that guy who obviously loves you and live happily ever after. Give him a house full of babies and forget you ever met me."

"I can't."

"Yes, you can, and you will. Once the organist starts playing 'The Wedding March,' and your daddy takes that first step to escort you down the aisle as your guests and bridal party gawk in awe at your beauty, you'll focus your eyes on your fiancé and realize *he* is your future. Tyson James Maxwell Junior will become a lost memory to you, vanishing into the forgotten abyss."

"That will never happen. I will always remember you."

"Well, you shouldn't. It won't benefit you at all."

I heard a female speaking to Tyson in the background before his phone faded into a muffled state. I could hear him responding, but I couldn't make out his words because he'd placed his hand over the mouthpiece to prevent me from doing so. He had moved on with someone else, and he'd advised me to follow his lead. He was right. There was no denying it. My fantasy had officially come to an end.

"Well, this is it, babe. This time tomorrow night, we'll be husband and wife and on our way to Tahiti." Collin leaned in and kissed my lips softly. "I can't wait."

"Neither can I."

"The rehearsal and the dinner went off without a hitch, don't you think?"

I nodded. "Everything was perfect. I'm going back to my condo for my final night as a single lady to relax."

"So, you're really not going to join your friends and attendants to party the night away?"

"I need my beauty rest for our big day. I'll probably do some more packing and cleaning too. I have a bottle of Hennessy and a couple of Redbox movies to keep me company. I'll be fine."

"Say what? Did you say, *Hennessey?*"

"Yes."

"Since when did you start drinking that shit? Isn't that what all of the rappers and black athletes drink?"

I wanted to spit and curse at Collin for his stereotypical thinking, but I remained calm. "I don't know. I tasted it at Connections one night when I was hanging out with some fellow law students, and I liked it. I've been drinking it from time to time ever since."

"Well, all right, then, *Sheniqua!* You go right ahead and drink that Henny. Do you smoke Black & Mild cigars too?"

"Stop it, Collin. That's not funny."

He pulled me into a warm embrace. "Lighten up, babe. I'm only acting silly because I'm excited about marrying you tomorrow."

"Cool. Just be on your best behavior at the bachelor party tonight."

"Don't worry. I will. We're going to get toasted and enjoy a few strippers from the Porcelain Doll."

"No touching, Collin. I'm serious."

"I'll keep my hands in my pockets. I promise." He looked into my eyes and smiled. "I love you, Mal."

"I love you too."

"I'll see you at the altar."

"I'll be there."

Chapter Thirty-five

Tyson

"Don't cry, princess. It's gonna be all right." I rocked Genesis in my arms as I held her close to my chest.

"It had to be the pizza, Ty. I think it may have been too greasy for her with all the cheese and sausage. I won't feed it to her again until she's older."

"Yeah, I think you're right. No more pizza for baby girl until she's 21."

Pilar sat down next to me and rubbed the baby's back. She stopped crying immediately. My princess knew her mama's touch. We sat on the sofa quietly for several minutes before I realized Genesis had finally fallen asleep. I made up my mind at that moment that she'd just experienced her last battle with gas. In the morning, Pilar and I were going to take her to see her pediatrician. Luckily for us, Dr. Oyedokun took walk-in patients on Saturdays from eight o'clock in the morning until noon. Pilar, Genesis, and I would be the first ones at her office tomorrow.

"I can take her, Ty. If it's okay with you, I want her to sleep with me tonight so I can monitor her."

"Cool. I need to crack the books anyway. But first thing tomorrow morning, we're going to take her to see Dr. Oyedokun. Be ready at seven sharp."

"Okay. We'll be ready."

"I'll probably be sleepy as hell because I'm about to study all night. The bar exam is a month away."

"And graduation is two weeks before that. How do you feel, Ty? You're at the threshold of fulfilling your dream."

"I'm excited. Mama sent out a bunch of invitations, and she's planning a big cookout. I can't wait to cross that stage with my law degree. Make sure you sit close to the stage and hold Genesis up so she can see her daddy taking his stroll."

"I will." She reached for our daughter. "I'll take her now. I'm exhausted. We'll see you in the morning."

"Good night," I said, handing the baby over.

I picked up my laptop from the coffee table and logged on to my study website to take a practice test on legal ethics in Georgia. The first dozen or so questions were rather easy, so I coasted along feeling confident. All of my many long nights of studying were paying off. I frowned when I got stuck on a question that didn't make sense to me. It was a trick question for sure. I opened a new tab so I could check it out on Google. About ten minutes into my research, my cell phone rang. Absentmindedly, I answered without checking my caller ID.

"Yeah?"

"Tyson, *please* come and hang out with me. I *need* to see you."

"Mallorie, what the hell is wrong with you? You're getting married tomorrow. Stop acting crazy."

"You don't understand. I'm losing my mind. I don't know if I can do it!"

"Have you been drinking?"

"Maybe."

"Empty the bottle of whatever you're drinking into the kitchen sink. Then go to bed. You'll feel much better in the morning. Every bride wakes up feeling excited and refreshed on the morning of her wedding. You're just experiencing cold feet right now. Sleep it off."

"*Nooo!* I won't stop drinking, and I can't go to sleep until I see you. Are you coming? Because if you aren't, I may call off my wedding. I need closure from you. You owe me that much, damn it!"

"Look, Mallorie, I don't know what the hell is wrong with you, but you need to pull your shit together. Your fiancé doesn't deserve to be stood up at the altar. And think about all the money your daddy has dropped on your wedding. Don't ruin your life over some whack-ass fantasy. I care too much about you to let you do that."

"You care about me?"

"Yeah, I care about you. You're a great girl who deserves a hell of a lot more from a man than I can give you. Promise me you won't call off your wedding."

"I won't call off my wedding *if* you come over and spend one hour with me. That's the deal, Tyson. I won't have it any other way. You'll come here for an hour, or there will be no wedding. It's up to you."

"Thanks for coming."

"You didn't give me a choice," I spat, walking past Mallorie in disgust. I was one pissed-off brotha.

Boxes were packed and stacked all over the place. I walked to the den and sat down on the love seat. Mallorie went into the kitchen. I had no idea why. I wasn't going to be at her spot long. She had asked for an hour of my time to talk, and that's all I was going to give her. My watch was already ticking. She had exactly fifty-nine more minutes to say whatever the hell was on her mind. After that, I would be out of her life for good. I swear to God, Mallorie would *never* see me again.

She finally entered the den with a bottle of Hennessey in one hand and a glass in the other. She placed both on the coffee table and sat down next to me. "I'm sorry for calling you with my problems, Tyson. I just didn't know who else to call. No one knows about you except Camden, and she's at a club with the rest of the girls in the bridal party." She reached for the liquor bottle. "The least I can do is offer you a drink for showing up."

I shook my head. "Nah, I'm good on that. Talk. That's what you said you wanted to do, Mallorie. I'm listening."

"Did I ever mean anything to you besides a fuck buddy?"

"You're a nice girl, and we had a good time while it lasted. I guess we were friends."

"You were more than just a friend to me. I considered you my liberator."

"That was then. It's time to live in the *now* and re-connect with reality. And that includes your beautiful wedding tomorrow to a cool cat. You two will build a home and a family and enjoy a nice life together."

"I don't know if I'll be happy, and that terrifies me, Tyson."

"No one but *you* can determine what your happiness is. But you need to give it a fair shot with this man, Mallorie. Don't fool yourself into thinking there's a huge population of great guys out there who're standing in line to make you or any other woman their wife and the mother of their babies. It ain't so. No man on the planet will ever be 100 percent of what you desire or need. But if a dude is willing to give you 75 to 80 percent of his heart and anything else he's got, you better take it and run. God didn't create perfect people, so no relationship will ever be perfect. The idea is only make-believe. Trust me. I know."

"You're right." She smiled and tossed her hair over her shoulder. "You usually are."

"I've lived through some shit that taught me a lot. We're all seeking happiness and contentment, but we've got to be realistic in the process."

"Thanks for the advice. You just talked me down that aisle."

She reached out and hugged me, and I felt the naked silhouette of her body underneath her Matt Ryan jersey pressing against my muscles. *Just one last time for the road,* I silently rationalized as I took her hand and placed it on my hard dick. She must've been thinking the same thing because the stroking began slowly before she eased her hand inside my sweatpants and underwear to take full possession of Thunder. Within minutes, we both were butt-ass naked, and I was reaching inside my wallet for a condom. But she took it from me and held on to it while she bathed Thunder with her mouth.

It was our final time together, so I relaxed and allowed Mallorie to feast on my dick, getting it primed for our farewell fuck. Tomorrow would be a new day. It would be the beginning of her new path to happiness with her beau, and I would spend some much-needed time trying to figure out how to find mine. Either way, we had taught each other some things over the past few months about life, love, expectations, and happiness. Everything Mallorie and I had shared would always be our swirl secrets.

"Tyson, your phone is ringing." Mallorie shook me a few times. "I swear I wasn't nosy, but I couldn't help but notice Genesis' picture and name on your ID screen."

I sat up straight on the love seat and took my phone from Mallorie's hand. It was after two in the morning. I wanted to punch myself in the face for falling asleep after we'd had sex. I pushed the power button on my phone. "What's up?"

"Genesis woke up screaming about fifteen minutes ago. I tried to nurse her and rock her back to sleep, but she wouldn't take my breast. She's crankier and fussing more than ever, Ty. And when I checked her diaper, I realized she'd had a bowel movement. It was hard, black, and *bloody!* I don't know what to do!" Pilar let out a blood-curdling scream, and my heart dropped to my stomach. "Now, she's vomiting, Ty! Oh God! My poor baby!"

"Hang tight, Pilar. I'm on my way. I need you to calm down and call Dr. Oyedokun's answering service. Tell them to get in touch with her and have her meet us at Eggleston Children's Hospital. Then call Mama and Khadijah. They'll want to know what's going on. I'll be there shortly."

She sniffed and released a sigh. "O-okay. B-but . . . but hurry, Ty! I'm scared!"

"I'm on my way."

I ended the call and looked at Mallorie. She was standing in front of me with my keys and tennis shoes in her hands. The expression of genuine concern on her face gave my heart comfort. I damn sure needed it too. My baby was sick, and that alone was turning my world upside down. I jumped in my clothes and slid my feet into my tennis shoes. Mallorie knelt and tied one while I worked on the other.

"Genesis is going to be okay, Tyson. You're a Christian man. Pray for her and rely on your faith. I'll do the same."

I ran to the front door. Mallorie was on my heels. I turned around to face her with my hand on the knob. "Congratulations, Mrs. Cartwright. Have a wonderful life." I kissed her on the forehead and turned to leave.

"Goodbye, Tyson. I wish you nothing but the best."

Chapter Thirty-six

Tyson

"*Intestinal obstruction?* That sounds pretty serious, Doc. Can you fix it? Please tell me you can."

"It *is* serious, Mr. Maxwell, but, yes, I *can* repair it. Dr. Oyedokun and I have located the blockage. Thank God there's no permanent damage to your little one's intestines. That means I won't have to remove any part of the tract. I simply need to unblock the passageway. I've done it hundreds of times before with success. With the help of God, I can do it again."

Pilar rested her head on my shoulder and whimpered her gratitude to heaven. She was an emotional catastrophe. But she had calmed down a lot since I'd found her in her underwear on the floor in our living room rocking Genesis and crying like death was upon us. I had to pry the baby from her arms. Then I went into her bedroom and found something for her to wear to the hospital and dressed her. It was hard to do while my baby girl screamed and kicked in her bouncy chair. The scene would go down in history as the worst experience of my life. I fought to maintain my composure, but, eventually, my emotions broke through the dam. I cried like I was in deep mourning all the way to the hospital. Actually, all three of us did.

"How soon will you perform the surgery?" Mama asked, rubbing the top of my head as she stood above me.

"She's about to be prepped now while she's asleep. Her auntie is keeping a watchful eye over her." Dr. Samba, the pediatric surgeon, turned to Pilar and me. "Parental consent forms need to be signed, granting the anesthesiologist permission to put Genesis under. I need your consent to perform major surgery on your baby as well."

"Major surgery means you're going to have to cut her little tummy open, doesn't it?"

"I'm afraid so, Mr. Maxwell. It's the only way Genesis will ever experience full relief."

"*Oh nooo!*"

I wrapped my arms around Pilar and pulled her closer to me. She buried her face in my chest to stifle another scream. I felt my heart shred into a million tiny pieces as I digested Dr. Samba's words. Genesis, my precious year-old baby girl, was about to go under the knife. This wasn't supposed to be happening to my munchkin. I wanted to tackle something or someone, but I pulled myself together and cleared my throat. "Where are the papers? I'm ready for you to make my daughter better."

"Khadijah, I loved your brother with all my heart. I never meant to hurt him. I was so damn young and stupid. But I loved him, though, and I still do."

"Why did you cheat then, Pilar?"

"I was so lonely back then. I was looking for the attention and affection I wasn't getting from Ty. Chad just happened to be there when I needed to feel special. But it was only twice, Khadijah. I *swear* on my daughter's life that I was only with Chad two times."

"So, it wasn't a full-blown affair?"

"Not at all. How could it have been? We didn't live in the same city or state, for that matter."

"Wow! Tyson made us all believe you and the guy were seriously involved."

"That's not true, and I tried to tell Ty that. But he wouldn't listen."

"He was hurt and angry, Pilar. You put him at risk when you slept with another man without protection."

"I *never* did that. The damn condom broke. I swear that's what happened. I value my life. I wouldn't have jeopardized my health or Ty's."

"I believe you. I should've known better, and Tyson should have too," my sister said, looking me directly in my eyes.

Pilar's back was to me as I stood under the waiting room's doorjamb. So, she had no idea I had returned from the hallway where I'd called and spoken to my daddy and Bailey. I'd been standing there speechless for a while listening to Pilar tell Khadijah all the things I'd never allowed her to say to me. And if she had told me, I wouldn't have believed her. Up until this very moment, my anger over her cheating had been more important than why she'd done it or how it had all gone down.

"I tried to be honest with Ty," Pilar continued through sniffles and tears. "But he was so damn angry at the time. I could feel his hatred for me every time I looked into his eyes and whenever he spoke to me. All the fussing and crying wasn't good for the baby or me."

"No, it wasn't."

"So, after a while, I gave up. The truth was no longer important anyway. I had cheated on the love of my life, and that was all that mattered." Pilar blew her nose on a crumpled tissue before she said, "You know I didn't have to tell Ty I had been unfaithful at all. But I loved him, and he deserved to know the truth. It would've killed him if I'd given birth to a child who belonged to another man, and he discovered it after the fact. I refused to take that risk. So, I came clean a few days after I'd told him we were going to have a baby. And I lost him forever. I haven't been with another man since."

I walked away and hurried down the hall because I had heard more than enough. My mind and my heart were too full to take in another word.

"Tyson, I want you to take Pilar home to eat and shower. She needs to rest too. Khadijah and I will stay here until Dafiq brings Mama and Auntie Darlene to visit."

"Nah, I ain't leaving. Pilar can drive my truck home, but I ain't going nowhere."

Mama got up and walked across the waiting room to stand in front of me. "You *and* Pilar are going home. The doctor said the surgery was a success. She doesn't expect Genesis to wake up anytime soon. And if she does, your grandmother and great-auntie will be here with her or your sister and I will. No matter what, my grandbaby will see a familiar face whenever she opens her pretty little eyes."

"I can't leave, Mama, so, please, don't try to make me."

"I've spoken, Tyson James Maxwell Junior. Now, wake Pilar up and get your ass out of here *now*."

I stood and walked over to the reclining chair where Pilar sat sleeping in a very uncomfortable position. I shook her, and her body jerked straight up as if she'd been shocked by electricity. "Let's go eat and change clothes. Mama arranged a watch schedule for Genesis until we get back."

"Can't we just grab something from the cafeteria downstairs? I want to be here when the baby wakes up."

"That may be later on tonight, Pilar," Mama explained. "You'll be back here by then. Go home, take a long, hot shower, eat something, and try to sleep for a few hours. Genesis will not be left alone. Someone in the family will be here every minute until you and Tyson return. Go on now, honey."

While Pilar was catching a few winks, my body was cruising on autoenergy, and my mind was flooded with all kinds of thoughts. After we shared a meal of fried chicken wings and homemade waffles in complete silence, we washed dishes together like old times before calling the hospital. Dafiq answered the phone in Genesis' room and informed us that all of her vital signs were stable, but she hadn't stirred yet. Then he handed the phone to Granny. We spoke briefly to her and Auntie Darlene before we decided to rest. But I couldn't fall asleep no matter how hard I tried. I had drunk three beers, checked my emails, and even read a few verses in the Bible and the Koran to strengthen my faith. But sleep remained my enemy.

I couldn't stop thinking about everything I'd learned from ear hustling on Pilar and Khadijah's conversation. The mother of my child loved me, and she'd never stopped. There had been no "affair" between her and Chad. My brain was still reeling from that revelation. And my heart had softened. I snatched the covers from my body and got out of bed. My fucked-up thoughts had already caused me more pain than was necessary. I wasn't going to allow insanity to hinder me again. I left my room and went down the hall to bang on Pilar's door. I needed to talk to her.

"Wake up! We need to talk!" I banged again, impatient out of my mind.

Pilar opened the door in a panic. "What's wrong, Ty? Did your mother call? Is Genesis awake?"

"I was a fool, Pilar. I was a mean and stubborn fool that refused to hear you out. I'm so sorry. Please forgive me. I am so very sorry for the way I've treated you. My anger and sadness got the best of me because you were my heart, and I loved you more than I loved myself, but you had cheated on me. It was partly my fault, though. I wasn't attentive to your needs, and I had messed around on you many times. I'm sorry. I love you so much. I never stopped loving you."

I gathered Pilar in my arms and captured her lips with mine in a long overdue kiss that gave me a natural high. The nearly two years I'd spent resenting her for being unfaithful to me dissipated with every twirl of my tongue as it mated with hers. I intended to love away all the pain my rage and stupidity had caused her. I had acted like a goddamn fool toward Pilar for tipping out on me when I had all but given her a license to do it by neglecting her and taking her for granted.

My hands explored Pilar's flesh feverishly. Her body was exquisite. It was softer and warmer than I remembered. Her natural scent mixed with a hint of the strawberry-kiwi body wash she'd used since college still lit my fire. How had I denied myself the pleasure of intimacy with the only woman I had ever loved over the only sin she'd ever committed against me? It was like heaven, holding her in my arms. I lifted her off her feet and carried her to the bed. I pulled back to search her eyes. I needed to see if there was still a place in her heart for me. The lust, passion, and *love* that shone in her orbs told me it wasn't too late for us. Our hearts were still connected. It was true. Pilar's love for me had never died. And I still loved her. I'd attempted to suppress it and will it away, but it was yet alive.

I undressed Pilar slowly, kissing every inch of her flesh as I exposed it. The need for my hands to reacquaint with the body that had carried and birthed my daughter was powerful. When she was fully unclothed, I marveled at her glistening, taut skin and her voluptuous hourglass figure. I picked her up again and placed her in the center of the bed. I removed my checkered boxers, which was my single article of clothing, and joined her on the bed. I lay gently on top of her kissing her like there'd be no tomorrow. She purred as my fingertips explored, caressing her skin. I placed butterfly kisses along her neck and lowered to her breasts.

I traced both areolas with the tip of my tongue before I took one hardened nipple into my hungry mouth and suckled it. The stream of sweet, warm breast milk surprised me. I'd forgotten Pilar was a nursing mother. I had been too caught up in sizzling passion and lust for my one and only. My brain was on strike because my heart and body had taken full control. My mouth abandoned her breasts to kiss her belly and dip my tongue into her naval.

Pilar arched her back and grabbed a handful of my loose locs. "Mmm . . . Ty . . . mmm . . ."

I slid farther down her body and grazed her pubic hairs with the tip of my nose, taking in the potent scent of her pussy. One deep intake of her unique feminine fragrance caused Thunder to jump to full salutatory status and throb with need. I kissed the lips of her vagina repeatedly and licked the fine hairs that covered them until she parted her legs wide—throwing a thigh over each of my shoulders—for my easy access. The instant the tip of my tongue engaged Pilar's clit, my salivary glands excreted with appreciation. The familiar taste of the only pussy I'd ever eaten was deliciously sweet. My greed kicked in. I wanted to drink every damn delectable drop. I flicked, sucked, and twirled my tongue over the stiff bud, causing a heavy flow of Pilar's honey to slide down my throat. The pussy was drenched with her juices and hot. The scent and taste of it chipped away at my resolve as I devoured it from the inside out and from its top to the very bottom.

Pilar's hands clutched the back of my neck, and her hips raised high off the bed. She worked her pussy rhythmically, grinding it against my face in perfect coordination with the strokes of my tongue. The arch in her back grew deeper, and her entire body started to quiver. I pressed my tongue firmly against her clit and held it there, sending her into the orgasm to surpass all others. It was massive.

"*Tyyyyyy!*" The sound of my name in high pitch bounced off the four walls. I was sure our neighbors didn't appreciate the echo.

I crawled up Pilar's body and kissed her lips tenderly. Her tongue latched on to mine, which was covered with the taste of her sex. Every muscle in my anatomy was tense with anticipation. I needed to get inside of her right away, or my heart would stop beating. I grabbed Thunder and rubbed him up and down her clit. The heat and wetness at her opening caused my meat to buck. I closed my eyes and inhaled as I entered Pilar inch by hard inch. The homecoming was sweet. Thunder was exactly where he belonged and where he had always wanted to be.

"I love you, Pilar. Damn, I love you, girl."

"I love you too, Ty, and I always will."

We rocked and stroked each other slowly at first, kissing, and caressing our way back to familiarity. Pilar's walls were so tight, juicy, and hot that I felt my soul drift outside my body. A Negro was honored that she'd saved herself. Making love to the mother of my child after so long gave my life new meaning. The deeper my penis penetrated her body, the closer I felt to euphoria. And the way she responded to me confirmed that we were meant to be together. Each time her walls hugged my dick and released it, I knew we were a perfect fit inside and outside the bedroom.

The love we shared and the satisfaction being exchanged caused us to pick up the pace. Buck for buck and stroke for stroke, we gave each other the healing our bodies and hearts had thirsted for. Our enjoyment went far beyond the physical. I felt our souls reconnect the second Pilar's body began to writhe underneath mine. She released liquid love all over my dick as she panted and sang my name like an '80s love song. I continued pumping in and out of her, determined to give her the maximum sexual pleasure she deserved.

And once my baby love was fully satiated, I allowed my body to follow hers over into the land of ecstasy. My nut was a million measures above combustible. It was *earth-shattering*. I released all of the love, passion, and semen that had stirred within me inside of Pilar until I was completely empty. And then I rolled over onto my back with her body covered in perspiration in my protective embrace. I didn't ever want to let her go. I welcomed the weight of her body on top of mine. It felt natural and comforting. I was sated beyond my wildest dream. Visions of Pilar, Genesis, and me together as a real family floated through my mind before I drifted off to the most peaceful sleep I'd had in almost two years.

Chapter Thirty-seven

Tyson and Mallorie

It was a good thing that I had left Pilar's bedroom door open. Otherwise, I wouldn't have been able to hear my cell phone ringing in the living room. I sat up in bed with her sleeping like a baby in my arms. Careful not to wake her up, I eased her body to rest on her side. Visions of us making love brought a smile to my face. *She loves me!* Just the thought of it made my heart dance as I left her bed to answer my phone. I had no idea what time it was. I only knew the sun was giving way to dusk because of my view through the front window.

"What's up, Mama?"

"How is Genesis?"

My head jerked backward involuntarily at the sound of the familiar voice. I snatched the phone from my ear to look at the screen. It was Mallorie all right, and the time was ten minutes after six in the evening. She should've been in postmarital bliss right about now at her wedding reception and not on the phone talking to me.

I looked over my shoulder nervously before I whispered, "What the hell is your problem? You shouldn't be calling me. You're *married!* I'm about to hang up on your crazy ass and block your damn num—"

"Wait, Tyson, please. You don't have to do that. I'm never going to call you again. I only reached out today because I was concerned about Genesis. How is she?"

"She's fine. Now, I have to go. Goodbye, Mal—"

"I didn't do it. I didn't get married. I couldn't go through with it."

I nearly choked on my next breath before I composed myself. "Hey, that's *your* problem. It has nothing to do with me. I'm about to shut down communication between us forever."

"Collin didn't deserve a wife like me. He's too good for me and my issues. So, I never showed up at the church. I didn't call or leave a note. I just didn't show up. I'm at the airport. I need to get away. I'm going someplace to find myself. Then maybe I can figure out what and who will make me happy."

My ears were ringing from Mallorie's insanity. I took a seat on the couch. "You need to go and find your man, girl. He loves you. It may not be too late to fix things between you two. Go to him, Mallorie. Explain that you got cold feet. Tell him you still want to marry him. Y'all can hop on a plane tonight and get married on some island or even your honeymoon spot."

"I don't know if I should do that, Tyson. I'm sure Collin is pretty upset. He'll never accept cold feet as an excuse for what I did."

"You'll never know what the man will accept until you try."

"I'll think about it."

"You should because it's time for you to live in the *real world* again. The fantasy is long gone. I've reunited with Pilar, the mother of my child. We're a family now, and I won't let anything or anybody come between us. Go and find Collin, Mallorie. Goodbye." I ended the call.

"Who is *Mallorie*, Ty?"

I turned my head quickly to face Pilar. She was standing a few feet behind me with her hands on her hips, and she wasn't happy.

"I was no choir boy when we were apart, Pilar. I got around a little bit. I can't lie to you, baby. But from here on out, it'll be just you and me. All my bullshit with other women and my anger toward you are all behind me."

"You didn't answer my question. Who is Mallorie?"

"Come here, Pilar." I waved my hand, motioning to her. "Let's sit down and talk. I swear I'm about to tell you *everything*. I'm done with secrets."

I sent God a silent prayer of thanks when my love made steps in my direction. She sat down on the sofa, and I took her hand into mine. I was ready to come clean with her about my latest secret . . . the *swirl* secret.

Collin's car was parked in the driveway of what was supposed to have been *our* new home. An unfamiliar black BMW was right behind it. I assumed it belonged to his friend, Matthew. After ending my phone call with Tyson, I felt empowered and confident that a heart-to-heart talk with Collin was in order. But my anxiety level spiked as I sat in my SUV with wild thoughts racing through my brain. I had no idea where his head was after being stood up at the altar. He was calm and calculated by nature, but traumatic events often robbed people of their God-given personalities and turned them into monsters. There was no doubt in my mind that Collin was hurt and disappointed by my behavior. I wouldn't be surprised if he was angry. But I wondered if his love for me would allow him to cast all that aside in order to have a civil conversation with me.

Besides a heartfelt apology, I didn't know what else I was going to say to him. But one thing I knew beyond a shadow of a doubt was that I wanted to give him . . . *us* . . . a fair chance. How would I ever know what kind of life we could have together if I never tried? Collin was the only man who'd ever expressed his love for me. All the others had been nice and attentive enough, I guess. But only *he* had gone the distance, committing his heart to me and asking for my hand in marriage.

Tyson's unexpected entrance into my life had only been a distraction from the course I had decided to take. I would forever thank my lucky stars for the opportunity to live out my fantasy, but that was all it had been. And now that it was over, reality was staring me smack dead in the face. Somewhere inside the two-story brick home standing before me, there was a man who had asked me to become his wife and bear his children. Up until an hour before we were to pledge our lives to each other, I'd had every intention of honoring him with my heart, but something inside of me unraveled. I couldn't explain it. I just couldn't force myself to walk down that aisle although I had promised Tyson I would. So, I'd chosen the coward's road. I sneaked out of my parents' home, where a glam squad was pampering all of my wedding attendants and me with makeovers, expensive champagne, and scrumptious hors d'oeuvres. I eased out of my bedroom undetected, leaving everything behind and sped to the airport.

I cried because of my many regrets on the drive. I was confused and had no clue where I was going. I just wanted to get away from Collin to save him from the beast that was Mallorie Elizabeth Whitaker. An amazing guy like him could do so much better than me. I also cried for my parents. I had yet to make them proud of me. Maybe it was simply impossible for me to do so. I was such a disappointment to them, and I was helpless to change it.

After I parked and arrived at the Delta kiosk, I drew a mental blank. I couldn't think of a single place on the globe to purchase a ticket to. I ran into the bathroom like a bat out of hell in tears to call Tyson, and after speaking to him briefly, I accepted his advice. That was why I was parked outside of the home Collin and I had purchased to create a family and raise our children in. I wiped my tears away, determined to make that dream come true. Like Tyson had told me: the fantasy was long gone. He had moved on past our secret association to reunite with the mother of his child. I needed to do the same with Collin, the man who adored me.

I removed my keys from the ignition and found the shiny golden one that would unlock the door to the house and hopefully, to my future with Collin. I was going to be happy and content with him and our kids even if it would kill me. I'd much rather die trying than to live without ever making a serious attempt at all. So, I exited my truck with my heart pounding a million times a second. My legs felt like they were laden with steel on my short walk to the front door. To say I was nervous would've been an understatement. I inserted the key into the lock and entered the house with soft baby steps. I smelled food cooking, so I made my way to the kitchen. I almost went into cardiac arrest when I saw Kiyomi bent over looking inside the oven, wearing a short red kimono.

"*Kiyomi?* Oh my God! What the hell are you doing in my house?"

She turned, and her slanted eyes sliced straight through me. She smirked and asked, "Is this *really* your house, darling?" She tossed the spatula she'd been holding on my green granite countertop. "This *could* have been your home, but you fucked up. You left a good man at the altar, you selfish, ungrateful bitch. You tore his soul from his body and now, you think you can just waltz in here and reclaim what you feel entitled to? Well, you're wrong. Your *ex*-fiancé is in good hands now—so, you need to leave."

"Collin!" I ran out of the kitchen, screaming. "Collin, where are you? How could you do this to me?" I headed up the winding staircase.

Collin met me face-to-face on my ascent. "What are you doing here, Mal?"

"What the hell is *Kiyomi* doing here?" I looked over my shoulder through a heavy flow of tears and saw her at the bottom of the stairs. "She is not supposed to be here, Collin! Make her leave *now!*"

"*I* was there for him when *you* humiliated him. How dare you—"

"Kiyomi, thanks for being a friend when I needed you, but I'm going to have to ask you to leave now."

"But I—"

Collin held up his hand. "Kiyomi, just grab your stuff and leave, please. I'm begging you."

Epilogue

Tyson

Six months later . . .

Pilar swatted my hand away when I palmed her ass. That thing was perfectly round and as soft as a pillow filled with feathers. My baby definitely had back. I pulled her closer to me and continued swaying to the beat of the music. My life was too good to be true. This time last year, the only thing that made me smile from deep down within was Genesis. Now, I was genuinely happy and satisfied with every aspect of my life. My daughter was healthy, and her mother and I were madly in love. I had aced the Georgia bar exam on my first attempt, and I was working a dream job at my daddy's law firm with a salary that afforded me the finer things in life. Never in my wildest imagination had I envisioned myself working with him, but shit happens. He and I were much closer now that he had left Lorna. Pops was doing his damnedest to make up for all the lost time he'd spent away from Khadijah and me when we were kids. The three of us were bonding, and Bailey spent time with us as often as possible.

I grinned like crazy when I looked over at Mama and Dafiq dancing. He placed a tender kiss on her lips, and she lay her head on his chest after she blushed like a schoolgirl. My heart was filled with pure happiness for them. They hadn't wasted much time tying the knot after their short courtship. I guess they realized life was much too short to allow time and opportunity to slip away. Their small and intimate wedding ceremony had been one I would never forget. It had brought out my romantic side. I was tempted to contact a judge and have him hitch Pilar and me up right away. But it was Mama and Dafiq's special day, and I was enjoying every minute of it. Furthermore, I had made a fat contribution to the reception, so I wasn't about to leave until the champagne fountain was dry, and the dee-jay had spun his last record.

I twirled Pilar around and dipped her way down low. She squealed and giggled before I pulled her sexy body upright again. She kissed me with enough fire to jump-start Thunder. But I forced him to stand down until I got my baby home. Then I was going to be all up in her like we were Siamese twins joined by our genitalia. We had christened every room in our apartment since we'd been back together. It was kind of like we were making up for lost time and getting it all in before we were to move out in sixty days. We had found the perfect house in the Buckhead area, and we'd been approved for a reasonable mortgage. We were just waiting for everything to go through escrow.

"Check out Aminata, Ty. She's looking at Dafiq like he's the last piece of fried chicken on the table at Sunday dinner. I feel sorry for that man. She's going to fuck him into her submissive slave."

"I don't think he'll complain. Just call that Negro *Toby*."

Pilar and I cracked the hell up over my joke. Then I looked around the ballroom until my eyes landed on Granny bouncing Genesis on her knee. Mamie Lee looked elegant in a silver beaded evening gown. My heart fluttered at the realization that four generations of my family were gathered under one roof, celebrating Mama's big day.

"I feel like a billionaire, baby. I'm rich with a good life. You and Genesis bring me so much joy. I love you, girl."

"I love you too."

"Yeah, I know, and you'll have an opportunity to show me just how much when I get your ass to the crib."

Pilar

"It's been a while, Ms. Turk. It appears that a lot has happened since I last saw you peeping at me from the feminine hygiene section on aisle two a few months back."

"It *has* been a while. How are you, Dr. Moye?"

"I'm well. Thanks for asking. How have you been?"

"Life is good."

Julian gave me a half smile. "I can tell."

"How so?"

"Well, first of all, you're glowing. And that huge piece of bling on your finger is blinding the hell out of me." He paused and rubbed his chin as if contemplating his next words. "Your prescriptions tell me a lot too. How far along are you?"

"We just found out for sure yesterday that I'm expecting. I'm ten weeks according to my doctor."

"Congratulations. Pregnancy and engagement agree with you. Do you need a consultation on how to take the vitamins or the iron tablets?"

"No, thank you. I was anemic when I carried Genesis too, so I know exactly what to do."

"Great. Well, take care of yourself."

"I will." My feet wouldn't move. I couldn't walk away from the pharmacy counter because there was so much I wanted to say to Julian. But he was at work, so I didn't have a lot of time. Therefore, I decided to say the most important thing. "I'm sorry for how things went down between us. It wasn't my intention to lead you on. Life is just funny like that sometimes."

"There's no need for an apology, Pilar. I believe everything in life happens for a reason. Your heart wasn't available to me because it still belonged to your child's father. Apparently, you guys were destined to be together. I wish you well."

"Thanks. That really means a lot to me."

Julian

As I watched Pilar walk away, I knew I had made a wise decision by ending our brief friendship before it even took off. In my opinion, she had never looked more radiant before today. Love and happiness had a way of bringing light to even the very darkest lives. One day, I wanted the same things God had blessed Tyson Maxwell with. My man had a beautiful woman who loved him endlessly, an adorable daughter, and another child on the way. The guy had it all. But I wasn't jealous of him, though. I had faith that my season was just around the corner, and I was ready to take flight and receive every blessing coming my way. There was a good sista out there waiting for a serious brotha like me to scoop her up and add sunshine to her world. My heart was open to whomever God had created just for me.

I wondered if Khadijah, the gorgeous and sophisticated med school student I'd met last week was the future Mrs. Moye. We hadn't spent any time together yet due to our crazy schedules, but I was enjoying getting to know her over the phone. She was very intelligent and deep. The sista had goals and definite plans for her future. I was going to chill and take it slow with the sassy sista to see where our friendship was going. She had impressed me so much already that this Christian man wasn't even tripping over the fact that she was Muslim. So, I planned to chill, take it slow, and enjoy the process.

Mallorie

"I'm going to hang up now so you can finish studying, Mal. I want you to do well on the bar this time."

I frowned because I hated to be reminded about how stupid I was. Yes, I had flunked the Georgia bar exam, but it wasn't because I didn't know the material. My state of mind at the time had been the cause of my failure. I was an extremely disturbed creature back then. After my canceled wedding and the Kiyomi scandal, I went into complete isolation. I literally checked out on everybody. I ended up on the psychiatric ward of Presbyterian Medical Center in Charlotte, North Carolina. My depression and anxiety were so severe that the doctor kept me in the hospital for twenty-one days. How the hell was I supposed to pass a major exam after my discharge when I was emotionally unstable and on powerful medications?

"I've been studying all day, Collin, and I feel very confident. The North Carolina bar seems like it's going to be easier than Georgia's. And I'm in a much better frame of mind now."

"Yeah, you tell me that every day. I'm tired of hearing it already. It's a damn shame that running away from home, abandoning your family and the man who loves you has brought you so much peace and happiness. Do you ever think about your poor mother, Mal? What about your father and Godfrey? And how do you think it makes *me* feel to know you're living a rock star's life without me?"

"I imagine you feel the same damn way I felt when only hours after what would've been our wedding, I discovered you had fucked my longtime friend and bridesmaid."

"Don't even go there, Mal! I won't allow you to go there because you have no right! I almost lost my fucking mind at the church waiting for *you*, my bride and the woman I wanted to spend the rest of my life with—but you never showed up! You ran away like a death-row inmate fleeing execution! Every damn night when you say your prayers, you should thank God that I even still talk to you. Most men in my situation wouldn't give you the time of day!"

"I had cold feet, Collin! I told you that. If I could do it all over again, we would be married right now. But I can't!"

"How am I supposed to believe that when you're up in Charlotte and refuse to come home so we can work it out? If you ever gave a damn about me, you would come home *right now*, Mal! Leave that itty-bitty studio apartment and come back to Atlanta to the home that we bought together."

"I will not return to Atlanta, so stop asking. I care about you, Collin. You damn well know that!"

"Do I? How am I supposed to know that you care about me when you skipped our wedding?"

"I made a *mistake*, Collin! And you paid me back by fucking that slut, Kiyomi! What the hell were *you* thinking?"

"I thought that my life was over because the woman I loved didn't want to marry me! You broke my heart. Don't you understand? I was totally humiliated. I wanted to die!"

I choked back a sob when visions of Collin standing at the altar, dressed in his black, designer tux appeared in my mind's eye. He hadn't deserved the pain or embarrassment I'd caused him. Now, I was eternally indebted to him for even dialing my number once a day. "I'm sorry," I apologized once again.

"In spite of what you did and why you did it, I still love you, and I want you to be my wife someday, Mal."

I didn't know how to respond to Collin's declaration. I cared very deeply for him, but I wasn't in love with him. Intense therapy had forced me to come to terms with that, although I'd already figured as much the night he proposed to me. However, Dr. Connolly, my psychologist, had encouraged me to maintain a relationship with Collin because he felt the odds were in our favor for a healthy romance if we sought couples counseling. But first, forgiveness was in order on both sides. I had to forgive him for sleeping with Kiyomi, the slut, and he needed to free me from the guilt of being a runaway bride.

Honestly, I understood that Collin had needed someone to comfort him after I'd left him hanging on our wedding day. Sex with a warm and willing body had more than likely helped to ease the stress and calmed his raging emotions at the end of the day. But why did his comforter have to be *Kiyomi,* of all women? Julie had been spot-on about that whore.

"I'm tired of having this same argument every day, Collin. Let's go to counseling."

"I don't have a problem with that. You should make an appointment for us as soon as possible, and I'll be there. As a matter of fact, if it's okay with you, I'd like to visit you this weekend."

I smiled a heartfelt smile because after all the hurt and shame I'd dragged him through, there was still a tiny space in his heart with my name on it. A handsome, successful fellow like Collin could have any girl he wanted, but he still wanted *me*.

"Sure. Come on up. I would love to see you. It's been a few weeks since your last visit. I miss you."

"I miss you too, babe. I'll see you on Friday afternoon. I can't wait. We're going to get past this roadblock, Mal. I promise."

"Anything is possible."

"That's true. I love you, Mal."

"Me too."